Praise for the Miss Julia series

"A charming, fun adventure with new relatives, old secrets, and a will putting Miss Julia and the Abbotsville regulars in a true Southern mess. I loved it!"

—Duffy Brown, bestselling author of the
Consignment Shop Mysteries

"The memorably droll Ross has a gift for elevating such everyday matters as marital strife and the hazards of middle age to high comedy, while painting her beautifully drawn characters with wit and sympathy." —*Publishers Weekly*

"Ann B. Ross develops characters so expertly, through quirks, names, and mannerisms that they easily feel familiar as the reader is gently immersed into the world Miss Ross has created. . . . A delightful read." —*Winston-Salem Journal*

"Miss Julia is one of the most delightful characters to come along in years. Ann B. Ross has created what is sure to become a classic Southern comic novel. Hooray for Miss Julia, I could not have liked it more."

—Fannie Flagg, author of
The All-Girl Filling Station's Last Reunion

"Yes, Miss Julia is back, and I, for one, am one happy camper."
—J.A. Jance, author of *Cold Betrayal*

PENGUIN BOOKS

MISS JULIA WEATHERS THE STORM

Ann B. Ross is the author of nineteen novels featuring the popular Southern heroine Miss Julia, as well as *Etta Mae's Worst Bad-Luck Day*, a novel about one of Abbotsville's other most outspoken residents: Etta Mae Wiggins. Ross holds a doctorate in English from the University of North Carolina at Chapel Hill, and has taught literature at the University of North Carolina at Asheville. She lives in Hendersonville, North Carolina.

Miss Julia Weathers the Storm

ANN B. ROSS

PENGUIN BOOKS

PENGUIN BOOKS

An imprint of Penguin Random House LLC
375 Hudson Street
New York, New York 10014
penguin.com

First published in the United States of America by Viking Penguin,
an imprint of Penguin Random House LLC, 2017
Published in Penguin Books 2018

ISBN 9780735220485 (paperback)

THE LIBRARY OF CONGRESS HAS CATALOGED THE
HARDCOVER EDITION AS FOLLOWS:

Names: Ross, Ann B., author.
Title: Miss Julia weathers the storm / Ann B. Ross.
Description: New York, New York : Viking, [2017]
Identifiers: LCCN 2016056691 (print) | LCCN 2017003001 (ebook) |
ISBN 9780735220478 (hardback) | ISBN 9780735220492 (ebook)
Subjects: LCSH: Springer, Julia (Fictitious character)—Fiction. |
BISAC: FICTION / Contemporary Women. | FICTION /
Mystery & Detective / Women Sleuths. | GSAFD: Mystery fiction.
Classification: LCC PS3568.O84198 M586 2017 (print) |
LCC PS3568.O84198(ebook) | DDC 813/.54—dc23
LC record available at https://lccn.loc.gov/2016056691

Printed in the United States of America
1   3   5   7   9   10   8   6   4   2

Set in Fairfield LT Std
Designed by Cassandra Garruzzo

This book is for Miss Julia's friends everywhere.
You keep her—and me—going, and we thank you for it.

Miss Julia Weathers the Storm

Chapter 1

"*Good* morning, ladies." Sam, beaming with his usual early morning smile, came into the kitchen greeting Lillian and me. My second husband—so different from the first one—was a man of warm good humor from the time he got out of bed until he got back in it. That had been somewhat of a surprise to me, having been accustomed to steering carefully around a bristly, short-tempered husband every morning for forty-something years. Having watched my step and my words for that long had turned me into a woman of cool temperament with few smiles—and stiff ones, at that—before coffee was poured.

"Mornin', Mr. Sam," Lillian said as she stood beside the stove. "Eggs 'bout ready."

"Good morning," I responded but without the bouncing eagerness with which he started the day.

"Julia," Sam said as he sat at the kitchen table, "I have had an epiphany."

"A what?"

"An epiphany. You know, a sudden flash of enlightenment." He accepted the cup of coffee I'd just poured, then said, "Well, maybe it's more of a bright idea. What do you think of going to the beach for a couple of weeks?"

"The *beach*? Why, Sam, you and Lloyd and Mr. Pickens just got back from the beach. Why in the world would you want to go back?"

"That wasn't a beach trip. We went deep-sea fishing and stepped from a dock to a boat and back again every day without being on the beach at all. No, I'm talking about renting an oceanfront house on one of the islands out from Charleston and just enjoying the sun and the waves and the ocean breeze. And there'll be shopping in Charleston and a lot of good seafood dinners—a real vacation for everybody, especially you. You've done nothing this summer but worry with Miss Mattie's affairs. You need a break, sweetheart.

"And, think of this, Julia. Think of sitting out on a screened porch overlooking the Atlantic and watching the sun go down."

I looked at him from under lowered brows. "More like watching the sun come *up*. Last I checked, we'd be facing east."

He laughed. "Just testing you, honey. But what do you say? Lloyd and Latisha will be back in school in a couple of weeks, and August is always a slow month. Let's rent a huge house and take everybody."

"*Who* everybody?"

"Everybody who wants to go—the Pickens family, the Bates family, Lillian and Latisha, Miss Wiggins, if you want, you, me, and Lloyd, and anybody else you want to ask."

"My word, Sam, you'd need a hotel for a crew like that."

"No, no. I've been looking online, and there're a few big houses—nice houses—still available. How many bedrooms would we need?"

"One for you and me, for sure. I'm not sharing with anybody else."

He laughed again, passed the cream pitcher to me, and thanked Lillian as she set his plate before him. "Let's count them up. I think five bedrooms would do it, though six might be better. Maybe put all the children together in one—they'd like that, wouldn't they?"

"Probably so, to start with at least. Then there'd be little feet pattering all over the house looking for their mamas. But, Sam," I went on, "August is an active hurricane month. What if we're there when a hurricane blows in?"

"Honey," Sam said, smiling with indulgence at my concern, "we'd pack up and leave long before it hit the coast. I tell you what—I'll check the Weather Channel every day and keep you fully updated."

I smiled and nodded. Then, realizing that Lillian had been noticeably silent during all this, I said, "What do you think, Lillian? Would you and Latisha like to go?"

"Yes'm, I guess we could," she said, busying herself at the sink.

"Latisha, she never seen the ocean, so she would. But me, I could pro'bly take it or leave it." Latisha, Lillian's great-grandchild, had lived with her for a number of years. Bright as a new penny and full of energy, she kept Lillian hopping, so it occurred to me that Lillian herself could use a vacation—not just days off, but a real get-out-of-town vacation. Sam's bright idea suddenly seemed made to order.

"Well, what about James?" Sam asked, bringing up the touchy subject of the man who'd worked for Sam before we married and who now cooked for Hazel Marie and Mr. Pickens. "Think he'd want to go?"

"Nobody never know what he want," Lillian mumbled as she ran water into the egg skillet.

I shook my head at Sam, warning him off. "Let's just think about James. He can be hard to get along with at times."

"That be the truth," Lillian agreed with some force.

"Well," Sam went on with unflagging enthusiasm, "the first thing we have to do is find out how many want to go. Then I'll know how big a house we'll need. I'll start with Pickens and see what he says."

"All right," I said, "but, Sam, it's awfully late in the season to be looking for a rental. So I want to say right now that if you can't find a nice one, I'm not going. I don't want to either camp out or try to make do with the dregs of the rental market."

"Oh, I agree," he said, standing. "We'll do it right or not at all." And off he went, as happy as a clam—an expression I thought appropriate for the subject at hand.

"Come sit with me, Lillian," I said. "There's still some coffee in the pot." When she'd settled at the table, I went on, "Now tell me what you really think about this bright idea."

"Well, Miss Julia, I guess goin' to the beach won't never be my first choice—they's things in that ocean. But I'll go, 'cause y'all need somebody to cook, an' Latisha never let me forget it if she don't get to go."

"No, Lillian, I'm not thinking that way. I wouldn't ask you to cook three meals a day for as many people as Sam has in mind. That wouldn't be a vacation for you at all. I expect there're plenty of good cooks who hire out by the week for renters. No, I'm talking about your going just for the rest and the fun of it."

Lillian reared back at the thought. "With somebody else in the kitchen? No'm, I don't know 'bout eatin' somebody else's cookin' while I set around watchin'. I wouldn't know what to do with myself."

"Well, let's think about it. I don't want you having to cook for an army for days on end—we'd have to bring you home on a stretcher. Let's wait and see how many Sam can talk into going. To tell the truth, it wouldn't surprise me if nobody wants to go, and if that's the case, Sam's bright idea will get dim in a hurry."

Which, to be honest, wouldn't bother me at all. Oh, I'd hate for Sam to be disappointed, but let's face it—I hadn't lost one thing at the beach. My sweet, generous Sam, with his good heart and itchy feet, was always planning a trip to somewhere. Why, he'd even been to Russia, and a year or so ago, he'd wanted to float down the Rhine, and another time he'd gotten a bee in his bonnet about looking up ancestors in Scotland. And he always wanted me to go with him, although, as should be apparent by now, I wasn't the traveling kind.

So, considering the many times I'd turned him down while urging him to pursue his dreams, I felt that I could and should agree to a beach trip. What was it—two hundred or so miles from home? I could manage that for a couple of weeks, even though I am essentially a homebound, routine-loving, day-in and day-out kind of woman.

Ah, well, I sighed. For Sam's sake I could put up with a week or so of a house full of noisy children, occasional ill tempers, wet bathing suits, lumpy mattresses, and sand tracked in everywhere.

Maybe I'd never have to do it again.

Chapter 2

I found Sam in the library, which had once been the downstairs bedroom but was now decked out in Williamsburg paint colors, floor-to-ceiling bookshelves, and eighteenth-century furniture. Reproductions, but still.

Making a note on a pad as he put down the phone, Sam looked up at me. "I think the Pickenses will go. Hazel Marie's excited about it, but she has to speak to J.D. She'll call back after they talk it over."

I nodded, but as I started to speak, the phone on the desk rang. "Hold on, honey," Sam said, as he reached for it. "It's Binkie, returning my call."

I sat on the leather Chippendale sofa, mentally counting Hazel Marie, Mr. Pickens, Lloyd, and the twin toddlers. Five of them, with Sam and me making seven. Nine if Lillian and Latisha went, eight if Lillian didn't.

As Sam's conversation with Binkie went on in the background, I thought of my curly-headed lawyer. I hadn't seen much of her lately as the estate Lloyd and I equally inherited from Wesley Lloyd Springer—my first, unfaithful and unlamented, husband—had been perking along quite well in Binkie's capable hands, especially with Sam's occasional advice. She had taken over Sam's law practice when he retired to begin his tortuous way to writing a legal history of Abbot County.

Binkie Enloe Bates was married to Coleman Bates, a sergeant in the Abbot County Sheriff's Department, a union which had begun in my living room when she had come running in soaked to the skin by a sudden summer shower. Coleman, my roomer at the time, had been smitten at once, and from all evidence I could see, remained that way. Little Gracie was their daughter.

So the Bates family would, if they accepted Sam's invitation, make three more beachgoers. Either eleven or twelve in all, still depending on Lillian's decision.

Then my thoughts drifted from one possible beachgoer to another as an image of Hazel Marie's sweet face formed in my mind. I'd seen so little of her recently, having been taken up with settling the estate of an acquaintance who'd obviously thought more of me than I had of her. Not that I'd disliked Mattie Freeman; it was just that I'd hardly thought of her at all, and to have been named executor of her will had been both shocking and remarkably time consuming. To be away from the constant concern about getting her last wishes through probate and put to rest, as she had been, was something devoutly to be desired.

But, back to Hazel Marie, as Sam's conversation with Binkie went on; what a change in that young woman. Well, not so young, unless compared to some whom we won't mention. I recalled the first time I'd seen her—knocking at my door, looking to my mind like a street harlot, as she introduced the skinny, freckled-faced urchin beside her as my recently deceased husband's only child. Lord, what a shock to my system! Wesley Lloyd Springer had been the wealthiest, most dogmatic and upright member of the First Presbyterian Church of Abbotsville—when he spoke, Pastor Ledbetter listened.

And standing right out there on my front porch was his long-time mistress and illegitimate son; and as if that hadn't been bad enough, come to find out that half the town had known of his extramarital activities. And that half had not included me—talk about having to live something down! But I'd done it, taking both mother and child under my wing and into my home and daring the town to snub either them or me. Money talks, don't you know, and Wesley Lloyd had left plenty, even when shared with Lloyd. It hadn't taken long to change a number of tunes.

Over the years, though, Hazel Marie, under my tutelage, had evolved into a classic young matron, well thought of around town, safely married, and the mother not only of Lloyd—the light of my life in spite of where he'd come from—but also of twin toddlers, courtesy of Mr. J. D. Pickens, PI, who had immeasurably improved his standing with me by adopting Lloyd.

"Julia?" Sam's voice broke into my reverie. "You all right, honey?"

"Oh. Yes, just daydreaming. What did Binkie say?"

"Well," he said, patently pleased with himself, "it just so happens that both she and Coleman have some time off coming. They were halfway planning a camping trip, but she likes the idea of going to the beach. Little Gracie is just old enough to enjoy it. So Binkie will talk to Coleman and let me know. But she said to count them in."

I laughed. "Coleman will do whatever she wants. I just hope the sheriff's department can get along without him for a few days."

"He's well thought of over there, that's for sure."

"Sam," I said, thoughtfully, so as to indicate a change of subject, "I'm a little concerned about Lillian. I don't think she wants to go, even though I assured her that it would be a vacation and not two weeks of extra work. But she knows Latisha will want to go and she doesn't want to disappoint her."

"Then let's take Latisha with us, and Lillian can have some real time off."

"What a good idea," I said, even though I'd already thought of it. "But that means we'll have to be extra careful keeping an eye on her. All the other children will have mamas and daddies watching out for them."

"We'll set some rules, and the first one will be no going to the beach alone. But, Julia, how would she do without Lillian? I doubt she's ever spent a night away from her great-granny."

"She'll have Lloyd and she adores him, and besides, we'll make sure before we leave that she really wants to go. Actually, though," I went on, thinking it through, "it'll probably be the other way around. Lillian may not be able to spend a night away from her."

"Well, see what she says. Lillian needs some time for herself, and we'll all watch Latisha. She's never any trouble when she's here, so I'm sure she'll be fine." Then with a few clicks at the computer, he said, "Come over here, honey, and let me show you what I found."

I leaned over his shoulder to view the picture of a large yellow house with white trim. "Oceanfront," Sam said, "and three, actually four, stories. Two bedroom suites on the main floor on opposite sides of the house, four suites on the second floor, and a huge dormitory room on the top floor. Oh, and there're two maid's rooms with a bath on the ground floor. See, the house sits on pilings, so the main floor is really the second. That's to get the ocean breeze through the living space and to give an ocean view over the dunes."

"Uh-huh, and to protect it from high tides and floods," I said. "Well, it certainly has plenty of room and it looks nice. But, Sam, it must cost a fortune to rent."

"Pretty much," he said, amiably enough. "But well worth it to have us all together. We used to see a lot of the Pickenses and the Bateses, but we've let too many things get in the way. Their children will be grown before we know it, and, Julia, they're our only grandchildren. I want to get to know them before they're up and gone. In fact, we ought to make a beach trip something to look forward to every year. That's something they'll grow up remembering, and I want their memories to include us."

Hearing from him what I had often thought, I leaned over a little farther and kissed his cheek.

Although Sam and I had both had previous marriages, neither of us had been blessed with children and, to tell the truth, I'd never felt shortchanged by the lack. I'd always figured that the Lord had known what He was doing and, sure enough, He had. If my marriage to Wesley Lloyd had produced a child or two, there might not have been room in my heart for his yard child. So, even though at first the sight of that little boy—he looked so much like Wesley Lloyd, you see—had turned my stomach and made me ill for weeks on end, I was finally able to see his bright mind, his generous soul, and his indomitable spirit, none of which had come from his father. Add to that the fact that Little Lloyd, as we'd called him, thought that I'd hung the sun and the moon. Who could resist such wide-eyed devotion?

As the phone rang again, Sam answered it while I returned to the sofa to await the final count. Paying no attention to the one-sided conversation, I let my mind wander to what we might be letting ourselves in for. It's a fact that the best of friends can get on one another's nerves when cooped up together for any length of time. Taken one at a time in short spurts, the company of friends can be not only tolerated, but actually enjoyed. But herd them all together in a cramped space for days on end, and we might be headed for trouble.

Mr. Pickens, for example, was one whose company I avoided when I could. I concede, however, that in the past he had always responded when I'd needed him, although he was too bullheaded to follow directions or accept suggestions even when offered with the best of intentions. But Sam thought the world of him and so did Lloyd, and deep down, I guess I did, too. He was a good man to have around in times of trouble, but he wasn't what you'd call sociable. You didn't just drop in on Mr. Pickens on a social call or for some inane chat about the state of the world. He was always waiting for your real reason for visiting to come to light, sitting there looking at you with those black eyes of his and seeing right through you, which, I suppose, is a good skill for a private detective to have. I just wished that he wouldn't use it on me.

Anyway, living for two weeks in the same house with such mixed company as Sam was collecting would be interesting to say the least. We would all have to be on our best behavior or the consequences could be dire.

So, I, for one, determined to make the best of it by being pleasant, accommodating, and easy to please, regardless. And to that end, I began to plan a number of solitary walks on the beach, several lunches out, and numerous sightseeing trips to Charleston.

Chapter 3

The back door slammed and I heard Lloyd's voice from the kitchen. "Hey, Miss Lillian. Is Mr. Sam home?"

After a few minutes of mumbled conversation with her, Lloyd came into the library wearing a green-striped polo shirt and tennis shorts, his skinny legs ending in sneakers large enough to resemble flippers. I automatically smiled as I always did—he was such a pleasure to have around. Although he would be beginning his second year as a high school student, he was still thin, freckled, and inches shorter than his contemporaries. He couldn't help what he'd inherited from his father, but his great personality and generous heart were his own—nurtured, of course, by me.

"Hey, Miss Julia, Mr. Sam," he said with a smile that brightened the room. "Mama says we might all be taking a trip to the beach. Is that right?"

"Yep, we just might," Sam said. "What do you think of it?"

"What I think is count me in. They're having a tennis tournament with some ranked players at the Isle of Palms next week, and I'd sure like to see some of the games."

"Perfect," Sam said. "That's exactly where I'm looking to rent a house."

I patted the sofa for him to sit beside me. "How's your tennis going this summer?"

"Pretty good, I guess. I've really been working 'cause I'm going to challenge for the number two spot this year. My plan is to be number one my last two years."

"I'm so proud of you for making the team at all, especially in your freshman year," I said, getting a whiff of the sweaty, grassy aroma of an active boy as he sat beside me. "We enjoyed watching your matches."

"Well," he said with a wry smile, "I sure don't intend to stay in the number four spot for long." He twisted around on the sofa and faced Sam. "When will we be going, Mr. Sam? If we go, that is?"

Sam said, "I'm just waiting to see how many of us there'll be before confirming a house. But I'm hoping we can leave this coming Sunday and stay until a day or two before school starts."

"Wow, that would be super." Turning to me with a grin, he said, "Miss Julia, is your bathing suit a one-piece or a two-piece?"

"Neither, I'll have you know. Bathing suits aren't on my agenda, nor is going in the ocean at all." I declare, Lloyd seemed to be picking up Mr. Pickens's propensity for teasing the unwary. "Besides, somebody has to be the designated lookout, watchman, or whatever, and that'll be me."

"Oh, come on, Julia," Sam said, winking at Lloyd. "You'll have to go in a little bit."

"No," I said firmly, "my days of cavorting around in the ocean in the kinds of bathing suits they sell nowadays are over. Not," I added, "that they'd ever begun."

Lloyd and Sam started laughing. "Cavorting?" Sam said. "Honey, I'd love to see you cavorting in the ocean."

"Me, too," Lloyd said, then stopped laughing long enough to ask, "What is cavorting, anyway? I mean, what do you do when you cavort?"

"Look it up," I said, brushing back his sun-bleached hair. "I'm certainly not going to demonstrate. Now," I went on, rising from the sofa, "since you two are in such a teasing mood, I'm going to go talk to Lillian."

As soon as I stepped into the kitchen, Lillian turned and said, "Miss Julia?" just as I said, "Lillian?" We laughed at ourselves, as I pulled out a chair from the kitchen table.

"Come sit with me, Lillian. Sam has made a suggestion that I want to run by you."

"Yes'm, an' I got one, too." She hung a washrag on the spigot and came to sit at the table. "See, Miss Julia, I been holdin' off on tellin' you 'cause I know you need me here. But if y'all don't need me to go to that beach with you, then I can get it done without takin' extra time off."

"Get what done? Lillian, are you having a problem?"

"No more'n I been havin', but the doctor, he say I got to go ahead an' do it or I'm gonna get crippled, which I just about already am."

I was stunned. "Crippled? Lillian, what in the world?"

"It's this ole bunion what's been botherin' me for years, an' he say it got to come off." She stuck out her left foot for me to see, although I'd long known that every left-foot shoe she owned had a slit along the side of it. I'd never thought much of it since she also wore down the heels of both shoes, so that they became, more or less, like the currently popular flip-flops.

"Oh, for goodness' sakes," I said. "Of course you must have it done. You should've told me before it got so bad. Just what has your doctor told you?"

"Well, the doctor, he say he do it in Day Surgery, so I don't have to stay in the hospital, but he say I might not wanta do much walkin' for a day or two. Then he gonna put on what he call a walkin' cask, so I can get around a little. But, Miss Julia, that won't be no help with Latisha. With her around, I'd need me a runnin' cask. That's why I been waitin' for school to start 'fore lettin' him operate so she be outta the house most of the day."

"Oh, Lillian, you should've told me. You could've already had it done. But that settles it. I'm not going to the beach. I'm going to stay right here and look after you and Latisha. Or, even better, we'll send Latisha to the beach with Sam, and I'll be your nurse."

"Miss Julia," Lillian said, glancing away, "I don't wanta hurt your feelin's, but I jus' as soon you go on to the beach an' let Miss Bessie do my nursin'. She already say she bring some meals an' help me get aroun' for the first few days, an' she try to keep her eye on Latisha, too. So I jus' as soon have her help out, if it's all the same to you."

"Well, if that's the case and if you're sure, then here's another proposition. You call the doctor and set up a time right away to have it done—the sooner the better, because I want to take you to the hospital. Then if you'll have Miss Bessie to look in on you, Sam and I will take Latisha to the beach, and that will give you almost two weeks to get back on your feet. Literally."

Lillian lowered her eyes, but I thought I saw the glint of tears. "I don't know, Miss Julia. Latisha, she be a handful, an' I hate for her to be actin' up and ruinin' ev'rybody's vacation."

"Listen," I said, putting my hand on her arm. "It would be a pleasure to take Latisha to see the ocean for the first time, and she is always perfectly behaved when she's here with us. Besides," I went on with a smile, "who in the world would dream of acting up with Mr. J. D. Pickens and Sergeant Coleman Bates around?"

"Well, that be the truth," Lillian said, a smile playing around her mouth. "Mr. Pickens, when he swivel them black eyes on you, you straighten up an' fly right. Maybe they work on Latisha, too."

"I have no doubt that they will. Even I watch my p's and q's around him. Okay, Lillian, it's settled. Set up your appointment, pack Latisha's things, and she'll go to the beach while you recuperate from your bunionectomy. This is going to work out for everybody, and I'm going to tell Sam that he should have more bright ideas like this one."

"Yes'm, 'cept I hope I don't have to have no more operations when he have another one."

On my way back to the library I met Lloyd on his way out. "I'm going home to start packing," he said. "This is the best idea yet, and I can't wait."

"Well, hold on a minute," I said. "I've just learned that Lillian has to have a bunion removed from her foot, so she's going to have that done while we're gone. That means we'll be taking Latisha with us. Is that all right with you? She loves you to death, you know, and she'll probably make every step you make the whole time."

"Aw," he said, grinning, "I don't mind. She can chase balls while I hit 'em. Besides, I could give her some lessons, too. I'll take an extra racket for her. Oh, and," he went on as if he'd just thought of something, "Latisha can help me collect shells for Mama. She just bought a hot-glue gun for her crafts, and J.D. says it's a worse menace in her hands than an Uzi."

"Well, whatever," I said, unsure of the reference. "But looking for shells will give Latisha something to do and keep her busy. I expect, though, she'll want to tag after you wherever you go. So if it gets to be too much, let me know and we'll find something for her to do. Maybe," I said, thinking it through, "I could take her shopping for school clothes. That would be fun, wouldn't it?"

"Maybe for her, but I'll pass. But, Miss Julia, is Miss Lillian gonna be all right? I kinda hate to go off if she's having an operation."

"Yes, it worries me, too. I offered to stay and be her nurse, but for some reason she seems to prefer Miss Bessie—that's a friend who lives down the street from her. I really can't understand it, but, let's face it, my cooking repertoire is quite limited, and Miss Bessie is an excellent cook."

"I'm sure that's it, Miss Julia," Lloyd said. "I expect Lillian's looking forward to some good eating. Besides, she'd probably rather have you looking after Latisha than serving her tuna-fish sandwiches every day."

"Oh, you," I said, smiling. "I can do better than that." But, I mentally conceded, not a whole lot better. It behooved me to be content with Latisha-sitting and leave Lillian's care in the hands of a better cook.

"Julia," Sam said as I went back to the library and before I could tell him about Lillian, "do you realize how hard it can be to do something nice for some people? Both Pickens and Coleman are up in arms insisting that they contribute to the rental. And I don't want them to. It's my idea, and I want to do it. Yet they both say they won't go if they can't help. And all I wanted was to do something nice for them and their families."

"Well, Sam, here's a solution for that. You take care of the house and tell those two that they're responsible for the food. Maybe they can each take everybody out one evening while we're there. By the time they pay for eleven or twelve shrimp dinners, they'll feel they've contributed plenty."

Sam laughed. "And they can go grocery shopping to stock the kitchen for breakfast and lunch. Good idea, Julia, that'll make them feel they're pulling their weight, all right."

With that settled, I told him about Lillian's upcoming bunionectomy and how our trip to the beach would give her time to recuperate. "So," I concluded, "Latisha is ours for the next couple of weeks. I just hope we're not biting off more than we can chew."

Chapter 4

Ever since Sam had mentioned asking Etta Mae Wiggins to go with us, I'd been going back and forth about it. It would be the perfect way to repay her in some small way for all she'd done for me. Besides, I enjoyed her company. On the other hand, though, I didn't know how she'd feel being the only single woman among a group of couples. And I feared that it would be too easy to saddle her with babysitting, or, at least, that she would feel that looking after children was the reason she'd been asked.

But, finally, I decided to run the risks and ask her. I would just have to keep an eye out and see to it that she didn't become the live-in nanny. Not, I assure you, that Hazel Marie and Binkie would deliberately take advantage of her, but then again, as willing to be helpful as Etta Mae was, it would be easy to do. I'd have to see that it didn't happen.

So I called her. "Etta Mae? It's Julia Murdoch. How are you?"

"Oh, Miss Julia!" she said, sounding just as happy as she usually did to hear from me. "I'm fine, but how are you? Is everything okay?"

The question saddened me in that it indicated that the only reason I would call would be if I needed something from her.

"Everything's fine, Etta Mae. I just wanted to tell you that Sam and I, and a few others, are going to the beach for a couple of weeks, and we'd love for you to go with us. Would you be able to take time off from work? We're leaving this Sunday, and I know it's short notice, but that's the way Sam does things. Would you like to go?"

"Would I like to go!" she exclaimed. "Oh, my goodness, yes. I'd *love* to go! Wait a minute, let me pull off to the side of the road. I'm in the car on my way to the next patient. Hold on a minute."

Etta Mae was a licensed practical nurse or a nurse's aide or a trained-on-the-job employee—I wasn't sure which—of the Handy Home Helpers and made in-home visits to shut-ins and the elderly.

"There," she said into the phone. "I'm parked now. Do you really mean it? You want me to go with you?"

"I certainly do mean it. Etta Mae, Sam is renting a huge house with enough room for an army. Hazel Marie and her family are going and so are Binkie and Coleman and their little girl. Oh, and Lloyd and Latisha, but Lillian has to have a bunion removed, so she won't be going. Do you think you could put up with a crew like that?"

"Could I ever! And I could help, too. I mean, with the cooking and the children and whatever else you need."

"No, Etta Mae, I'm not asking you for that. I'm asking you to go as our guest."

"Your guest," she said, almost in wonder. Then she heaved a deep sigh. "That's about the nicest thing I've ever heard. But, Miss Julia, I can't. I really appreciate it, but I just can't go."

"You can't get the time off?"

"Oh," she said, somewhat ruefully, "I'd *take* the time if that's all it was. No, you remember me telling you about Miss Irene Cassidy? Well, she died a few days ago."

"I'm sorry to hear that," I said, recalling the fragile diabetic patient who had so concerned Etta Mae with her promise to leave something to her in her will. "But why should that stop you?"

"Well, her funeral is at the end of next week—Friday, I think— and I feel I oughta go. Well, actually, I go to the funerals of all my patients. The ones that die, that is. They're putting off the funeral until next week to give a relative time to get here. He's overseas or something."

"That's very thoughtful of you, Etta Mae. I'm sure the family will appreciate your being there. But, listen, we'll be staying for two weeks. So why don't you plan to leave from the funeral and drive on down? That'll give you more than a week to lie on the beach and eat all the seafood you want."

She didn't say anything for a few seconds, and I gave her time to think about it. "Would it be all right if I did that? I mean to come in the middle of your vacation?"

"Of course. By that time we'll probably be sick of each other, so your charming self would be most welcome."

She laughed. "Uh-huh, I bet."

"Maybe I shouldn't ask this," I said, assuming that Etta Mae's obligation to go to the funeral was because she was a beneficiary of her patient's will. "But have you heard what Mrs. Cassidy left you in her will? I hope it was something lovely and something you have no qualms about accepting."

"No'm, nobody's said anything, but Miss Irene's sister went to the lawyer's office right after she picked out a casket. I know, because I drove her there. And picked her up afterward, and all she talked about was getting that relative home so they could get things divided up. I think, Miss Julia, it's exactly the way you said, that Miss Irene meant to do it but forgot it. Or just had second thoughts.

"But it doesn't matter," she went on as if the world had suddenly settled on her shoulders. "Whatever she did or didn't do shouldn't affect what I do, and I'll go to her funeral out of respect."

That, I thought to myself, was the voice of someone who'd been disappointed too many times.

"Well," I said briskly, "we'll count on you joining us sometime next Friday evening. Let's check in with each other the day before, so we'll know what time to expect you. And I'll ask Sam to text you the address. You have our phone numbers. Now, Etta Mae, no matter what happens, I want to see you at that house on the beach. I will be mightily disappointed if you don't get there."

She laughed a little. "I'll try my best, and thank you, Miss Julia. I'm so excited I can hardly stand it." Then she added, "Man alive! A trip to the beach!"

After hanging up, I decided that I was going to see to it that Etta Mae had a vacation she'd never forget. Then, before I forgot about it, I went to tell Sam that we had another beachgoer, albeit one who'd be there only half the time, and that I hoped he'd meant it when he said to invite anyone I wanted.

He had, because he was delighted that Etta Mae would be joining us. "Oh, good," he said, "I *like* Etta Mae."

"Sweetheart," I said, smiling at him, "you like everybody."

"Hazel Marie?" I whispered when she answered the phone. I was in our bedroom upstairs, not too far down the hall from the office where Sam was working on his book. "Can you talk?"

"Yes, I think so," she whispered back. "Why, what is it?" Then, as if suddenly realizing how odd my question had been, she said, "But, Miss Julia, nobody but me can hear you over here."

"Oh, I know," I said, speaking up. "I just don't want anybody on your end to hear what you say."

"Well, nobody's around right now. Granny Wiggins and the little girls are out in the yard. She's trying to tire them out enough for a nap. What is it, Miss Julia? Is anything wrong?"

"No, not wrong, exactly. It's just something I'd prefer not to share with half the town." I took a deep breath and plunged ahead. "Hazel Marie, I don't have a thing to wear at the beach and, furthermore, I don't even know what to buy. I need your help."

"Oh!" she said, perking right up. "You want to go shopping?"

"Not particularly, but I have to. Will you go with me? I don't even know what I'll need, but I have a feeling it's going to be nothing that I'll want."

She laughed. "Well, you'll need sundresses or at least short-sleeved dresses, a couple of bathing suits, and some pants and shorts—"

"Stop right there. No shorts. And no sundresses or bathing suits, either. I don't plan to go in the ocean or to expose myself unnecessarily. Think of something else, Hazel Marie." What no one seemed to understand was that as age had crept up, certain areas of my body had crept down. I had no desire to make those areas open for public viewing.

But when it came to problem areas and helpful beauty aids of any kind, Hazel Marie had solutions for every situation. "I know just what you need," she said. "And the look is quite fashionable now. It'll be perfect for you."

"I'm almost afaid to ask."

"We'll find you some capris. You know, they're pants, but usually fairly loose and they're longer than shorts but shorter than long pants. They'll be perfect for everyday wear and for wading in the ocean. If you're so inclined."

"I'm not. But what do you wear with them? I tell you, Hazel Marie, I cannot wear those sleeveless, low-cut, tight-fitting T-shirts that I see all over town."

"Well, you're in luck there, too," Hazel Marie said. "Everything is loose and flowing now, some even with sleeves. You can wear those on the beach and out to dinner, or anywhere. Another possibility would be some mid-calf leggings. . . ."

"No leggings, Hazel Marie."

"Well, not leggings, exactly, but capris with narrow legs. Wear them with a tunic top, and all you'd need for a really good look would be a couple of pairs of sandals."

"No flip-flops."

"Okay," she said, laughing. "You can get plain sandals for the beach, but you'll be amazed at how fancy sandals can be today. You'll love them. But you'll need a pedicure, Miss Julia, something up-to-date and colorful that you might not wear on your fingernails. You should go shopping first, then you'll know what color to get."

"They Lord," I said with a roll of my eyes which she couldn't see. Then, sighing in defeat, I asked, "Would you mind going with me, Hazel Marie? I don't even know where to start."

"Sure, let's go first thing in the morning. I know just the shop you need, so it won't take long to have you decked out for the beach. But go ahead and make a pedi appointment for tomorrow afternoon, and you'll be all set."

Set. Yes, I thought, but for what? I was not looking forward either to shopping for the beach or to the beach itself. But, for Sam and for our nominal grandchildren, I would brace myself and do as I always did under less than optimum conditions—grit my teeth and get through it.

"Oh, *Julia!*" LuAnne Conover wailed my name as soon as I answered the phone. It was late afternoon, not long before Lillian would call us to dinner, and I'd already planned an early bedtime to prepare myself for the morrow's shopping trip.

"LuAnne? What's wrong?" Not that I particularly wanted to know because LuAnne was forever finding molehills that exercised her out of all proportion.

"Oh, Julia, you won't believe this. *I* don't believe it, but I have to because it's been thrown in my face. Oh, Julia, I have to talk to you. You're the only one who'll understand. Can I come over? I can't talk about it on the phone."

"Yes, of course. But, LuAnne, it's almost dinnertime. Don't you want to wait for a better time?"

"*I can't wait!* I'm at my wit's end. I have to talk to you, to *some*body, *any*body, or I'll go crazy."

"Well, don't do that. Come on over and we'll talk."

She blew her nose, sniffed, then said, "I don't want Lillian or Sam or Lloyd or anybody else you have going in and out of your house hearing it."

I took a deep breath, blew it out, and said, "LuAnne, Sam *lives* here. Lillian works here, and Lloyd is always welcome. I can't very well turn them out."

"Oh, I know," she said, offhandedly. "But I don't want any of them to hear a word, although . . ." She broke down and sobbed. ". . . everybody already knows, and it's killing me, Julia. It's just killing me."

And she sounded as if it really was. "Oh, LuAnne, honey, you want me to come to you? I can be there in fifteen minutes."

"No, don't do that. I have to get out of here. I'm on my way, but, Julia, find a place where we can talk without anybody hearing us."

LuAnne and her long-retired, game-show-watching husband, Leonard, had joined the downsizing fad a few years back and lived now in a cramped condo up on the side of the mountain. It had a view, but to my mind that was all that recommended it, especially since Leonard was underfoot all day, every day. Why, once when a criminal was on the loose and the sheriff issued a shelter-in-place lockdown order, Leonard was already in compliance.

The more I thought of LuAnne's distress on the phone, the more disturbed I became. Knowing that it would take a few minutes for her to get into town and to my house, I hurriedly walked upstairs to let Sam know what to expect when she came.

"We'll talk in the library, Sam, and I know she'll want the door closed. So just go ahead and eat dinner if she stays that long, and—I hate to ask this—but you and Lillian better stay out of sight. LuAnne is really upset."

Sam smiled. "I'll sneak from room to room in my stocking feet. She won't know I'm around. But, Julia, what do you think is wrong?"

"I don't have a clue. But you know how LuAnne is—she can get upset over things that aren't worth a hill of beans to anybody else. But from the way she sounded . . . well, I don't know. I keep thinking of the boy who cried wolf, and I don't want to ignore the possibility that LuAnne's wolf might be real this time."

Chapter 5

When I opened the door for LuAnne, my first thought was that this time the wolf was indeed real. She was a wreck, her face tear-streaked and stricken looking, her hands trembling, and instead of openly crying, she whimpered with each shuddering breath.

Although we actually had little in common as far as interests went, LuAnne and I had been friends for as long as I'd lived in Abbotsville. She was a short, full-breasted woman who made it her business to know everything about everybody, and to tell it to anybody who would listen. Yet she was also kindhearted, the first one at the door of anyone who was ill or who had suffered a loss. I thought the world of her, but I will admit that a little of her company went a long way.

I reached out to her and drew her in. "Come in, LuAnne. Let's go to the library."

"Is anyone . . . ?"

"Don't worry about it. Sam and Lillian are in the kitchen, and all the doors are closed."

I led her down the hall, past the closed doors of the living room, dining room, back hall to the kitchen, and downstairs bathroom, and into the library. Then I closed that door behind us.

"Sit right here," I said, aiming her for the sofa near the fireplace. I sat beside her and took her hands in mine. "Tell me what's wrong. You look as if the world has come to an end."

"Mine has," she said, her lips trembling as the floodgates opened. I dashed across the room to the desk for a box of Kleenex.

Waiting as the tears streamed down her face, I saw her shoulders hunching over as deep sobs shook her body. I was moved in spite of myself. Not that I'm that skeptical or lacking in compassion, but I had been through too many of LuAnne's agonies before this. And as often as not, just as I would begin to sympathize with her for whatever subject she was then exercised over, she would suddenly drop it as if it had never bothered her. I'd finally learned my lesson and had more recently taken her sudden upsets with large grains of salt. The more upset she became over some small slight or careless word, the less credence I gave her response to it.

But this. This was different. She was shaken to her core. Was she ill? Terminally ill? Or was Leonard? Had the vagaries of the stock market wiped them out? Was foreclosure looming ahead?

"Oh, Julia!" she wailed, leaning her head on my shoulder. "Only you will understand. But don't tell anybody, please, please, don't tell anybody. Except . . . except everybody already knows!"

"Knows what?" I took her shoulders and straightened her so that she had to look at me. "What does everybody know, because I don't."

She sniffed loudly and wetly. I handed her a Kleenex and when she'd used it, she said, "Well, maybe you don't. You didn't even know about Wesley Lloyd."

"Wesley Lloyd? What does he have to do with it? He's been dead and gone for years."

"I know," she said, sniffing again. "That's why you're the only one I can talk to. You've been through it, and although I thought you were crazy at the time, at least you survived. I don't think I will." And the tears started again.

Oh, my goodness. Was she telling me that Leonard, *Leonard Conover*, was doing what Wesley Lloyd had done and gotten himself *involved*? Impossible to imagine, even as I tried to visualize Leonard Conover in the throes of passion. And failed.

"Julia," LuAnne said, dabbing at her face with the Kleenex, "I've always believed that the wife always knows. If she doesn't do anything about it, it's because she doesn't *want* to know. But that's not true, is it? You really didn't suspect Wesley Lloyd, did you? I mean, even if he was losing interest in . . . you know. Because I thought Leonard was just getting older and, to tell the truth, it suited me fine. I mean, after a certain age, the less the better, don't you think?"

"Well, I guess," I said, hedging as I thought of my steady Sam. But she was absolutely right when it came to Wesley Lloyd Springer. I recalled the sense of relief I'd felt as his demands became less and less frequent. I had assumed that tapering off was merely the natural course of a long marriage. That's the way it had been for me but, as I later learned, not for him.

"But, LuAnne," I said, "I can't believe that Leonard has, well, you know."

"Well, believe it, because he has." LuAnne was beginning to get over her spasms of grief. She sat up straighter, wiped her face again, and said, "I'd like to wring his neck. After all I've done for him—cooking and washing and cleaning and encouraging and going to church and keeping up with our social obligations and buying his clothes and paying the bills. . . . Why, Julia, if it hadn't been for me, we'd have nothing! I mean, the man has no ambition, no get-up-and-go, no drive to get anywhere in life. You know that. Everybody knows it."

I nodded, because I did know it. Leonard Conover was the epitome of a nonentity. The only social skill he had was showing up on time when he was supposed to be somewhere, and that was because LuAnne got him there. I had often wondered at the differences between the two of them, but had assumed that his silent fade into the background was because LuAnne more than made up for it with her outgoing and relentless personality.

The tears had begun streaming down LuAnne's face again as tremors shook her body. Between sobs, she said, "I've given my whole life to this marriage, and, Julia, this is how he treats me. I can never hold my head up again. Everybody will be laughing. *At me!* Not at him. Oh, no, they always laugh at the one who's hurt, not the one who does the hurting. Oh, Julia, I don't know what to do!"

"Well, wait, LuAnne," I said, trying to make some sense of her predicament. "Let's look at this reasonably. First of all, are you sure? It could just be gossip with no truth to it at all."

"*I wish!*" she shrieked, making the hair on my head stand up. "He *told* me, Julia! He *admitted* it! Just came right out and said he needed *solace*! Can you believe that? He throws me away for *solace*!"

That was a new one on me. As many reasons as there might be for looking beyond one's own bedroom, solace, comfort, or consolation wouldn't normally head the list. Unless, of course, a dull, ineffectual man was married to a whirlwind like LuAnne.

"Go back to the beginning, LuAnne. Did he just come out with this announcement, like, over breakfast? I mean, what brought the subject up?"

"He told me because I asked, that's what happened and, no, it was over lunch—which I, as usual, had made for him. And served it to him on a TV tray so he wouldn't miss reruns of *Cops* on Spike or whatever he was watching." LuAnne mopped at her face, blew her nose, and went on. "It started with a phone call. I answered as I always do, and this woman whispered, *whispered*, Julia, in a hoarse-sounding voice, 'Why don't you let him go? He's no use to you. He gives it all to me and has for years and years.' Then she hung up." LuAnne sniffed, loud and long. "I was stunned. I couldn't believe I'd heard it right. But as I stood there with the mayonnaise knife in my hand, I knew I *had* heard it right. So I marched right into the living room and told Leonard. And I *laughed*! Can you believe that? I laughed because I didn't believe it and thought somebody was playing a joke. Or had gotten a wrong number. Or something."

"What did he say?"

"He just mumbled something like, 'She shouldna done that.' And I just stood there and said, 'What? *What!*' Because it hit me then that he *knew* who'd called and wasn't all that surprised. He said, 'I'll tell her not to call again.' Now doesn't that just beat all? And I said, '*Who?* Who're you going to tell not to call again?' And all this time he'd not taken his eyes off the television, but then he glanced up at me—he was still in his recliner and I was standing over him—and he said, 'A friend. Just a longtime friend.' And I screamed, '*Longtime? How* long? And how much of a friend is she? And what does she give you that I don't?' That's when he said *solace*. And sorta tacked on at the end that it had nothing to do with me, and he'd make sure she didn't call again. Oh, Julia, I am devastated. Just devastated. How am I going to live with this? He didn't say anything about giving her up, much less offering an apology." She blotted her face again and went on. "Not that I would've accepted it, but the gall, Julia. The *gall*! It was as if he expected me to just go along with it because, I guess, I had one job—feeding and looking after him—and she had another. And never the twain should meet. Or something like that."

By this time I was almost as shaken as LuAnne. Who would've suspected such complacent arrogance from Leonard Conover? I couldn't wait to tell Sam. He'd be shocked.

It was time for me to say something but, I declare, I was barely able to think. In some ways, I was reliving the shock to my system when I'd learned of Wesley Lloyd's faithlessness, recalling how I'd regretted that he was where I couldn't get my hands on him. Dead and buried, maddeningly safe from the slings and arrows of a spurned and humiliated wife.

But Leonard was still around, and outrage and indignation for LuAnne's sake welled up in me. "You *can't* just live with it, LuAnne," I said. "I mean, now that you know about it. But one question: When does he see her? As far as I know he's pretty much of a homebody."

"Oh, he goes out occasionally. Every Thursday, he goes to lunch with some people he used to work with. Then he goes to the library. *Library*, ha! He just lugs books back and forth. I've never seen him read them." LuAnne clasped her hands in her lap. "But, see, Julia, *I* go out all the time. I'm always home at mealtimes because that's my job, but now I see that I really don't know what he does when I'm gone."

I nodded, for that was true. LuAnne volunteered for any number of good causes, mostly, I'd always assumed, because she was bored to death at home. As who wouldn't be with Leonard ensconced in a recliner with the remote in his hand?

"So what're you going to do?" I asked softly and with great sympathy. "Binkie is a good lawyer if you want to talk to her. And Mr. Ernest Sitton is, too, if Binkie is too close a friend."

"I don't know. I can't even think. All I know is that I can't go back there. Julia," she said, grabbing my hand and looking at me with eyes gone wide and wild, "I might kill him."

And I believed her. As impetuous as I knew LuAnne to occasionally be, I believed her. So at that point, I opened my mouth and said something that I lived to regret.

Chapter 6

"Why don't you go to the beach with us?" I said, and at her raised eyebrows, went on. "We're leaving Sunday for a couple of weeks at the Isle of Palms. Listen, LuAnne, it will get you away for a while and give you a chance to decide what you want to do." And also, I thought but didn't say, prevent you from committing great bodily harm on Leonard, thereby keeping you out of jail.

"I didn't know you were going to the beach." LuAnne gave me a hurt look as if I'd been keeping something from her.

"It just came up. Sam decided that he wanted to get everybody together and go somewhere before school starts."

"Everybody?" she asked. "Who all's going?"

"Oh, the Pickens family and the Bates family and Lloyd, of course. And Latisha because Lillian needs some time off."

"Then you don't want me tagging along. You'll have your hands full entertaining everybody. And I don't want to end up sleeping on a sofa."

I suppressed a sigh of exasperation. "Several things, LuAnne. First, I don't intend to be entertaining anybody. They'll all be on their own. We may have a few meals together, but other than that, everybody will entertain themselves. And Sam is renting a large house with six bedroom suites. You won't be sleeping on a sofa.

"Look, LuAnne, the best thing you can do right now is to get away from it all. That way you'll be able to weigh your options and decide what you want to do."

"But what will I do between now and Sunday? I can't go home. I can't spend four more days with him." She shuddered. "Or four more nights, either."

"You can stay here," I said, wondering just how deep I was getting in. "Lloyd won't be using his room. He'll be busy packing and helping his mother get the twins ready for the trip." Lloyd essentially had two homes, his mother's and mine, and he came and went between them as he wanted.

"Well," LuAnne said, almost as a child putting up one excuse after another, "I can't just stay. I don't have any clothes with me."

"You'll have to go home and get them. Obviously," I said, almost as a mother parrying the excuses. "You can do that. Just go home, get what you'll need for the next several weeks, and get out of there. And at the same time, you can tell Leonard that he's on his own. You don't want to leave without telling him. He might report you as a missing person."

"Huh!" she said. "He won't even notice till it's time to eat. But, Julia," she went on as she raised another objection, "what if he has that woman come in while I'm gone?"

"All the more you'll have to use against him, if it comes to that."

"But I don't *want* her in my house. It's my *home*! The only one I have." And the tears gushed out again.

"That's why you need to get away and decide what's best for you, LuAnne. But here's another thing," I went on, consumed now with curiosity. "Who *is* she?"

"That's just the thing!" she cried. "I can't imagine who it is. He never goes anywhere to meet anybody. And, let's face it, Julia, he's no great catch—he's seventy-eight years old, he's all out of shape, he has no conversation to speak of, and he has no interests and no opinions, and frankly, he's boring. I mean, who in the world would want him?"

I'd been asking myself the same thing.

"Well, here's something else," I said. "How long has it been going on? If it's a recent thing, it could just be the last fling of an aging man. For reassurance purposes, don't you know. And if that's the case and you *want* him back, I expect something like getting away for a few days would be all you'd need to do. But that's for you to decide."

"I can't decide anything right now," she said, leaning back against the sofa. "I'm just overwhelmed with it all. But," she went on, sitting up, "you're right, Julia. I need to find out how long it's been going on and who she is. I need to know what I'm up against. And," she said, getting to her feet, "I'm going to find out right now. I'm going back up there and give him a chance to come clean and ask forgiveness. And then, I'm going to hold my head up high in this town if it kills me, and, besides, it's the Christian thing to do, isn't it?"

"Well, backing him into a corner might not be a good idea. Why don't you—"

"No," she said firmly, "why should I have to leave my home? *He's* the one in the wrong, so why should I have to move out? He can either admit everything or he can leave and move in with *her*. We'll see how she likes *that*."

"LuAnne, I'm not sure about giving him ultimatums. They could backfire on you, especially since you're up in the air about what *you* want."

"I'm not up in the air about anything. I want my home, and I want him out of it. And I want her name, and I want a complete admission—dates, times, frequency, and how much he's spent on her. I want it all, Julia, because otherwise I'll never be able to hold my head up in this town again.

"Anyway," she said with a huge sigh, "thank you, Julia, for listening and understanding. I feel better now. I'm going back to our condo on the mountain—where, I remind you, he promised me we'd have a lovely retirement—and I'm going to have it out with him."

"Well, if you're sure," I said, standing with her. "But both invitations stand. You're welcome to come here for the next few days and to go to the beach with us."

After seeing LuAnne out with, I admit, some doubt as to the wisdom of what she was planning to do, I hurried to the kitchen. I found Sam still at the kitchen table, half of a slice of apple pie in front of him as he turned a page of the newspaper.

"Lillian's gone?" I asked.

"Yes, she called her doctor as you suggested, and he wanted to see her right away. But, Julia, that old car of hers is in bad shape— took forever for the engine to turn over. We need to do something about that, but, here," he said, standing, "she left a plate in the oven for you. Come sit down. I'll get it."

"I'm worried about her car, too. But stay where you are. I'll get it. I'm not even sure I can eat anything. Oh, Sam, you're not going to believe what's happened. I'm so upset about it." But not so upset that I was unable to retrieve my plate from the oven, pour a glass of tea, sit at the table, and begin devouring my long-delayed dinner.

Sam smiled, put down the paper, and said, "Take your time. I might not believe what's happened to LuAnne, but then I rarely believe everything I hear."

"Well, prepare yourself, because this is going to shake you. Leonard Conover is having an affair."

Sam's eyebrows went straight up. "I don't believe it."

I had to laugh, but abruptly stopped when he frowned and said, "But you know, I did hear a few rumors some years ago. I discounted them and never gave it much thought after that."

"Years ago? And you didn't tell me?"

"As I said, I didn't believe it then and find it hard to believe now."

"I know. I'm the same way. But, Sam, some woman called LuAnne and told her to give him up, and when LuAnne confronted him, he as much as admitted it. Said he needed *solace*. Can you believe that?"

"I'll take the Fifth, if I may. But when I think of what it might be like to live with LuAnne, solace makes a strange kind of sense. And I *like* LuAnne."

"I know you do, and I'm counting on it. Because I've invited her to stay here with us until we leave Sunday. And then go on to the beach with us." I gave him a sideways glance to see how he would take that announcement. "See," I hurried on, "she really needs to get away so she can think clearly. And everybody will be so busy going to and from the beach and watching out for children that one more person won't make a difference. I know I should've talked to you first, but . . ."

"Honey, you don't need my permission for anything you want to do. And, of course, she's welcome to come here and to go with us if she wants to. But, listen, don't leave me hanging. Who is this remarkable woman who's able to lure Leonard away from the television?"

"Nobody knows! I mean, I don't, and LuAnne doesn't, although she thinks everybody's talking about it." I leaned forward, hoping he had the answer. "When you heard those rumors years ago, who was he supposed to be seeing?"

"I'm not sure a name was ever mentioned. I have a vague recollection that it was somebody who worked with him. In the same office or area or something. Work related, anyway. But don't go on that, Julia. Obviously it wasn't important enough to stick, and it was a long time ago."

Leonard had been retired for so long that I could barely remember what he'd done when he wasn't. Some civil service job, I thought. Local civil service—that is, a county job in the annex to the courthouse, it seemed to me.

"That would make sense though," I agreed, nodding, "because, really, he never went anywhere but to work, and when he went out socially, it was always with LuAnne. It would be hard to connect, unnoticed, with another woman in a social setting. I mean, of the kind we have."

"Right," Sam said, smiling, "no one could accuse us of being a fast crowd, could they? Where's LuAnne now?"

"She's gone home to confront him and demand some answers. She wants to know *who* and *for how long*. And, Sam, she seemed to have herself well in hand when she left, but the more I think about it, the more concerned I get. At one point, she threatened to kill him. What if I just let her go and she actually *does* it?"

"Oh, I doubt it'll come to that. If anything, she'll give him a good tongue-lashing. Which he deserves and which will make her feel better. Because, let's face it, Julia, I doubt she has too many options, financially speaking. She'll realize that, and, as likely as not, they'll have it out with each other, and it'll all blow over."

I smiled at my sunny, optimistic husband who always kept me anchored with his plain good sense. And hoped he was right.

Chapter 7

"Oh, by the way," Sam said, "I confirmed that house—the one I showed you online. And everybody's on board to go. Your suggestion about the food makes them feel they're contributing."

"Well, good. And we leave Sunday?"

"Yep, we can't get the house keys till three that afternoon. If we leave no later than midmorning, we can stop for lunch in Columbia, and get there in plenty of time for a swim before dark."

"Hmm," I said, laying my knife and fork across my plate, then realized that I was signaling only myself. So I got up and began clearing the table. "I can't wait. But, seriously, Sam, this is an extraordinarily generous thing you're doing. And I'm looking forward to it."

Just as I'd rinsed my plate and put it in the dishwasher, the doorbell rang. Glancing at Sam, I murmured, "Oh, my," and hurried to answer it.

LuAnne, tear streaked and pitiful looking, stood there on the porch surrounded by three suitcases, two full shopping bags, and an armful of hanging clothes. It must've taken her five trips between her car at the curb and my front door.

"Oh, LuAnne," I said. "Come in. Come on in, honey. Just leave everything. Sam will take your bags upstairs."

"No, I'll take them. I can't face Sam. I can't face anybody. Please don't let him see me." And with that, she picked up one suitcase and, loaded down with it and the armful of clothes, she headed for the stairs. There was nothing for it but that I follow her with another heavy suitcase and one of the shopping bags filled with shoes. And make another trip for the rest of her things after getting her settled in Lloyd's room.

"Make yourself at home, LuAnne," I said, holding my back

after that last trip up the stairs. "The bathroom is right through there, and there's plenty of room in the closet. Now, have you had supper?"

"No, but I can't eat," she said, sitting on the side of the bed, her hands clasped in her lap. "I just want to go to bed and try to forget it all."

"That might be the best thing, but it's barely seven o'clock and still light outside. You'll be awake before sunup. Come on downstairs and sit with Sam and me." As she started shaking her head, I went on. "You might as well face it now. You can't avoid him for the next few days or when you ride with us to the beach. Come on, LuAnne. Let's see some of that high head holding we've been talking about."

She managed a smile at that, but said, "I'm going to take a sleeping pill and sleep for twelve hours straight. That's all I want to do—sleep for twelve hours and forget it all."

"Well, that's understandable, I guess. But, LuAnne, did you talk to Leonard? Did you find out who the woman is?"

She seemed to scrunch up into a ball, as the tears started again. "He wasn't there. He's with her, whoever she is."

I blinked, thinking that she was probably right. But I said, "Not necessarily. I expect he went out to get something to eat. Which means he's already missing you. Now, listen, LuAnne," I said in a bossy way because I knew she needed a firm hand, "I'm going to bring you something to eat, then you can crawl into bed and sleep as long as you like."

The shower turned off just as I returned with a tuna-fish sandwich and a glass of iced tea. Placing the tray on a bedside table, I noticed a small bottle half full of pills beside the lamp. *Take one for sleep*, I read on the label and wondered if she'd already taken that one.

When she came out of the bathroom, she was ready for bed in a long, cotton gown that looked as used as some of mine.

"Oh, Julia, you shouldn't have," she said, eyeing the sandwich. "I'm just not hungry."

"I know, but try a little. You can't sleep on an empty stomach."

"Well, I'll try, but not too much. It might keep the pill from working. Or maybe I should take another one after I eat, just in case." Then she yawned, but managed to go on. "I just want to sleep and forget it all. These pictures keep running through my mind—you know, pictures of them together."

"Come on, get in bed. I'll fix the pillows for you. You're already half asleep now." So I bustled around, turning off lights except the one by the bed, checking the bathroom, which she'd left in good order, smoothing the covers for her, urging one more bite of sandwich, then taking the tray from her lap.

"Slide on down," I said, removing some of the pillows. "I'll leave you now, but if you need anything in the night, our room's just across the hall, and I sleep on the far side of the bed."

"Thank you, Julia, for being so kind to me." LuAnne yawned again as she curled up under the sheet and light blanket. "I'll make it up to you. In the morning. I know I'll feel better in the morning."

"I know you will, too. Good night, LuAnne," I said, switching off the lamp and palming the bottle of sleeping pills. "Sleep tight."

I don't know how long Sam and I had been asleep but the room was as black as pitch when I felt a hand on my shoulder and a hoarse whisper in my ear.

"*Julia*, you asleep?"

"What? What. LuAnne?" I sat up, disoriented and dazed. "Uh, no, I'm awake. What is it?"

"I don't want to wake Sam," she said. "Come downstairs."

She eased out of the room as I, still half asleep, struggled into a robe and bedroom slippers. Following LuAnne down the stairs, I wondered if she'd been looking for more sleeping pills. The bottle was in my bathroom, safely hidden, where it was going to stay for the duration.

She was pacing up and down the length of the library when I got there. One lamp was on, so I could see her robe swinging as she strode back and forth.

"What's wrong, LuAnne? You couldn't sleep?"

"No, I couldn't. Not long enough, anyway. I'm going to get something stronger tomorrow. Today, I mean."

"What time is it, anyway?"

She slewed around, her robe billowing out behind her. "I don't know. Around three, I think." She stopped in front of me. "I had the worst dream, Julia. I dreamed that she was in *my* bed with Leonard, and I can't stand the thought that they've just been waiting for me to leave. I played right into their hands by packing up and leaving."

"Oh, no, I wouldn't think so."

"Well, whatever they think, it's not going to work. I'm going up there, Julia, and I'm going to wait and see her come out. Then I'll know who she is. You'll go with me, won't you? I mean, I might need a witness."

Witness to what? "I'm not sure that's a good idea. Why don't you—"

"Oh, I'm not going to *do* anything. I just want to see her with my own eyes. I won't even get out of the car. We can park beside the front hedge and wait for her to come out. Nobody'll know we're there."

She looked at me with those pitiful tear-filled eyes and, against all common sense, I said, "Well, okay. But no getting out, and no confronting anybody. Promise?"

"Of course. I don't want a public spectacle any more than you do. I just want to see who it is. Come on, let's go."

"*Now?* LuAnne, it's the middle of the night. Let's get a couple more hours of sleep, then go."

"You don't understand these things, Julia," LuAnne said, as if she did. "She'll come out and be gone long before daylight. She's been carrying on under the radar for who knows how long, so she knows how it's done. She won't risk being seen in the daylight."

"Wel-l-l," I said, wondering how we'd see who she was in the dead of night. "Then I guess we'd better get some clothes on."

"Oh, come on. Nobody's going to see us. And think of this: you can jump right back into bed when we get back. Or," she went on, "you can nap while I watch."

So, against my better judgment—which isn't better if you don't use it—both of us, in washed-thin gowns and cotton robes, slipped out of the house and into LuAnne's car. I'd had the presence of mind to leave a quick note for Sam on the kitchen table—no details, just *With LuAnne, back soon.*

And off we went with a screech of the tires, which should've warned me of LuAnne's state of mind. It was the fastest trip up the mountain I'd ever made, but at that time of night there was no traffic. As we approached the top of the mountain, LuAnne dimmed the headlights to low beam, murmuring that she didn't want to be conspicuous.

She guided the car through the open gates into the small group of condos clinging to the side of the mountain; then, scaring me half to death, she turned off the headlights and crept around a curve. The condos were all close to the street. Only a few feet of walkway led to the front doors, which is what you get when you build so near the edge.

Easing off the street onto a narrow strip of grass, LuAnne scraped the side—my side—of the car against a high, thick hedge that ran along the front of a line of cookie-cutter condos. Every ten or so feet, the hedge opened for a short walkway to a front door. LuAnne nosed the car to the edge of the third opening and came to a stop with the headlights still off and the engine still running.

"Here we are," LuAnne said. "She'll have to come out right in front of us. We'll see her, no doubt about that."

We sat for a few minutes as the night settled around us, while I hoped there were no security guards.

"The idea!" LuAnne suddenly fumed. "Here I am outside my own house. I've a good mind to go in there and pull her hair out! And his, too. If he had any." Then before I could issue a word of caution, she said, "Put your window down, Julia. It's getting hot in here."

I did, and got smacked with branches from the hedge springing inside the open window. Holly bushes, I realized, and rolled my window up. Getting hot was better than getting scratched.

LuAnne turned off the engine, and the night got even quieter as the sultry air wafted in from LuAnne's open window. Unlike most condo communities, this mountainside street had no street-lights or security lights that would diminish the spectacular views of the town lights below. All I could see were darker shapes of hedge, tree, mailbox, and a few parked cars against the darkness of the night. There might've been a moon and stars somewhere, but not where we could see them nor where we could see anything by them.

Hoping that LuAnne would muster the wisdom to remain unseen and unheard, I scrunched down in the seat and put my head back. I was convinced that our vigil would be a long, boring exercise in futility. Only a fool would bring in another woman on the first night his wife was gone.

But then I thought again of whom we were dealing with—Leonard Conover—and tried to keep my eyes open.

Chapter 8

"Julia! Wake up!" LuAnne whispered as she leaned over the steering wheel, peering into the dark in front of the car.

"What is it?" I sat up, rubbed my eyes, and tried to see what she was seeing.

LuAnne whispered, "I heard something. The front door just opened—I've told Leonard a hundred times to fix that squeak. And somebody's mumbling. I think she's coming out."

We both leaned forward, straining to see out the windshield, listening as hard as we could. Then I distinctly heard a door close and the scrape of a shoe on concrete.

LuAnne grabbed my arm. "She's coming!"

And somebody was. I saw a dark shadow emerge from behind the hedge and step onto the street directly in front of our car.

"It's her!" LuAnne screeched as she switched on the headlights. The whole world lit up.

LuAnne flung open her door just as the figure in front of us threw up her arm, shielding her eyes—and her face—from the glare of the headlights. I reached for LuAnne to hold her back, but missed—she was already out the door, losing a bedroom shoe in the process. The figure turned on a dime and sprinted down the street, quickly outrunning our low beams. LuAnne, panting and crying, but unwilling to wake the neighborhood, skipped and hobbled down the street, her untied bathrobe flying out behind her.

"Wait!" I called, but not very loud. "Wait, LuAnne!" Pushing to open my door, I was blocked by the thick hedge. Giving that up, but anxious to stop LuAnne, I scrambled for her open door. And would've made it except for the console. I ended up half in and half out of the car, my paper-thin gown snagged and tangled on the gearshift.

Grabbing the steering wheel to straighten up, I caught sight of

LuAnne stumbling and hopping into the dark beyond the range of our lights. Then the interior lights of a car some yards ahead came on, and I heard the slam of a door. And watched as it sped off.

Finally untangling myself, I saw LuAnne stand for a minute looking forlornly after the car. Then she slowly turned and hobbled back, stopping to pick up her lost shoe, then sliding into the car with the glint of frustrated tears on her face.

"Did you get the license number?" she asked.

"Uh, no. I didn't think to. I was too busy trying to get out. Who was it, LuAnne? Did you recognize her?"

"No, she covered her face, the shameful hussy! And she was *fast*, Julia. She was in that car and gone before I could get to her." LuAnne took a deep breath, then said, "Well, one thing's for sure. I'm signing up for a fitness class after this."

She leaned her forehead against the steering wheel for a minute, then asked, "Leonard didn't come out, did he?"

"No, not that I saw. But if we sit here much longer with the headlights on, he might. Let's get out of here, LuAnne."

She nodded, turned the ignition, put the car in gear, and, with a great deal of scraping and scratching against the hedge, eased the car onto the street. I hated to think of what a new paint job was going to cost.

Contrary to what I'd feared, LuAnne drove slowly and sedately back down the mountain toward my house. After all, what was the hurry now? The woman was obviously long gone, and LuAnne had missed an opportunity to identify her.

"Julia," LuAnne said tightly, as if she'd been holding it in for some time, "Leonard is *not* a gentleman. I hope you noticed. He didn't even walk her to the car."

Well, horrors, as Sam would say. Certainly, a man who is not a gentleman is a poor bargain, especially if you're married to him, but I would've expected LuAnne to have been exercised by Leonard's more pressing deficiency. Like, for instance, the lack of common sense.

Because, if you want to know the truth, no one with any sense would want to get crosswise of LuAnne Conover. She was the best of friends, willing to go the extra mile for anyone, but if you ever crossed her, she'd never forget it. Nor would anyone else because she'd talk about you till the end of time.

The sky had turned gray by the time we pulled to the curb at my house. The sun had yet to come up, but it was well on its way, and I was feeling the lack of sleep.

As we entered the kitchen through the back door, LuAnne said, "Put the coffee on, Julia. I'm too wound up to go back to bed."

I wasn't, but I plugged in the coffeepot, which Lillian always left ready to perk, and soon LuAnne and I were sitting at the table with cups of the hot brew. I wadded up my note to Sam, somewhat relieved that he hadn't seen it. I would tell him about our night's work, but the fact that he was still in bed and hadn't seen my note saved him from hours of worry.

After a few sips of coffee, LuAnne started airing all her grievances again. She went over everything that had happened the day before and during the night, righteous indignation building in every word. I sat and nodded, injecting an "uh-huh" every now and then, but she needed no input from me.

Then, hearing Sam stirring upstairs, she quickly stood up and said, "I'm so tired I can't see straight. I'm going to bed, Julia, if you don't mind. I may just stay there all day."

"Do that. It's just what you need," I agreed. "I have to check on Lillian, then I'm going shopping with Hazel Marie. You're welcome to go with us if you'd like."

"*Shopping?*" she said. "How could I go shopping with my head about to explode? You don't understand what I'm going through. Shopping is the last thing on my mind." She looked up as we heard Sam start down the stairs. "I'll hide in the library till he comes in here, then I'll sneak upstairs. I can't face him or anybody else until I can hold my head up again."

I sat at the table, holding a now empty coffee cup, wondering if LuAnne was going to spend the next two weeks lurking behind doors, slipping in and out of rooms, and hiding from everybody. I could understand wanting to avoid explanations and overly sympathetic eyes, but this could get ridiculous. LuAnne would be living with three families plus Latisha in one house, so how she expected to steer clear of all of us all the time, I didn't know.

"Good morning," Sam said as he entered the kitchen from the dining room. "You're up early this morning, sweetheart. Didn't you sleep well?"

"More like, did I sleep at all." I gave a quick laugh, then hurried to the back door to let Lillian in. Which was just as well, because one telling of the night's work would suffice.

"What y'all doin' up so early?" she said on her way to the pantry to put up her pocketbook—the one that was the size of a duffel. "You not goin' to the beach today, are you? An' I hope you know what you doin' 'cause Latisha 'bout to go crazy. That chile beside herself, she so excited."

"No, no change of plans. We won't be leaving until Sunday. Now, Lillian, I want to know what the doctor said. You saw him yesterday, didn't you?"

"Yes'm, but I got to get breakfast on."

"Breakfast can wait," Sam said. "Tell us what he said."

"Well," Lillian said, leaning against the counter of the peninsula, "he say he fin'lly gonna get to take that ole bunion off, an' he gonna do it first thing come Monday morning."

"*Monday!*" I cried. "But I won't be here." Abruptly sitting back down, I looked at Sam and said, "Well, that decides it. I'm not going. I'm staying right here so I can look after Lillian. She needs me."

Before Sam could respond, Lillian walked over to the table, looked down at me, and said, "Miss Julia, you know I love you to death, but you don't know too much 'bout nursin' an', I tell you the truth, I jus' as soon you go on to the beach. Miss Bessie an' me plan to watch ev'ry show on the teevee, an' we might play us some gin rummy, an' sleep late in the mornin' an' go to bed late at night, an' who knows what else we get up to. You jus' go right on to that beach. Takin' Latisha with you an' watchin' her be the best help I can get."

"She's right, Julia," Sam said. "Having Latisha taken care of will help Lillian more than anything else you could do."

It took me a few minutes to put aside the image of myself as Florence Nightingale ministering to the sick and ailing, but I knew that Latisha was always Lillian's chief concern, and if I could relieve her of that, then I would indeed be helping her. I will admit, however, to feeling a tiny bit hurt that she preferred Miss Bessie's nursing skills to mine.

Chapter 9

"I just love to shop," Hazel Marie said as we left Abbotsville fairly early Thursday morning. We were on our way to that perfect shop in south Asheville even though I'd much rather have been in bed. "It's my favorite thing to do."

She'd come by for me driving that huge vehicle that looked more like a bus than a car—the very thing for a large family except there was no trunk. Long and wide and high off the ground, it had taken extreme exertions on my part to climb up into it. A step stool would've helped. Sitting up behind the steering wheel, Hazel Marie looked like a Barbie doll driving a long-haul truck, but I'd seen her zip that vehicle into a parallel parking space like nobody's business.

"Well, it's not my favorite thing," I said, stifling a yawn and recalling with envy the sound of LuAnne's snoring as I'd passed Lloyd's room on my way downstairs. "But I appreciate your going with me. I just hope I can find something that's not only decent but something that I'll like."

"Oh, you will. This shop has lovely things, but, Miss Julia, you have to be willing to try them on. They look a whole lot better *on* than they do on a hanger."

"Whatever you say, Hazel Marie. I'm entirely in your hands, but I reserve for myself the final decision of what to buy." Then I yawned again.

She laughed, then said, "You must not've gotten your nap out last night. Didn't you sleep well?"

I took my time answering, because I could hardly contain what I'd learned about Leonard Conover—still remarkably unbelievable to me. LuAnne had made me promise not to tell anyone, while at the same time loudly bemoaning the fact that everybody already knew.

So I pondered what I should do and finally came down on the side of telling it. I reasoned that we would all be living together for some time, and with the way LuAnne was acting, questions were going to arise. And also, I will concede, I was dying to tell it.

"Hazel Marie," I began, "have you heard anything, well . . . *unsavory* about Leonard Conover?"

She glanced at me then quickly back at the interstate on which we were risking our lives. "Mr. Conover? No, I don't think I've heard anything savory or unsavory. Not lately, anyway. Why?"

"Well," I said, then stopped to enjoy the thrill of telling something so incredible. "It seems that he's been engaged in a long-running affair."

"Oh, that. I heard that years ago."

"You *did*? And didn't tell me?"

"I didn't tell anybody," she said, smiling. "Except J.D., of course. I tell him everything. But I didn't believe it then, and I don't believe it now. I mean, I just can't imagine Leonard Conover doing such a thing."

"Well, imagine it, because I saw it with my own eyes."

"You *did*?"

I should've known better than to tell it while she was driving. I grabbed hold of the door handle as the car veered off the lane onto the wide shoulder. Hazel Marie quickly corrected our trajectory, and I started breathing again.

"You mean to tell me," Hazel Marie demanded, gripping the steering wheel, "that you actually witnessed the . . . the *act*? Who with? I mean, who was *he* with?"

"That's the big question." And I went on to tell how LuAnne had been determined to find out, and how we'd huddled in a dark car for half the night just to get a glimpse of her, and how that hadn't worked out even though the woman had walked right in front of us in full glare of the headlights.

Hazel Marie reacted to my tale pretty much as Sam and Lillian had. That is to say, she was more concerned about my part in

LuAnne's escapade than about our catching Leonard in the act. Or, more specifically, in the afterglow of the act.

"Don't worry," I said, waving off her concern, "I didn't even get out of the car. I just went to keep LuAnne company. But the reason I'm telling you about it is that I've invited her to go to the beach with us—you know, so she can get away and clear her head. So don't say anything to her."

"Oh, goodness, no," Hazel Marie said. "I wouldn't bring it up for the world. And you know J.D. won't. He forgets everything I tell him, anyway."

She came off the interstate and after a few turns pulled into a shopping center, found a parking place, and stopped. "The shop's right down there," she said, pointing to the right.

After two hours of trying on, frowning at my image in a mirror, and discarding the very thought of wearing such things, Hazel Marie took over. She selected five outfits from the discard pile, told the clerk that we'd take them, then ignored my complaints. We left the shop with two shopping bags full, so that, like it or not, I had a beachwear wardrobe.

Then we went to a shoe store, and she'd been right—sandals came in every color and style you could imagine. The first pair she picked out had wedge heels higher than any dress shoes I owned. I could barely stand in them, much less walk. It took a while, but I finally agreed to two pairs, neither of which had any heels to speak of nor did they have straps that wound around my ankles. I was relieved to make the choices and be through with shopping.

"You'll be better dressed than most of the people you see," Hazel Marie assured me as we got in the car and started for home.

"I'm more concerned with being *fuller* dressed," I said, with a tinge of sharpness. "Anyway," I went on, "I do thank you for taking the time to come with me. You must have a dozen things to do to get ready."

She laughed. "You wouldn't believe what it takes to get ready to go anywhere with twins. Thank goodness we have the SUV, but even so we may have to put some things in your trunk."

"Whatever you need," I said. "And speaking of that, who's going to ride with whom?"

"Well, as soon as Lloyd learned that Latisha was going, he said he wanted to ride with you and Mr. Sam and her." Hazel Marie laughed. "Apparently she entertains him better than the twins do."

"That brings up a problem. I doubt that LuAnne will want to ride with anybody but us, and she may wear a sack over her head even then. She's been hiding from Sam for the past twenty-four hours as it is. So I was thinking Latisha could go with us—there's plenty of room in the backseat for the two of them, and LuAnne won't have to hide her head. Latisha won't know or care what's going on with her husband."

"Well, be prepared for a fuss about that," Hazel Marie said. "I'm pretty sure she'll want to ride with Lloyd. We can put them in the third seat back there." She waved toward the back of the car, I mean bus. Or truck, or whatever it was. "So what about this: we'll take both children plus the twins, and LuAnne can go with you and Mr. Sam. That way, if you don't mind, we can fill up the rest of your backseat with baby stuff."

"That's fine with me, if it is with Mr. Pickens. He may not appreciate driving what amounts to a school bus."

Hazel Marie laughed. "Don't worry about J.D., Miss Julia. He's pretty well domesticated by now. He can tune out crying, fussing, wet diapers, and you-name-it."

She took the Abbotsville exit, as visions of an afternoon nap danced in my head. But Hazel Marie had other things on her mind. "I kinda hate to bring this up," she said, "but is LuAnne going to be hiding from us the whole time we're there? It could really put a damper on everything if we have to tiptoe around to avoid seeing her. Or her seeing us."

"Believe me, I know it. But I think when we get down there, she can do whatever she wants and so can everybody else. Which, for me—if she keeps acting like that—will be to just leave her alone."

"Okay," she said as she turned onto Polk Street and approached my house. "I just wanted to know what and what not to do. I wouldn't want to say the wrong thing and make matters worse. I'll have to warn J.D., too, because the first thing he'd say to her would be, 'What's Leonard up to? Didn't he want to come?'"

"Oh, Lord," I said, "don't let him do that! She'd probably tell him exactly what Leonard is up to, and tell it in great detail and we'd never hear the end of it. Believe me, he'd get sick and tired of hearing it. Which is just about where I am, but, Hazel Marie, I do sympathize with her. It's such an upheaval, you know, of her whole life. As hard as we find it to believe, it's even harder for her. I mean, she knows even better than we do that he's not God's gift to women, so it's hard to get her head around the idea that somebody thinks he is."

"I understand," Hazel Marie said, nodding as she pulled to the curb in front of my house. "Well, here we are. I'll help you carry things in, and I want to see every one of those outfits on you during the next two weeks."

"Yes, ma'am," I said, smiling, relieved to get off the subject of wandering husbands. Hazel Marie and I had a somewhat unnerving history in which such extramarital gamboling had changed our lives. For the better in the long run, I might add, but it was a subject that we generally stayed away from. So I changed it.

"Hazel Marie," I said, stopping halfway out of the car, "would you mind calling Binkie and telling her about LuAnne? I mean, so neither she nor Coleman will ask about Leonard?"

"Oh, sure, I'll do that," Hazel Marie agreed. "But don't forget, you have a pedicure appointment this afternoon. You want me to go with you?"

"Thank you, but no. I can manage on my own. No telling what color I'd come out with if you went with me."

She laughed, gave me a hug, which she was often wont to do, and helped me carry the bags of beachwear and sandals into the house.

After crawling up into Janelle's Spa-Pedicure chair, I was finally able to make up for some of the sleep I'd been missing since 3 a.m. The chair was like a recliner, only higher, more mechanized, and perfectly adjustable to one's sleep-deprived body. I stretched out on it and gave in to the long, rolling massaging action that ran from the back of my neck to below my knees.

Janelle Woods, who'd been doing my nails for years, was her usual soothing self. "Just lie back and enjoy it, Miss Julia," she said. And when she lifted one foot after the other and lowered each one into a pan of perfectly heated water, tension oozed out of me from one end to the other.

As my feet soaked, I vaguely heard Janelle ask, "Do you know what color you want?"

"Oh, anything suitable for sandals," I murmured without opening my eyes. "Something colorful, maybe, that I wouldn't wear on my fingernails." And I was out like a light for the following thirty minutes or so.

Take my advice: don't ever fall asleep while a pedicurist is working on you. I couldn't believe what I saw when Janelle woke me.

"*Purple!*" I exclaimed, aghast at the sight.

"Well, not exactly, but kinda," she said. "Don't you like it? It's a favorite OPI color. It's called Do You Think I'm Tex-y."

My eyes rolled back in my head, but I didn't have time to have it changed. *At least,* I thought as I looked down at my purple-tipped toes, *one pair of sandals will cover them, and maybe, very likely in fact, Sam will appreciate the name if not the color.*

Chapter 10

After two days of packing, repacking, loading cars, telephoning to check on the other travelers, deciding who was riding where, making sure that Lillian would be cared for, and constantly reassuring and encouraging LuAnne, Sunday morning arrived. With all the planning and preparing we'd been doing, I was more than ready for that good, long rest that Sam had promised if and when we ever got to the beach.

It was, however, somewhat strange and disorienting to be missing Sunday school and church, which is where we could ordinarily be found on most Sundays of the year. Cars of faithful churchgoers were turning in to the parking lot across the street, and I had an urge to run out to explain why we weren't among them. Still, we so seldom missed being in our usual pew that I felt justified in taking one Sunday off to begin a well-deserved vacation.

Mr. Pickens had come over the evening before and loaded half of our backseat with two suitcases stacked on top of each other, a huge package of diapers on top of them, and a shopping bag full of toys on the floorboard. I had assumed we'd have room in the trunk, but LuAnne seemed to be taking everything she owned.

"I might decide to stay," she told me. "I might get down there and decide that I can do just fine without Leonard."

I just nodded, declining to argue or to point out that she was leaving her car in our driveway, as well as what it would cost to stay on even though the season was almost over. She would have no friends nearby, no job, and, if Sam had been correct, little or no money to support herself. But LuAnne was not in any emotional condition to listen to reason, so I nodded again and asked if she wanted to take a pillow with her.

"What do I need a pillow for?" she asked with a sniff. "Half the backseat is taken up with somebody else's things. I'm going to be cramped up the whole way as it is."

"No more than anybody else, LuAnne," I reminded her, refraining from pointing out that she was getting a free vacation even though the ride would be shared with a one-hundred-forty-count package of Huggies that kept sliding off the suitcases.

I declare, between comforting and reassuring both LuAnne and Lillian, I had a good mind to take a Greyhound all by myself. Lillian had come to the house the evening before planning to fry up several chickens for us to take with us. It had been all I could do to talk her out of it.

"We'll be stopping for lunch in Columbia for barbeque, Lillian. Everybody's looking forward to it. And really," I went on, "there's no room in the cars for a Styrofoam container full of ice and fried chicken."

"You might wish you had that chicken when you get to the beach," she said. "You goin' to a house that don't have nothin' to eat in it."

"Well, that's Mr. Pickens's and Coleman's problem. They're in charge of the food."

"They Lord!" Lillian said, laughing as she threw up her hands. "You depend on them two, you likely be eatin' b'loney sam'iches."

I laughed. "You may be right, but they'll have a mutiny on their hands. Now look, Lillian, I'm going to call you Monday afternoon to see how the surgery went, so if you need anything I want you to tell me. We'll have three cars among us, so I can be back here in about four hours. And," I went on, "you have a key to the house, so feel free to use it if you'd be more comfortable here."

"No'm, Miss Bessie an' me, we already got our plans, an' she say she gonna keep me so busy I won't even miss Latisha."

"Well, I'll put Latisha on the phone several times as we check on you. And, Lillian, we'll take care of her, don't you worry about that. How's she doing, anyway, now that we're almost ready to go?" My fear was that Latisha, once it really sank in that Lillian wouldn't be going, would back out at the last minute.

"Oh, she so excited, she want to know why you can't go tonight 'stead of tomorrow. She already over at Miss Hazel Marie's, 'cause when Mr. Pickens come by an' say it easier to pack the car tonight, an' he say why don't Latisha spend the night at their house, she jump in his car without hardly sayin' "Bye, Granny, see you later.'"

In an effort to distract her from missing Latisha before Latisha was even gone, I changed the subject. "Now, Lillian, remember that all you have to do is present your insurance card at the hospital when you get there. It will cover everything, including your surgeon and so forth. There should be no extra charges at all, and if there are, I'll speak to the insurance company myself."

Actually I was pleased that she was finally getting to use her insurance. I'd been paying the premiums for years, so it was high time she got some good out of it.

Sam, eager to start the vacation that he'd arranged, swung out of bed at five o'clock Sunday morning. I moaned and turned over, dreading the long drive before us. Of course I couldn't go back to sleep—Sam was too excited for me to dawdle in bed. He wanted me to be up and just as thrilled as he was, so I crawled out of bed and began to try.

To my amazement, LuAnne was already up, dressed, and sitting at the table drinking coffee when I got to the kitchen.

"Goodness," I said, as she was not known to be an early riser. "What are you doing up so early?"

"I have something to do before we leave." She turned her cup around in the saucer without looking at me.

Oh, me, I thought, *what's she up to now?* Deciding not to ask for specifics, I poured coffee for myself, took a seat at the table, and waited for LuAnne to tell me. Because she would, sooner or later.

Sam came bustling in, stopped at the sight of us sitting silently at the table. "Anybody cooking anything?"

"Not yet," I said, putting off the effort to get up and do it. "I will in a minute, but it's still early."

"Well, don't. I'll get us some sausage biscuits. Then we won't have to clean the kitchen."

"Oh, that's good. Thank you, Sam. I'll try to be awake by the time you get back."

He laughed, gave me a quick kiss, and left for McDonald's.

As we heard the car crank up, LuAnne looked at me with tear-filled eyes. "You're so lucky, Julia."

"Believe me, I know it. I sometimes wonder how I'm so fortunate as to have both Lloyd and Sam."

"And a few million dollars, too," LuAnne said with an edge of sharpness. "Don't leave that out."

LuAnne was not basically an envious woman, but every once in a while she couldn't help herself. I figured most of her resentment was aimed at Leonard for being a poor provider rather than at those of us in better financial situations. But I couldn't let her remark pass unnoticed.

"I *do* leave that out, because I didn't get it through luck. I *earned* every cent of it, LuAnne. You think you have it bad with Leonard, well, if you'd lived for forty-some-odd years with a man like Wesley Lloyd Springer, you'd know what bad is." Actually, I'd gotten hotter about it than I'd intended, but the idea that I'd sat complacently by while good luck in the form of financial assets drifted down around me just irked me no end.

LuAnne quickly backtracked as she always did when she overstepped. "I didn't mean it that way, Julia. I guess I should be glad that Leonard hasn't fathered a child. At least," she amended, jerking upright, "not that I know of. Surely he hasn't. You don't think he has, do you, Julia?"

"No," I said, comforting her with a pat on the arm. "I think the woman who called you would've told you. And, by the way, LuAnne, what did she sound like? Old? Young? Could you tell?"

LuAnne shook her head. "No, she whispered like she was making herself sound hoarse. But you're right, Julia. I think she would've told me just to throw it in my face. But I'll tell you one thing, I could never do what you did about Lloyd. However," she said, standing, "that's neither here nor there. I have to run home before we leave. I won't be long."

"You're going back? *Why?*"

"There're a few things I forgot. And, who knows? It might be my last time ever." She set her cup and saucer in the sink, picked up her purse, and started out the door.

"Well, hurry back," I said, refraining from arguing with her. "Sam wants to be on the road no later than ten."

It was nine forty-nine Sunday morning, and we'd eaten sausage biscuits; Sam had checked all the windows and doors of the house, reset the thermostat, made sure everything was turned off, packed last-minute odds and ends into the car; and instead of being in our pew in the church across the street, we were waiting on the front porch for LuAnne to get back. Coleman had called thirty minutes before, saying that they were leaving and would see us at lunch in Columbia. Hazel Marie had called right after that to say they were heading out as well. And still no sign of LuAnne.

Turning to Sam, I asked, "What if they all get to the beach before we do? Will they have to wait on us?"

"I figured we might get separated, so I called the rental office. They'll give Pickens and Coleman keys if they get there before we do. Which looks highly likely."

"Well, I don't know what to do, Sam," I said, feeling that I had to apologize for my tardy friend. "I've called and called, and no-body answers. I hope she hasn't had an accident. You think we should drive up there?"

"No, we might miss her coming or going. Don't worry about it, honey. She'll show up and we'll be on our way."

"Well, I'm going to have to go to the bathroom again if she doesn't soon get here."

My kindhearted, easygoing husband laughed, even though I knew he was anxious to get on the road. He checked his fancy latest release in cell phones and said, "Here's a text from Lloyd. He says they're almost down the mountain and looking forward to barbeque for lunch."

"Text him back, if you will, and ask how Latisha's doing."

He did, then read me the response. "He says, 'Latisha bouncing, twins throwing up, Mama mopping up, J.D. laughing.'" Sam stopped, then said, "Uh-oh, didn't know he knew that."

"What? What does he say?"

"He ends it with 'snafu.'" Sam laughed. "I guess that sums it up fairly well." Then he told me what snafu meant, somewhat freely translated, I suspected.

Before I could react to Lloyd's shocking knowledge of army code, LuAnne drove up and parked in the drive. "Here she is," I said, rising. "At last."

LuAnne, holding a plastic grocery sack, rushed across the front yard, calling, "I'm sorry, I'm sorry. I know I'm late, but I'm ready. Let's go, let's get out of here. But first," she said, stopping to take a breath, "I better go to the bathroom. Come go with me, Julia."

I rolled my eyes just a little, although by this time I wasn't averse to another trip. Sam unlocked the front door for us, and we hurried to the hall bathroom.

"Wait, Julia," LuAnne said, holding me back. "I'm not in that much of a hurry. It took me a while, but I want you to see what I found."

"Leonard wasn't there?" I stared at her, picturing her rummaging through everything in their house for the past two hours, looking, I supposed, for evidence. As if she needed further proof after Leonard's admission.

"No, he's probably in church, the old hypocrite. But look at this."

LuAnne reached into the grocery bag, pulled out a handful of black mesh, and held it out for me to see.

"A hairnet?" I asked, frowning.

"That's what I thought! You can't imagine what went through my mind at finding a hairnet. But look."

"Oh, my word!" I gasped, as LuAnne, with thumb and one finger, gingerly shook out, then dangled in front of my face a familiar shape made of black net and lace. "Is that what I think it is?"

"It most certainly is. A pair of black lace step-ins and it was in Leonard's shaving kit, would you believe? It's the one place in the whole house that I never clean or replenish. I mean, why would I? He never goes anywhere. But there this thing was, all wadded up next to his razor and his Mennen's shaving cream."

"I don't suppose they're yours, are they?"

"Absolutely not! In the first place, I don't wear black underwear, and I certainly don't wear that size!"

They were spacious, all right, and I found myself marveling at Leonard's taste in women.

Chapter 11

As Sam aimed the car toward the interstate, LuAnne curled up in her half of the backseat, making good use of the pillow she hadn't wanted, and gave every indication of avoiding conversation. She'd barely spoken to Sam, who had been his normally solicitous self, welcoming her, and making sure that she was comfortable. It was going to be a long, silent drive, but Sam had thought of that as well.

"I picked up some CDs, Julia," he said, pointing to a sack in the footwell. "See if there's anything you want to listen to."

"What a good idea," I said, although I would miss the lively conversations that he and I would've normally had. I don't know why being enclosed in a car so encouraged us to talk, but it did. Not that we didn't talk at home—but somehow the close proximity of two bucket seats loosened our tongues. We told jokes, discussed friends, analyzed politicians, spoke of spiritual matters, and, in general, set the world aright. But not this time with LuAnne in the backseat and a black thundercloud surrounding her. As it was, I couldn't even tell him about the step-ins she'd found in Leonard's shaving kit, a subject that would've certainly engendered a lively discussion.

So we listened to a book on CD about a feisty woman who speaks her mind, hitches a ride on a Harley—at her age, too—and serves open-faced cucumber sandwiches on a silver tray.

By the time we pulled into the parking lot at Piggy Park in Columbia, I was more than ready to stop. In the two hours since we'd left home we'd passed two rest stops, either of which would've suited me, especially the second one. But LuAnne had slept the whole way, and I hadn't wanted to wake her by stopping. So while Sam placed our orders, LuAnne and I, with a great deal of anticipation, adjourned to the ladies' room.

Being close to forty-five minutes behind the Pickens and the Bates families, we missed having lunch with them. But as soon as we'd parked, Sam had talked to Lloyd on his fancy phone and learned that they were well on their way to the beach. The babies, he'd told Sam, were sleeping in their car seats, Latisha was coloring, and his mother was napping. J.D., he said, had the radio turned low to Rush Limbaugh, but not quite low enough. J.D. was talking back to him.

Sam also checked in with Coleman and Binkie, who were ahead of the Pickens car—they'd had only one child to see to at lunchtime, while Hazel Marie had had four.

By the time we were back on the interstate heading southeast, LuAnne was showing signs of rejuvenation. As well she should after consuming a large pulled-pork barbeque sandwich with coleslaw, French fries, half of my onion rings, and a pint jar of tea— lemoned and sugared. She was ready to talk, and talk she did. Far from hiding her head and her shame as she had been doing, she let it all out.

"Sam," she said, leaning forward as far as the seat belt allowed, "thank you for lunch and for inviting me to the beach. I appreciate all you and Julia are doing for me in my time of need. But I have to ask. Did you know what Leonard was doing? Have you heard any talk about him? I mean, I know that you keep up with what's going on in town, so I want to know what people are saying and what they think of him and, let's be honest, what they think of me. Because I know in cases like this, the wife is usually to blame. I mean, not actually, but people *assume* that she's to blame. And I want everybody to know that I have catered to Leonard Conover, hand and foot, for all these years, and this is the way he repays me."

"Well—" Sam began, but she wasn't finished.

"Now I know you're no longer practicing law, but you haven't forgotten what you knew when you were, so I want to know if I can sue that woman—whoever she is—for something. Like alienation of affection or something."

As Sam opened his mouth to reply, LuAnne kept right on going. "On the other hand," she said, "I think Leonard is losing his mind. I mean, he can't remember a thing from one day to the next, so it could be early onset of Alzheimer's, couldn't it? Although at his age, you couldn't exactly call it early. Anyway, could I have him declared non compost mentis or something and have him committed? And if that happens, I will most certainly see to it that that woman has no access to him. Which is another reason that I need to know who she is, so if either of you have heard anything, anything at all, that would put me on the right track to her, I want to hear it."

"Well, LuAnne—" I began, but she wasn't through. Bless her heart, it was as if a dam had burst and all the fear and anger and general unsettledness that she was experiencing came rushing out.

"One thing's for sure," she said, giving in to the pull of the seat belt and sitting back, "I'm going to follow your advice, Julia, and hold my head up high. I'm not the one who's broken our marriage vows, and that brings up another problem. It says until death do us part, so does that mean I've vowed to stick with him regardless of what he's done? I mean, he's already broken *his* vows, so does that release me of mine or am I supposed to overlook everything and keep on putting up with him in sickness and in health, for richer or for poorer, and all the rest of it?"

"That's a conundrum, all right," Sam said, finally able to complete a sentence. "And, I'm afraid, one that only you can resolve."

"Well," she said, "I think Leonard needs counseling, except he won't go. But I really think he's sick. Nobody *normal* does such a thing, don't you think, Julia? I mean, you've been through the same thing. Didn't you think that Wesley Lloyd was sick? Mentally, I mean, not physically, because we know he was physically sick. After all, he did have a heart attack, but didn't you think he had mental problems, too?"

"I have no idea, LuAnne," I said. I did not want to discuss Wesley

Lloyd Springer's aberrations, especially with Sam sitting right there with us. Besides, Sam and I had talked it all out long before this and had come to the conclusion that as wayward as Wesley Lloyd had been while he was alive, he'd done both of us a huge favor in the long run. Sam and I no longer had need to bring it up, much less to talk it to death.

Which was exactly what LuAnne seemed intent on doing. I just wished she'd get off the subject of my former husband and quit comparing her current situation to what had once been mine.

"Well," LuAnne said, "there ought to be something I could do. It's just not right that he can do whatever he wants while I have no recourse but to put up with it."

"That's not true, LuAnne," Sam said, glancing in the rearview mirror at her. "You have several options, but they all depend on what you want in the long run. So you need to think it through very carefully." Sam stopped, then, as if gathering his courage, went on to say, "It might be a good idea to think about consulting a counselor yourself."

"*I'm* not the one who needs a counselor," LuAnne snapped, taking immediate umbrage at the suggestion.

"Oh, I didn't mean that you *need* one," Sam said quickly. "I just meant that discussing the situation with somebody who's completely objective might help you weigh all the options."

"Well," she said somewhat huffily, "I wouldn't want it to get around town that *I* was seeing a counselor. First thing you know, the talk would be all about me fooling around on Leonard. You know how the town is, Julia. No telling what they'd make of that. But, come to think of it," she said, suddenly switching gears, "maybe that wouldn't be a bad thing. Wonder what Leonard would do if he heard something like that? Because I have certainly had opportunities as every woman has at some time or another. Right, Julia?"

"Don't count me in on that, LuAnne," I said, trying to make light of the turn her thoughts were making. "I had only one opportunity, which was Sam." I reached for his hand on the console. "And I grabbed him while I could."

"Well, it's something to think about," LuAnne said. "Not that there's much to choose from in Abbotsville."

"There's always Thurlow Jones," I said, turning to look at her so she'd know I was teasing. I was referring to the town's most eligible bachelor, if, that is, you could overlook his outlandish behavior and general state of dishevelment.

"Huh," she said dismissively, but I saw a smile at the corner of her mouth. "On the other hand, it might not be a bad idea for you to imply something, Julia. I mean, just to put a question in the minds of one or two that I haven't been averse to a little romance. The town would take it from there, and we'd see how Leonard liked that."

All of a sudden I realized that she might not be teasing and hurriedly tried to tamp down her aspirations in the romance department. "Oh, you don't mean that, LuAnne. Your reputation is spotless, and you don't want to ruin it just because Leonard has ruined his. You have to rise above it and show that you're better than that."

"I'll think about it," she said, curling up in her corner of the backseat again. "Maybe I'll talk to Pastor Ledbetter. I know he'll give me good advice."

Oh, Lord, I thought, because if the pastor gave her the same advice he'd given me, she would not be happy.

Chapter 12

Pastor Ledbetter's advice had turned me inside out. I'd listened to a long lecture on my marital duties, the primary one being submission to my lot as a betrayed wife who should have a forgiving heart that would leave retribution to the Lord. Bitterly resenting the advice, I was angered to the point of considering divorcing Wesley Lloyd *in absentia* because by then he was beyond my reach.

Leonard, however, was near at hand, and LuAnne was not an easily appeased person. She would not—perhaps could not—merely throw up her hands and leave him to the Lord. She'd be compelled to do something, and it was what that something might be that worried me. My hope was that two weeks away from the fray would give her time to rein in her temper, as well as her impulse to maim, cripple, mutilate, or permanently disable her solace-seeking husband.

By this time, an hour or so beyond Columbia, I had begun to discern the gradual change of scenery as we neared our destination. The land was noticeably lower in grade, the highway at times elevated above reed-filled, black-water swamps. Long stretches of slender pine trees on both sides of the roadway flashed past our windows, and I caught glimpses of streamers of Spanish moss as we sped along. I knew from former visits to the coast that outside our air-conditioned interior the atmosphere would be heavy with humidity, filled as it was with swamp and paper mill odors, as well as the distinctive aroma of low tide and stranded fish that meant we were close to the ocean.

"Here we go," Sam said, turning onto the curving exit ramp to I-526 East that took us over the spectacular cable-stayed bridge that took my breath away as well. A few more miles brought us across some less notable bridges and finally to the long, straight street that led to the gated north end of the Isle of Palms itself.

"LuAnne," I said, looking back at her, "are you awake? We're almost there."

She pushed away the bulky package of Huggies that had slid on top of her and struggled to sit up. "Well, finally. I hate long trips and I'm glad this one's over. Except now we'll have to lug in all the luggage and this blamed pack of diapers that I've fought with the whole way."

"Well, you can stretch out in a nice, big bed tonight," I said, refusing to be drawn into her complaints, knowing that she'd have even more to complain about after the sleepless night she was bound to have. I mean, she'd slept most of the day, which in itself was a cause for concern. LuAnne was a goer and a doer. She didn't take naps or sit down to rest, yet sleep was all she'd done and apparently all she'd wanted to do. That, I supposed, was her way of dealing with the turmoil in her mind—just close up shop and put it all off till later.

After a quick stop at the rental office to sign papers and pick up extra keys, Sam drove another mile or so, then turned into a deep yard. "Here we are," he said, parking the car between the Pickenses' large vehicle and the Bateses' smaller version.

I looked up at the looming yellow house, noting that the back, with its screened porch, faced the street so that the front would have the ocean view. Latticework covered what I'd call the basement floor, while outside stairs led up to the main floor. Getting luggage inside would not be an easy job.

But then Coleman and Mr. Pickens came clamoring down the stairs, welcoming us, and yelling to the children to stay where they were. With such willing hands to unload the car, LuAnne and I made it easily up the stairs in spite of stiff joints from sitting most of the five hours it had taken to get us there.

The children—Little Gracie, Lily Mae, Julie, and Latisha— danced excitedly around as we walked into the huge center room that ran from the back of the house to the front. A well-appointed kitchen lined the back wall, separated from the large living area by a monstrous island. You could stand at the back wall of the room, look across the island, the many feet of wooden floor filled with sofas, chairs, rugs, and tables—plus an outlandishly large televison set—then through the windowed front wall, across the screened front porch, and see the horizon beyond dunes, beach, and a few miles of Atlantic Ocean.

"Miss Lady!" Latisha yelled, pulling at my hand. "Miss Lady! You oughtta see that big ole ocean. I never seen nothin' like it!"

"You've already seen it?"

"We sure have! First crack outta the box, Lloyd's daddy took us down there. And then made us all come back an' stay here inside. Look like forever, too, 'cause I'm ready to go back."

"You'll have plenty of chances, Latisha. Oh, hey, Little Gracie," I said as the little, curly-headed girl—so much like Binkie—sidled up close. "Are you having a good time?"

She nodded solemnly, while the Pickens twins stopped hopping around and stood back to eye LuAnne with suspicion. I declare, Mr. Pickens could never in this world deny those two little girls. With their black eyes and soft, black hair, there was nothing at all of Hazel Marie about them. But maybe outwardly favoring their daddy meant that they'd inherited their mother's sweet nature. Which would be much more of a blessing than the other way around.

"Where's your mother?" I asked Lloyd, touching him lightly because I couldn't help myself. He was standing among the younger children, grinning at us.

"She's gone to the grocery store with Binkie," he said, gently separating himself from one of his sisters who was clamped onto his leg. "We're all about to starve."

"I thought that was your daddy's job—his and Coleman's."

"Mama had second thoughts," Lloyd said, laughing. "Binkie, too. She said no telling what they'd come back with." Lloyd took my hand and said, "Come on, Miss Julia, I'll show you your room. Mama said if you didn't like it, she'd change with you."

He led me to the large bedroom suite to the left of the center room, and at first glance I could tell it was more than adequate. In fact, I was quite pleased with it—Sam had certainly fulfilled his promise.

"This is really nice," LuAnne said. She'd followed us into the room and was now opening closet doors. "But where will I sleep?"

"Well," Lloyd said, "Mama and Binkie looked at all the rooms, then they decided who would sleep where. Mama and J.D. have the suite across the way there because it has a little room next to it for the twins. Binkie and Coleman took the room above this one, and the room behind it will be for Gracie and Latisha. Mrs. Conover, you have the room above Mama and J.D.'s. You'll like it. It's real nice and it has an ocean view. But Mama said everything could be rearranged any way you wanted it. She just had to get unpacked so she could change the twins. They needed it."

"And what about you?" I asked. "Where will you sleep?"

"I've got the whole third floor," he said. "Except I have to keep the babies out. J.D. said he didn't want to see either one of 'em come tumbling down two flights of stairs. So that whole big space is just for me. But," he went on somewhat wryly but not at all ashamed to admit it, "if I get lonesome up there, I'll bunk out on a sofa."

"Lloyd?" Latisha said, frowning. "I'm not a baby, so can I come up to your room? I won't fall down the stairs, so can I come up?"

"Yes, you can," he said. "But entrance to the penthouse is by invitation only."

"I don't know what kinda house that is," Latisha said, "but I'll let you know when I'm coming."

By that time, the men had unloaded the car and now several suitcases, shopping bags, and the Huggies package stood in the living room, waiting to be distributed to the correct rooms.

Coleman wiped his face with his sleeve. "Man, it's hot out there. Still, too. Where's that ocean breeze you promised, Sam?"

"Low tide," Sam said. "It'll pick up in a while. Well, Julia," he went on, turning to me, "what do you think?"

"I think you've outdone yourself. The place is lovely, Sam, and perfect for us. Of course, though," I said, smiling at him, "I haven't been upstairs yet."

"Oh, you'll like it!" Latisha said, her piercing voice drowning out everybody else. "Come on, I'll show you." And up the stairs she raced with LuAnne and me following more sedately.

Mr. Pickens grabbed a twin in each arm as they started to follow us up the stairs. "Oh, no, you don't." He carried them to the front porch—screened in like the back one—and set them down in the middle of a pile of toys already unpacked and strewn around. All I could think of as we reached the second floor was what a time we'd have when we had to pack up and reload the cars.

Latisha showed us the room she would share with Little Gracie, announcing that it was as pretty as any you'd see on "that ole HGTV."

LuAnne, thank goodness, was pleased with her room and, I think, maybe a little stymied that she could find nothing to complain about. It was, in fact, equal to the master bedrooms downstairs except for having two full-sized beds instead of one king, which was perfect for LuAnne and Etta Mae.

Hearing Hazel Marie and Binkie come in downstairs, we hurried back down to see them. Everybody got hugged as if we hadn't seen each other in months while the men started bringing in groceries. Both Binkie and Hazel Marie raved over the house, thanking Sam profusely for his generosity.

Binkie said, "It's a thousand times better than a motel room with Gracie sleeping in the middle of the bed."

"Or," Coleman added, referring to their usual camping trips, "a pup tent with no room to turn over in."

Mr. Pickens had begun emptying grocery bags, setting out boxes, cans, and packages on the counter. He looked into one bag, then, holding it open, he sidled up to me. "Found your favorite here, Miss Julia. Wanta see?"

I glanced inside the bag to see a good many suspicious-looking cans. "Mr. Pickens," I said softly because I don't believe in publicly chiding anyone, "restraint is good for the soul. Don't drink that stuff in front of the children."

Those black eyes of his practically danced in his head. "I wouldn't dream of it. I'm saving half of it for you."

Chapter 13

I woke the next morning to the blare of cartoons on the television, the scream of "Mine!" from a child, the clatter of a spill of Legos, Hazel Marie announcing that breakfast was ready, and Binkie saying, "Let's all be real quiet so people can sleep." Too late for that.

I turned to see Sam awake, staring at the ceiling. So I said, "This is what we wanted, isn't it?" We smiled at each other, agreeing that indeed it was.

At the rumble of male voices in the center room, I stirred and said, "I should get up and help with breakfast."

"Oh, let's take our time and let the kitchen clear out." And that's what we did, emerging some while later to find Coleman filling the dishwasher. He'd already cleared the table and the island, working as efficiently as if he did it every day, which he probably did.

I had put on one of the outfits that Hazel Marie had chosen for me—a loose top and what she'd called capris that bared my legs from below my knees to my purple-tipped toes. Highly self-conscious from being so unusually clad, the worst was being without stockings. The stark nakedness of my bare, white shins and feet seemed to glow, and, for the first time, I could see the benefit of basking in the sun. If I could find a way to put the rest of myself in the shade, I determined to let the sun have its way with my lower limbs. Perhaps then they would at least *look* clothed.

The whole crew gradually collected in the living room, some carrying beach towels, some with sun hats, others with buckets and shovels for the children, some with bottles of suntan lotion, Coleman with a Styrofoam container filled with snacks and drinks, and every last one of them in various stages of dress. Or rather, undress. I declare, bare male chests seemed much larger than they did when shirt covered. I tried not to look—staring is so rude—at all the uncovered skin, male and female alike. Binkie and Hazel Marie were showing uncommonly wide expanses of it.

Sam, I have to say, held up well when compared to the younger men. Not that I was comparing, but when three half-naked men are right in front of one's eyes, well, one can hardly help but size them up.

The children, also clad in the briefest of clothing, could hardly contain themselves, so eager were they to get to the beach. Mr. Pickens snatched up the twins, their little ruffle-clad bottoms tucked under his arms. Yelling up two flights of stairs, he called, "Lloyd! Come on, bud! I'm surrounded by women down here."

"I think we've got everything," Hazel Marie said, calmly looking around. "Miss Julia, are you and Mr. Sam coming?"

We were still sitting on stools at the island finishing our second cups of coffee. "I'll walk down in a little while," I said. "I want to check on LuAnne first."

"Coleman?" Sam said, getting his attention. "There's supposed to be a couple of large unbrellas downstairs if you want them."

"Oh, we do," Binkie said. "They'll be shade for the children. I don't want anybody getting sunburned on the first day."

Latisha had been noticeably quiet, although she'd been milling around with the children as they waited for their minders to unlatch the screen door. Somebody had given her a bright blue bucket which she was holding close as she glanced several times out toward the ocean—with, I thought, anticipation but perhaps with a little apprehension, as well.

"Latisha," I said, motioning for her to walk over to me. "Are you looking forward to going in the ocean, honey? It'll be a lot of fun."

"No, ma'am, not for me it won't," she said as seriously as I'd ever seen her. "They's things in that ocean that I don't wanta see. I might wade a little bit, but Miss Hazel Marie told me that that ole beach is just covered with shells, so I'm gonna get me some. She wants some, too, so we might look for 'em together."

"What a good idea! When I come down, I'll help, too. We can

walk down the beach picking up shells and putting them in your bucket. Then when we come back to the house, we'll call your great-granny and see how she's doing."

"Okay, 'cause I could use some help. I'm plannin' to take me home a whole bunch of shells so Great-Granny can have some souvenirs of my beach trip."

Mr. Pickens looked around and began counting heads. "Okay, everybody, let's go. Stay together now."

And off they went with Lloyd bringing up the rear. He'd raced down the stairs at the last minute, waved at Sam and me, and headed out.

"Oh, Sam," I said as we watched them walk in a line over the dunes, Coleman and Mr. Pickens carrying the little ones, "I wonder if Lillian's surgery is over. I've a good mind to call her. You think she'll be home?"

Sam looked at his watch. "She's probably still in Day Surgery. I'd wait till after lunch. She'll be home by then."

I nodded, feeling that I should've been with her, but now that our multifamily vacation seemed to have gotten off to such a good start, I was also glad to be where I was. Everybody was in a happy, expectant mood, patient with the children, helpful with each other, and glad to be there. Then I remembered LuAnne.

Sliding off the stool, I said, "Let's go to the beach, Sam. I want to go before the sun gets too high."

"You want to see if LuAnne wants to go?"

I shook my head. "No, if she can sleep with all the noise we've made this morning, she probably needs it. Besides, I don't want to hover. I told her before we left home that everybody was on their own, doing whatever they want to do."

"Let's go then. Don't forget your sunglasses—you'll need 'em."

I must say that the beach was glorious, its white sand stretching from north to south as far as the eye could see, the waves breaking in a rush of whitecaps close to the shore, suntanned bodies dotted here and there, and the breeze playing havoc with my hair.

We found Hazel Marie and the little ones clustered under the open umbrellas, while Binkie and Coleman were out beyond the breakers. I saw two more familiar heads bobbing up and down with the waves—Mr. Pickens and Lloyd. Latisha was crouched down a safe distance from the encroaching waves, searching, I supposed, for shells.

"I'm going in with J.D. when they get back," Hazel Marie said. She brushed sand off Julie's back, then stuck a tiny shovel in her hand, saying, "See what you can dig up."

While Sam headed out into the ocean, I sat down in the shade and looked toward the sea. "Hazel Marie, are they too far out?"

She looked up, squinting in the glare off the water as she shaded her eyes with her hand. "No, J.D. said the tide's coming in so it's shallow for a long way out."

I took off my sandals, stuck my feet with their purple toenails out in the sun, and commented on the view. "Those waves look awfully big way out there."

"Yes," Hazel Marie said, "they're big, rolling ones, aren't they? J.D. says it's because there's a tropical storm down south."

"A *storm*? You mean a hurricane?"

"Could be, but it's a long way off. He says it'd have to pick up a lot of steam to reach us while we're here."

"Well, a storm anywhere is certainly worrisome," I said, somewhat disturbed by the thought. "Sam promised to check the Weather Channel every day, and he's not said a word about it."

Hazel Marie smiled. "Probably because it's not a threat to us."

"Not yet, anyway," I mumbled, then rose with some effort. "I think I'll take a walk with Latisha."

Latisha was eager for a change of scene. "I've already picked this place clean," she said, rattling the shells in her bucket. "I thought there'd be piles of shells everywhere, but, my gracious, you have to look for 'em. An' they're all tee-ninesy little ones. It'll take a million to do what I want to do."

Deciding it was better not to ask what she wanted to do, I took her hand and we began walking along the edge of the water, splashing through the foam as the waves came in. Latisha, saying that she needed her some sunglasses, pounced on every shell she saw. It didn't seem to matter what size, shape, or condition they were in, she picked up every one she saw. Her bucket was already more than half full.

"What're you going to do when you fill your bucket?" I asked, watching as she put another shell in it.

"I been thinkin' about that, an' I'm gonna empty this thing in a grocery sack every day, then come back down here and fill 'er up again."

"Good thinking," I said, smiling at her enthusiasm and relieved that it didn't extend to going in the water. "Well, let's turn back. It'll be time for lunch soon."

"That's what I'm countin' on," she said.

And by that time, I realized, so was I.

Chapter 14

After lunch, I took Latisha into the front bedroom, closed the door against the coming and going, the noise and confusion on the other side, and called Lillian.

Half expecting Miss Bessie to answer, I was pleased to hear Lillian's voice, subdued though it was.

"Lillian!" I exclaimed. "How are you? How did the surgery go? Are you feeling all right?"

"Hey, Miss Julia, how's Latisha doin'? She behavin' herself?"

"Latisha is just fine. She's right here and she wants to speak to you." Handing the phone to Latisha, I said, "Here, honey, tell your granny what you've been doing."

"Hey, Great-Granny," Latisha said, looking off into the distance as if she could see Lillian on the ceiling. "You oughta see this big ole ocean. Lloyd says it stretches all the way to China or somewhere."

Silence on Latisha's end.

"Yes'm, we eatin' pretty good."

More silence.

"No'm, I don't have a chance to bother nobody. Lloyd say he's gonna wear me out chasin' them ole tennis balls. Then I'll get in some time pickin' up shells, an' first thing you know, it'll be time to eat supper and then go to bed. And that's about it."

More silence.

"Yes'm, I will. Uh-huh, she right here." Latisha thrust the phone at me, saying, "She want to talk to you, an' I want some of that ice cream Coleman got for us." And off she went.

"Lillian?" I said into the phone. "Now tell me how you're feeling and how the surgery went."

"Well, Miss Julia," Lillian said, "I tell you what's a fact. I'm just settin' here 'bout to cry."

"What? Why? What's wrong, Lillian? Are you in pain? Didn't the doctor give you something? Call him. Call him right now or get Miss Bessie to call him. She's there with you, isn't she? Oh, Lillian, I can't stand it if you're not being looked after." I *knew* I should've stayed home.

"No'm, nothin' like that. I got some pain medicine for when I need it. No, I'm 'bout to cry 'cause I'm so happy that ole bunion's gone, an' on top of that, the Reverend Abernathy, he bring two big, strappin' deacons over here totin' in a big ole reclinin' chair that lays down and sets up and lifts my feet up an' keeps 'em up, just like the doctor tole me to. The onliest thing wrong is the doctor say I have to stay off my feet for a whole week. Then he gonna look at it an' maybe put on a walkin' cask, so I don't know how much work I can do for a while."

"That doesn't matter. You just get yourself well and take as long as you need to do it. And don't you worry about Latisha. She is perfectly behaved in every way. Now is there anything you need?"

"No'm, I don't need a thing. I'm just half layin' here in this big ole chair, feelin' like the Queen of Sheba. Miss Bessie, she in there cookin' turnip greens and cornbread for supper, so everything's jus' fine. An' best of all, that ole bunion won't be botherin' me no more."

After a few more reassurances from each of us—about her well-being from Lillian and about Latisha's from me—we hung up with a promise to talk again soon.

Walks to the beach, sandwiches for lunch, naps for the little ones— and for a few older ones as well—was pretty much the way the next day or so went, broken only by evening trips to seafood restaurants. Otherwise, I was occupied with sweeping sand out of the house, hanging up wet bathing suits, applying Noxzema to several sun-burned shoulders, finding plastic bags for Latisha's ever-increasing collection of shells, and occasionally just sitting on the front porch with LuAnne while the children napped.

Lloyd, taking Latisha with him, routinely walked to the tennis courts where they soon discovered that they could buy pizza slices for lunch. Latisha came back every day sated with pizza and worn to a frazzle from the tennis lessons that Lloyd put her through. She took a short nap in the afternoon but was always ready to accompany the others to the beach where she collected shells until time to go out for dinner.

One evening Hazel Marie and Binkie decided that we should eat in so the children, who'd become a little cranky, could get to bed early. Using huge pots, they boiled fresh shrimp and corn on the cob, then, after draining the pots, dumped everything on the large newspaper-covered table, which was soon piled high with shrimp shells. Coleman concocted a perfectly spiced cocktail sauce and Mr. Pickens made a salad, while Sam filled glasses with ice and tea. It was eye-opening for me to see how easily the men adapted to kitchen work.

And every day, the sky grew hazier and the waves grew larger.

"Sam?" I said one afternoon as the house quieted for nap time. "Are you watching the Weather Channel?"

"I'm on it," he said. "And that tropical depression has grown big enough to get a name and a category. Marty is on the verge of a catagory two designation. But, Julia, let's not worry about it. They're showing six different paths it could take, and only one would adversely affect us. It could go across Cuba and end up in Texas, or it could make landfall on Florida and go up into Georgia and Alabama. Or, more likely, it'll veer off to the northeast and stay miles from us. We might get a day or two of rain, but that'd be about it."

"I hope you're right, though I'd hate for it to be raining when Etta Mae gets here."

"It won't be," Sam said, though how he could be so sure was beyond me. Then he went on. "Have you figured out the sleeping arrangements? She'll be here Friday evening, won't she?"

"Or Saturday morning if she lets herself get caught up with the reception after the funeral. I'll call her tonight and make sure she's coming. And as far as sleeping arrangements are concerned, there're two full-sized beds in LuAnne's room so that's the obvious place."

"Hmm," Sam said. "Think that'll work?"

I sighed. "It'll have to. LuAnne knows that Etta Mae is coming, and she can count beds as well as I can. But," I said with another sigh, "I'd better confirm it before Etta Mae gets here. And if LuAnne pitches a fit about losing her privacy, I guess I'll have to put Etta Mae on the third floor with Lloyd. Although that's not such a good idea, so he'll have to sleep downstairs on a sofa. My goodness," I went on, "I thought I had it all worked out, and I did until LuAnne decided to come."

"How's she doing, anyway?"

"Actually, quite well. She's gone to the beach every day, and now she's shopping with Binkie and Hazel Marie. And, more important, she hasn't been sitting around bemoaning her fate."

"Maybe she's coming to terms with the situation."

"Whatever that means," I said with a sideways glance at him. "I can't imagine that she'd just live with it and let it keep going on, though that's what Leonard seems to expect her to do." I shuddered at the thought.

"Well," Sam said, "seems there're depths to Leonard that we've never suspected. He's the last man I would've expected to get himself in a situation like this."

I managed a wry smile. "LuAnne would certainly agree with you. As do I." I sat up as little heads began to appear one after the other over the dunes with Coleman and Mr. Pickens bringing up the rear. "Here they come. I better put out some snacks. They'll be starving."

Latisha was running ahead of the others and, as she reached the steps to the porch, began yelling at the top of her voice, "Miss Lady! Miss Lady! Look what I found!"

I met her at the screen door and opened it for her. "What is it? A real pretty shell?"

"Better than that by a long shot. I found some money! Can you believe they's money you can just pick up an' take home 'cause it don't belong to nobody? Look here, see? Lloyd told me what it is, an' that's what I'm gonna be lookin' for from now on. No need spendin' my time lookin' for shells that's not worth a red cent."

She reached into her bucket and held up an unusually perfect sand dollar, then reached back in to show me two more that were slightly chipped around the edges.

"Oh, Latisha," I said with the proper enthusiasm, "they are all beautiful. But be very careful with them—sand dollars break easily."

"Yes'm, Lloyd told me. I'm gonna take real good care of 'em, don't worry about that. I bet Great-Granny never thought there'd be money jus' layin' around waitin' to be picked up. Boy, is she gonna be surprised."

"I'm sure she will. But, Latisha, you know you can't spend sand dollars, don't you?"

"That don't matter. I got 'em an' I'm gonna keep 'em. Money's money to me. My teacher read us a book one time about pirates burying treasure on the beach, an' I'm bettin' this is part of it."

"That's wonderful, Latisha. Take good care of the one that's not chipped, because you certainly have a treasure." And a good imagination, as well.

The others had climbed the steps to the porch by this time and the little ones flocked around to see Latisha's great find. They weren't especially impressed with her wet, sandy bucketful of shells, so they looked and then walked away. Lloyd was grinning at Latisha's excitement, but he didn't—and wouldn't—ridicule her idea of treasure.

Chapter 15

Peace and quiet descended on the beach house that afternoon when Hazel Marie and Binkie took the little girls—including Latisha—to the movies, while the men, including Lloyd, went to a boat show. That left the house to LuAnne and me—the first time since being there that we'd had time alone.

We sat on the front porch in rocking chairs with glasses of lemonade on a table between us. A steady ocean breeze kept the heat from running us inside, while a few gusts now and then rattled the dry fronds on the palm trees.

"Julia," LuAnne said, "coming here was the best thing I could've done. I'm so glad you talked me into it."

I couldn't recall having had to exert much persuasion, but I nodded and said, "I hope it's been good for you. Getting away from a problem always puts things in a different light, don't you think?"

"It certainly has for me," she agreed. "And," she went on with a certain amount of satisfaction, "it has for Leonard, too. He's begging me to come home."

"You've talked to him?"

"Every day. He calls *me*, Julia, although I admit I called him first. I had to tell him there were some things in the freezer he could heat up. And of course how to heat them. I declare, I think the man would starve if he had to feed himself."

"Maybe you should let him," I murmured.

"Well, doesn't everybody deserve a second chance?"

"I suppose, but does that mean he's confessed everything and asked for a second chance?"

"No, it doesn't," LuAnne said, gritting her teeth. "And, Julia, I'd appreciate it if you wouldn't remind me. If I expect to ever get over this and put my marriage back together, it sure won't help for you to keep bringing up what he did."

"Well, I'm sorry," I said, stung by her jab at me. "I'm just concerned for you, LuAnne. If you try to overlook what he's done and pretend that everything's fine, it'll do nothing but eat away at you. Because there's no way you can just forget it happened."

She looked down at her hands, turned her wedding ring on her finger, then said, "I know that. But he keeps saying he's done nothing wrong and has no reason to confess or to ask for forgiveness. So it's up to me to decide if I can live with that. And I don't know if I can or if I can't."

She lifted her head and squinted out toward the ocean. "I know it's better to get it all out on the table," she went on. "But if he simply refuses, what can I do? He thinks our marriage is just fine."

"*Just fine!* When he's seeking solace from another woman? What about her, LuAnne? Do you want a third party in your marriage? I don't see you or any other woman being happy with that. I sure wouldn't be."

"Well, that's what you don't understand," LuAnne said with a tiny bit of smugness. "You never had a chance to confront Wesley Lloyd with what he did, so now you want me to do what you weren't able to do. You're reliving your problem through me."

I just hate it when somebody presumes to psychoanalyze me, but I did my best to brush it off. Sighing, I gave up and agreed with her.

"You may be right," I conceded. "But let me tell you this—if Leonard is smart, he'll never sleep well again. Because, LuAnne, if you let it fester inside, you're going to have fits of anger that'll come over you all of a sudden and no telling what you'll want to do. They used to come over me when I least expected them, and, I'll tell you, it's a good thing that Wesley Lloyd was already six feet under."

She didn't say anything for a few minutes, then her shoulders began to shake as she tried to muffle the laughter. Finally she laughed out loud. "Oh, Julia, you don't know how often I've wanted to skin Leonard alive. But I didn't know you felt that way about Wesley Lloyd. I mean, you're always in control. You never get mad, and you take things as they come without flying off the handle."

"Ha! You wouldn't believe some of the daydreams I've had about Wesley Lloyd—not recently, I admit, because I've put him to rest for good. But, honey, I've lashed him with a whip, pulled out all his hair, and turned him naked out of the house—all in my imagination."

She sputtered and said, "I've done every one of those things to Leonard, too, including braining him with an iron skillet. If Leonard knew what I've been thinking, he wouldn't want me within a hundred miles of home!"

We were both laughing by that time. But when LuAnne excused herself to go to the bathroom, I found myself wondering why we'd been laughing. There was nothing funny about her situation and certainly nothing funny about Leonard's denial of guilt.

I couldn't, for the life of me, figure out what the need of solace would entail, nor what was involved in the actual application of it, either. It was plain to me, though, that when a husband goes outside his marriage to have his needs met—be they for solace or whatever else—then that marriage is in trouble.

Yet LuAnne seemed to have decided that she might be able to live with sharing Leonard, the thought of which made me wonder just what either woman saw in him. I wouldn't have had him on a silver platter, but, I reminded myself, to each his own.

"Julia," LuAnne abruptly said as she came back onto the porch, "who am I kidding? There's no way in the world that I can just let it go on like this. And why would Leonard think that I could? It just doesn't make sense. *He* doesn't make sense."

"That's exactly what I've been thinking."

"Well, I wish you'd say so. It doesn't help if you just agree with everything I say. I need some options, some possibilities, not just platitudes and automatic agreements with whatever I bring up."

I declare, LuAnne was the most contrary woman I knew. She'd just slapped me down for saying what I thought, but the minute I agreed with her, she wasn't happy with that either. To tell the truth, I knew better than to get between a husband and a wife—whatever I said could come back to haunt me and ruin a friendship, as well.

"I'm just here to be a sounding board, LuAnne," I said, drawing back. "I'll tell you what I think when you want to hear it, but mainly I'll try to keep my opinions to myself."

"Well, don't do that! I may not agree with your opinions, but I do want to hear them. You might come up with something I never thought of because you've been through it."

"Not exactly," I pointed out. "I never had to decide whether to leave Wesley Lloyd or to put up with what he was doing. As you just reminded me, he was already gone, so I didn't have a decision to make. Listen," I said, putting my hand on her arm, "I hope you're praying about this. You're making a decision that will affect the rest of your life."

"Oh, Julia," she said, wiping away an overflowing tear, "I hate to admit this, but you know what it comes down to?"

"What?"

"Money. It comes down to money. If our retirement fund would support two households, or if I could support myself, I would leave him flat. I am so angry with him I can hardly stand it, and when he tells me that *she*—whoever *she* is—has nothing to do with me, I could strangle him. But . . . Well, wait." She jumped up, wiping her eyes, and ran into the living room, coming back with a box of Kleenex. "Sorry. I can't stop crying. Every time I think of the mess I'm in, I just start boo-hooing all over again.

"Anyway," she went on, mopping her tear-streaked face, "the thought of looking for a job just does me in. Who would hire me at my age? I'm not trained for anything and I can't do anything. Well, maybe I could be a lunchroom lady and wear a hairnet, but, Julia, I couldn't stand that. But the worst thing is thinking of being a *divorced* woman and knowing that everybody would know *why* I was divorced. I never pictured myself as a divorced woman—there's such an unfortunate aura about not being able to hold on to your husband. People always wonder what you'd done to ruin your marriage."

"Oh, LuAnne, I don't think that's true in this day and age. We know a lot of people who've been divorced, and we don't think anything about it."

"Maybe you don't, but I do."

"Well, think of this. I expect if we knew the real situations of a lot of people, there'd be a lot more who aren't divorced but who wish they were."

"I expect you're right," she said, surprising me with her agreement. "But I can tell you why they aren't—they can't afford it. It's too much trouble and it's too expensive. Like, for instance, I'd have to find a place to live because you know *he* won't move out. And did you know that when you rent an apartment you have to pay both the first *and* last month's rent at the same time? And then you have to pay a moving company, which means deciding what furniture I want and what Leonard will need, and it all gets to be too much."

"Well, if you really want my opinion, that's easy. If it were me, I'd leave him the recliner, the television set, and the remote. And take everything else. Oh, and," I said just as a reminder, "you could leave him that shaving kit, too."

"Hah! Do you know what he said when I asked about what I found in that thing? He said I shouldn't have been snooping around. Can you believe that? Snooping is what you do when you clean house—you don't clean *up*, you clean *out*. And throw away what you don't need, which is what I did with those nasty underpants."

Now, see, that's where LuAnne and I differed. I would've never thrown out such an obvious item of guilty evidence. I would've figured it would play a prominent role in any legal case I wanted to bring. But LuAnne didn't think that way. She went on the premise that if something wasn't around, it didn't exist and she wouldn't have to deal with it.

I wanted to tell her that that same attitude would work on Leonard, too. If she didn't have to put up with him every day, he'd soon fade away. Out of sight, out of mind, you know.

Chapter 16

Entering our bedroom to freshen up before going out for dinner, I found Sam sitting on the foot of our bed, gazing at the television set on the dresser.

"Watching the news?" I asked, thinking how out of touch with world events we'd been during our few days at the beach. And all for the good, if you want my opinion.

He smiled. "Just checking on Marty. It's still whirling around in the Caribbean, trying to make up its mind which way to go."

I sat beside him and watched as the meteorologist demonstrated on a map the storm's potential tracks, indicating to me that he didn't know any more about it than we did.

"It's pretty close to Cuba, isn't it?" I asked, trying to orient our position on the map. "Which means it's far from us."

"Right. And it's slow, which is a good thing for us. Except the longer it stays where it is, the stronger it gets."

"Oh, my goodness," I said, my attention heightened as the program switched to pictures of Floridians boarding up windows and emptying grocery shelves. "Sam, should we be doing anything?"

"No, honey. Even if it heads this way, we'd have several days to pack up and leave."

"I hope so," I said, laughing, "because the way everything's strewn all over the house, it'll take several days to pack up. Well," I went on as the weatherman relinquished camera time to the sports announcer, "I need to call Etta Mae and reassure her. I'd hate for her to come in tomorrow evening, then have to turn around and go home the next day."

"Etta Mae?" I said when she answered her phone. "Are you packed? Got gas in your car? We're expecting you tomorrow, you know."

"Oh, Miss Julia," she said, almost giddy with anticipation, "I am *so* ready. I can't wait to get there." Then, with a noticeable difference in tone, she said, "You still want me to come, don't you? I mean, your plans haven't changed, have they? Because if they have, it's all right."

"Our plans have absolutely not changed. We're all looking forward to having you. About what time do you think you'll be here?"

"Well, the funeral's at one, and I'll leave as soon as it's over, about two, I expect. So, I don't know, I should be there around six or seven, I guess. Maybe closer to seven, because I'll stop and get something to eat on the way."

"Call me when you're about an hour out and we'll wait supper for you. But, listen, Etta Mae," I went on, "I hope you won't mind sharing a room with LuAnne Conover. There're two full beds in her room and a private bath."

"Oh, I'll sleep anywhere, it doesn't matter to me. I wouldn't want to inconvenience Mrs. Conover."

"You won't, though she may inconvenience you. Just don't ask about her husband. She'd probably tell you about him all night long and you'd learn more than you ever wanted to know."

After a few more back and forth comments, including my telling her to be careful driving, we ended the call. I hung up and sat for a minute thinking of what a pleasure it was to do something for someone so openly appreciative.

Friday morning dawned gray and overcast, but hot as an oven. As the children gathered buckets and sunhats for their morning walk to the beach, Hazel Marie went around slathering suntan lotion on faces, shoulders, and arms. She had to chase down Lily Mae, who hid behind the sofa because she didn't like the feel of the lotion.

"Come on, now," Hazel Marie coaxed. "You don't want to get sunburned. We're taking some cookies with us, so you don't want to miss out on that, do you?"

Finally getting all the children thoroughly screened from the sun, she said, "Everybody else ought to use this, too. You can get the worst sunburns on a cloudy day." Hazel Marie knew what she was talking about, because getting a tan every summer had always been number one on her list of things to do.

Since it had never even placed on my list, I lingered at the house while the rest trooped across the dunes, towels dragging in the sand behind them. In a little while, LuAnne came downstairs, wearing what Binkie had whispered to me was a vintage bathing suit. Actually it was simply old because I could remember when a one-piece suit with a little skirt was the latest seaside fashion.

LuAnne announced that she was going to the beach because Marty was on the move and we might not have many more days to sunbathe. "And, Julia," she declared, "I'm not only going home with a tan, I'm going to lose weight. I've let myself get a little pudgy, especially around the waist, so I'm going to get back in shape."

Oh, my, I thought, now she's decided to woo Leonard back. Poor Leonard—being fought over by two women would certainly disrupt his television time.

With the house left to me alone, Sam having gone back to the boat show to take a second look at a fishing boat that had caught his eye, I poured another cup of coffee and sat on a sofa to watch a weather report.

From the graphics on the television screen, it seemed that Marty had ravaged Puerto Rico, then skirted Cuba and the Florida Keys during the night and was now churning along toward the northeast. With luck, it would continue on that course, sideswipe Bermuda, and head on out to sea. We would need that luck because it was now a category three storm, and people along the north Florida coast were continuing to be warned.

Suddenly I snapped off the television and sat up, listening more closely to what I thought I'd heard. I ran to the front porch just as Lloyd pounded up the stairs.

"Miss Julia! Come quick, you've got to see this!"

I think my heart stopped as images of one unspeakable horror after another flashed through my mind. "What? What is it?"

"Money, Miss Julia! Come on, hurry, you'll miss it." He grabbed my hand, tugging me toward the beach.

My first thought was that more sand dollars had washed ashore, but Lloyd knew better than that. Nonetheless, I trudged as fast as I could over the dunes behind him. Reaching the beach, I stood looking up and down the strand where people were racing along the water's edge, some stopping to bend down, others yelling as they waved something in the air. I saw not one soul lounging in the sun—they were all splashing along the water line, leaning over, searching, and grabbing at whatever was washing to shore. Binkie and Hazel Marie were at the water's edge holding the hands of the little ones but gazing off down the beach where the most activity was.

"Come on, Miss Julia," Lloyd urged. "Let's get closer. Have you ever seen anything like it?"

"Where's Latisha?" I asked as I hurried after him.

"She's with Coleman. They're right down here. Come on!"

When we reached the center of the activity, the excitement had almost died down. Sunbathers were gathering up towels and tote bags, many already hurrying across the dunes to get away from the beach. Coleman and Mr. Pickens stood grinning while Latisha, beside them with her little blue bucket, looked grim.

Lloyd said, "J.D., did you get any? Coleman, did you?"

"Nope," Mr. Pickens said. "We were afraid we'd get run over. Have you ever seen such scrambling?"

Coleman grinned. "Scrambling in the water, then scrambling to get away with what they found."

"Well, I think," Latisha solemnly announced, "that we oughta look around in case they missed some."

"Me, too," Lloyd said. "Come on, Latisha, maybe some washed farther up and we can find 'em."

I was finally able to get a word in edgewise. "What in the world was it?"

"Hundred-dollar bills," Coleman said. "Somebody found a couple of 'em washing in on a wave, then everybody started looking—and finding more and more. We think something—maybe a wallet or a pocketbook—fell off a boat somewhere." Then, after a moment's thought, he went on. "Maybe more like a strongbox or a duffel bag. There were bills floating around everywhere. Some people just paid for their vacations and then some."

"You're right about that," Mr. Pickens agreed, as both men professionally considered what had just happened. "A lot of money goes up and down Interstate 95. No reason it wouldn't go up and down the coastline, too."

"Why?" I asked. "I mean, where does it come from?"

"Smuggling," Coleman said. "Drugs, people, whatever."

"Oh, my," I said, understanding then why the apparently lucky ones had hurried away as fast as they had. Who would want to meet a smuggler looking to get his money back? "Lloyd," I said, calling to him, "you and Latisha come on back to the house. I expect the police will be here soon."

"Yep," Mr. Pickens said. "Probably the Coast Guard, too. Let's get everybody in. It's about lunchtime, anyway."

Chapter 17

The Great Money Haul took care of the morning, and it remained the subject of our conversation throughout lunch. Wild guesses as to the amount that had floated in were thrown around, but of course there was no way for us to know. Lloyd thought that it had to be millions. Hazel Marie said she'd seen one woman with both hands full of bills, and Mr. Pickens said that money in the aggregate looks like more than it actually is—a comment that put a lull in the guessing game.

The little girls were fussier than usual, having missed their playtime on the beach, so quiet didn't descend until they were put to bed for naps. By that time the day had brightened considerably after a cloudy start—all due to the antics of Marty, still off the coast of Florida. Even so, no one seemed inclined to go back to the beach—not even Latisha. She had dumped all her shells into the sink of an upstairs bathroom and was washing the sand from them.

Hazel Marie started a load of clothes in the washing machine, and Binkie decided to wash her hair. LuAnne had found a paperback book with a scantily clad, muscle-bound warrior on the cover, so she curled up on a sofa and began to read.

"Hey, everybody," Lloyd called as he stepped in from the front porch. "Cops are down on the beach, and I think the Coast Guard, too. J.D., can we go down and see what they're doing?"

"Sure," Mr. Pickens said. "Come on, Coleman, you're official, so maybe they won't run us off." And off they went.

Sam was reading a newspaper that he'd gone out to get, so I knew that he'd soon be occupied with the crossword puzzle. I fiddled around doing nothing much but glancing at my watch, thinking of Etta Mae. She should soon be out of the funeral and on her way.

I hoped that she'd enjoy her beach trip, although I still worried a little about her being the only single woman among us. Of course, LuAnne was temporarily—so far—a single woman, but she and Etta Mae had little in common.

Even with no eligible men around, I intended to see that Etta Mae had a good time. She deserved it, and as I thought of how much I actually owed her in terms of friendship and help on numerous occasions, I recalled the little use I'd had for her when we'd first met. She'd been a thorn in my flesh with her constant complaints about garbage pickup or lack of same, loud parties, and the generally poor upkeep of the Hillandale Trailer Park where she lived and which I owned, courtesy of Wesley Lloyd's demise. It had been Hazel Marie who'd suggested that I offer Etta Mae the job of manager of the park.

Unsure of the wisdom of encouraging the woman, I had reluctantly followed Hazel Marie's advice. I had to concede, however, that once Etta Mae took over the management, there was a noticeable improvement in the living conditions there.

The main reason for such a quick turnaround was the fact that Etta Mae's home was a single-wide hooked up to a rented space in the park, so she was on hand to see that things were run right. That single-wide, she'd said, was the only thing she owned free and clear, as it had been the settlement in the divorce from her second husband, and she had no intention of letting it go downhill in a trash-strewn trailer park.

The first thing she'd done was to evict the riffraff who'd been gradually moving into the park and who, according to her, had brought the park down to their own disreputable level. She'd made it clear that she had no use for such trash and wouldn't put up with them. She herself, she'd announced, had come from a long line of riffraff and knew how to handle them.

As I thought of these things, it occurred to me that Etta Mae might be able to give LuAnne some advice on living alone, although I couldn't envision LuAnne moving into a trailer park, no matter how well managed. Keeping up appearances was much too important to her.

After a while, the men came back to the house, full of what they'd learned from the law enforcement officers who were searching the beach.

"A yacht on the way to Miami got stranded, Miss Julia," Lloyd told me. "Right off the coast from here, maybe a little to the south, but too far out for us to see."

"What happened? I mean, how did it get stranded?"

"Blew a gasket or something, I guess. Anyway, it was just wallowing out there in the huge waves from the storm, so they had to call the Coast Guard. Boy, I bet they hated doing that!"

Coleman grinned. "Yeah, and hated having to get rid of their cargo, too."

"But," Mr. Pickens added, "it was either throw it overboard or be thrown in jail. By the time the Coast Guard boarded, it was just an innocent pleasure craft and the crew denied knowing anything about any kind of cargo. So they got towed in, and even though the officials were suspicious, they had no reason to hold the people on it."

"My goodness," I said, shocked at the waste. "You really think they just threw money overboard? I can't imagine doing such a thing."

Mr. Pickens's black eyebrows arched as he said, "Me, either. But somebody got rid of a pile of it—enough to show up all along the beach from below Sullivan's Island to here. No telling where it'll go when the tide turns. For all anybody knows," Mr. Pickens went on, thoroughly enjoying the possibility, "some of that money'll end up on the Jersey shore."

By that time the little girls had awakened and were now milling around in the center room with the rest of us. We'd had a few quick showers of rain spattering against the windows in gusts of wind, so no one was interested in sunbathing. To entertain them, as well as to add to the general noise, Binkie found a channel on the huge television set that was playing videos of what she called beach music.

Coleman cleared out the center of the room, grabbed Binkie, and they commenced dancing the shag. That delighted the little ones, and they began to dance along with them—not quite the shag, but twists and turns and shakes and whatever else they could think of that was inspired by the beat of the music.

Then Mr. Pickens took Hazel Marie's hand and began to demonstrate some moves that I didn't know he had in him. The children were thoroughly entertained to see their parents putting on a show, so squeals and laughter were added to the general mayhem.

When I saw the glint in Sam's eyes, I quickly busied myself in the kitchen. I had no desire to make a spectacle of myself trying to dance to a song about Leroy Brown.

Through all the whirling and twirling on the improvised dance floor, my eye caught sight of Latisha sitting apart as she watched the dancers. Surprised that she hadn't joined in, I noticed that she didn't look all that enthralled with the floor show. She looked, in fact, lost and lonely, so I threaded my way across the room and sat down beside her.

"Did you get your shells all cleaned up?" I asked.

"Yes, ma'am, and got some of the broke ones throwed out, too. I figured better to throw 'em out here than to tote 'em home and throw 'em out there."

"Good thinking," I said. "But what about your special sand dollars? Did you wash them, too?"

"No'm, I just wiped 'em with a washrag, then wrapped 'em up so they don't get broke. Great-Granny made me bring some socks in case we had to dress up, even though I tole her I didn't need no socks at the beach. But come to find out, I did need 'em 'cause that's what I used to wrap my sand dollars up in. Then I wrapped up them three socks in newspaper an' put 'em in a corner of my suitcase. So they ready to go when we leave this place."

"Are you ready to leave, Latisha?" My heart went out to her, well knowing the pangs of homesickness.

"I guess I could leave anytime, if it come down to it. But I sure do like that beach."

"Well, look," I said, pointing at the front windows, "the sun's coming out again. Let's you and me walk down to the beach and see what's going on. But first, would you like to call your Great-Granny and talk to her awhile?"

"No'm, I'll wait on that. She always ask me too many questions. I just as soon go for a walk. Maybe that big ole storm bring up some more sand dollars."

I took her hand and we moved around the gyrating children to the porch, then walked down the path to the beach. The breeze was stronger than usual, but not too bad. It was the sudden gusts, though, that tore through my hair, making me long for a scarf or a hat or something to hold it on my head. Maybe a helmet.

"Hey, wait for me!"

I looked back to see Lloyd running after us, so Latisha and I waited at the top of the dune.

"You're not dancing?" I asked, smiling as he caught up with us.

"Nope," he said, laughing. "The best dancers are already taken. I was just about to ask you, Latisha, but first thing I knew you were gone." He gave me a quick grin. "That left Mrs. Conover, so I decided I better get out of there."

I had to laugh at Lloyd's sense of propriety. He'd had a few years of attending cotillion classes and knew a gentleman's social obligations. To simply leave had seemed to him the better part of valor.

"Boy, the beach is just about deserted, isn't it?" Lloyd looked up and down the strand as he made his observation. "No cops, no Coast Guard, and no swimmers or sunbathers. Too much excitement this morning, I guess."

"Would you look at that," Latisha said, pointing south toward the pier. "What they doin' walkin' 'round like that?"

Coming our way, but still some distance away, was a trio of

figures in street clothes. As we reached the packed sand where the tide had receded, we could see that there were two men with their pants legs rolled up to their knees, carrying their shoes, while the statuesque woman, barefoot as well, had her shoes stuck one in each pocket of a windbreaker. The two men wore white dress shirts with ties loosened and flapping in the breeze. The woman was hampered by what Hazel Marie called a pencil skirt, a poor choice, it seemed to me, for a walk on the beach, or possibly a walk anywhere.

"Don't ask them, Latisha," Lloyd said. "Just pretend it's normal to swim fully dressed."

"Ha!" Latisha said. "That'd be pretty funny."

But the three fully dressed people didn't appear to be interested in swimming. They veered up near the foot of the dunes, walking unsteadily in and among the dune grasses and sea oats that grew in the soft, thick sand.

As we drew closer, the swarthier of the two men broke away and came toward us. "Afternoon," he said, his thick, dark hair blowing in the wind. He brushed it back with a gold-ringed hand, drawing my eye to the gold chain around his neck. "You folks live around here?"

"Just visiting," I replied. "And you?"

"Oh, we're just visiting, too. Heard there was some excitement around here this morning, so we decided to see if a bill or two got overlooked." He grinned to show that he knew how unlikely that was.

"Well," Latisha proclaimed, "you're lookin' in the right place, 'cause right about here's where I found mine."

I placed my hand on Latisha's shoulder to caution her about speaking to a stranger, but it was doubtful that she'd ever met one.

The man's eyebrows went up. "So you got some? How much, if you don't mind me asking."

I did mind. No well-bred person ever asks about money, either how much or how little, or whether it was found, earned, or inherited.

I sniffed and raised my head. "None," I said decisively. "We weren't even on the beach when it washed ashore."

"But, Miss Lady," Latisha said, tugging at my hand. "I found mine, remember?"

"That was something else, Latisha," I said. "He's not interested in that."

But, apparently, he was.

Chapter 18

"Is that right, little girl?" the man asked, peering closely at her as his companions glanced our way with disinterest. "How much did you find?"

"Three, but two's pretty messed up."

"That don't matter. The bank'll give you some good ones to replace them."

"It will?" Latisha said, frowning at the thought. "I didn't know that."

"Sure it will," he said. "Then you can buy yourself a scooter or something."

"I don't want no scooter."

Uncomfortable with his questions, I said, "Latisha is talking about something else entirely."

Then the man, having had enough of Latisha, turned to me.

"So you folks weren't at the beach when all the bills rolled in? Bet that was a disappointment."

Lloyd, who'd been digging his toes into the wet sand, then watching as the holes filled with water, looked up. He glanced at me and tilted his head to the side, indicating that he was ready to move on.

"Not especially," I said. "We saw enough of the mad scramble for money to stay out of it. So undignified, you know."

The woman, whose teased hair had been blown straight out to the side and was staying that way, which is what hair spray will do for you, had also had enough. With a roll of her eyes, she said, "Let's get on with it, Rob."

I, too, was ready to get on with our walk. The man—Rob, she'd called him—was much too interested in getting his hands on a few hundred-dollar bills, none of which we had.

"Well, nice meeting you," I said, taking Latisha's hand and starting on our way. Lloyd had already taken a few steps, but was still giving the three a quizzical once-over.

"Same here," Rob said in the dismissive tone that strangers use with each other. He caught up with his companions, and the three of them resumed their search for an errant hundred-dollar bill or two.

We walked on, stumbling occasionally in the wind gusts that seemed to be getting stronger. Lloyd kept turning his head to look back at the well-dressed but windblown beachcombers, checking, I supposed, to see if they'd found anything. I had my mind more on Etta Mae, wondering how far inland the wind gusts would go and hoping that her little car could withstand them. Latisha stopped every now and then to scrape sand from a shell sticking up from the wet sand, then moving on after deciding that it wasn't worth the trouble.

"I already got lots of shells better'n any I'm findin' today," she said.

"If you're not having any luck," I said, "why don't we turn back. Etta Mae will be coming in soon, and we should be there for her."

"Tell you what, Miss Julia," Lloyd said. "This wind's pretty strong. Why don't we cut across the dunes here? We'll come out near the hotel, and it'll be easier walking back to the house on the sidewalk."

"That's a good idea," I said, and that's what we did.

Lloyd, however, stopped at the top of the dune and looked back the way we had come. "They're still looking," he said as he hurried to catch up. "They're just about opposite our house. I'm just as glad they won't know where we're staying. That man was too nosy for my liking."

I frowned, wondering what he'd picked up that I hadn't. I mean, other than Rob's ill-bred interest in our financial standing and his penchant for jewelry. "Well, that's probably wise," I said. "No use advertising that we're renting the most expensive house around. You can't be too careful these days, especially with strangers."

"Not just strangers," Lloyd said, "but scavengers. Who ever

heard of hurrying here in street clothes to look for money hours later? It doesn't make sense."

But he made sense, so I picked up the pace when we reached the sidewalk, hurrying to reach the house that had two law enforcement officers temporarily in residence.

I combed my hair as best I could after our windblown walk, getting ready to go out for dinner. The children were restless with hunger in spite of the heavy snacks they'd had earlier. Sam had just finished insisting that we should go on while he stayed and waited for Etta Mae, when Lloyd sang out, "She's here!"

He ran down the back stairs to help with her luggage and soon they both came in, Lloyd with her battered suitcase and Etta Mae with a glowing smile on her face.

Hazel Marie and Binkie welcomed her with enthusiasm, while the children stood back and watched. Coleman and Mr. Pickens smiled at her, but restrained themselves from the hugs and kisses their wives were giving her. Surprisingly, LuAnne took it upon herself to lead Etta Mae up the stairs to the room they would share.

"We won't be but a minute," she said. "We'll just wash our hands." Etta Mae, I assumed, would want to do more than that after her long drive.

"Well, hurry up," Mr. Pickens said with a smile. I assumed that he'd had the same thought as I had. "We're about to starve."

We had to wait only about fifteen minutes before being led to a table on a screened porch at the back of the seafood house. It was worth the wait because we looked right out over the inlet where the shrimp boats were coming in for the evening. The little girls were entranced and, to tell the truth, so were the rest of us.

I had arranged to sit next to Etta Mae, wanting to make her feel comfortable and part of the group. While waiting for our orders, I asked about her trip.

"Oh, it was fine," she said, her eyes shining with the wonder of the late evening light on the water and the muscled men working on the boats. "I didn't have any trouble at all, but there sure was a lot of traffic."

"I think it's that way on Fridays every week of the summer," I said. "People coming down for the weekend. But how did the funeral go?"

"Well," Etta Mae said, frowning, "I guess it was as good as funerals get. I mean, it made me sad like they always do. I'm really going to miss her. She'd been my patient for almost two years, you know."

"Yes, I remember." I decided not to bring up that particular patient's promise to leave something in her will to Etta Mae. It was fairly obvious that the woman had not kept her promise and, even though Etta Mae was the least avaricious person I knew, I also knew that she couldn't help but be disappointed. I mean, when somebody promises something, they ought to either follow through or else not bring up the subject at all.

After eating enough fried fish, shrimp, crab, and scallops to raise the cholesterol count of everybody at the table, we shuffled out to our cars and headed back to the big yellow house. Latisha was sound asleep in our backseat by the time we got there, so she had to be walked up the stairs and put to bed. Coleman had Little Gracie over his shoulder because she, too, was out like a light.

The twins were just as sleepy, but were fighting it for all they were worth. Mr. Pickens carried them both in, and I don't know which of the three was the most grumpy. Hazel Marie was her usual serene self, following them into the bedrooms on the far side of the house and, I assume, putting the three of them to bed.

LuAnne, Etta Mae, and I sat up for an hour or so, letting our dinners settle. It was pleasant to just talk about nothing much between yawns, and especially pleasing to me that LuAnne had not objected to having a roommate. I'd fully expected to hear some complaints from her about sharing a room, especially with Etta Mae. LuAnne could on occasion feel just a little superior to those whom she considered beneath her in the social scheme of things. And ordinarily, Etta Mae would have qualified.

But perhaps, I mused, LuAnne was getting lonely. Granted, Leonard was not what I'd call good company, but she was probably used to having him around, even with his attachment to the television set. I expect, though, that LuAnne was at the point of considering poor company better than none at all. Whatever the reason, I was just glad that she seemed to be enjoying Etta Mae—as who wouldn't, I'd like to know.

The next morning brought a beautiful clear day, except for the bank of clouds on the eastern horizon, but the sunshine and the lowered wind put us all in good moods. The children were ready for the beach, and Etta Mae could hardly wait to get out in the sun. She was wearing a short cover-up over an eyepoppingly skimpy bathing suit.

As I stood by the sink rinsing breakfast dishes, I saw Binkie push Coleman against a kitchen counter and cover his eyes with her hand. "Eyes front, Buster!" she whispered fiercely to him, laughing as she did so. Coleman laughed, too, then he leaned down and kissed her full on the mouth. I kept rinsing cereal bowls.

Turning, I saw Mr. Pickens raise his eyebrows when Etta Mae's little robe gaped open. Hazel Marie, walking past him, gave him a pinch as she went.

"Hey, folks," Sam said, as they began gathering towels, suntan lotion, and all the other paraphernalia they usually took to the beach. "Listen up. Marty has stalled some way off the Florida coast and seems to be drifting out to sea. We're going to have a beautiful day, so everybody enjoy it—just in case."

"Oh, I can't wait!" Etta Mae said, her eyes shining. "I'm going to lie out in the sun all day long. I've just been dreaming about this."

Lloyd came clomping down the stairs from his room at the top of the house. His mother poured a glass of orange juice for him and put slices of bread in the toaster. "Come eat something, sugar," she said.

"Okay, thanks, Mom. Where's J.D.?"

"Right here, bub," Mr. Pickens said as he came from the bedroom. "What's up?"

As Lloyd slipped onto a stool at the island counter, he said, "You should've called me if you needed something from the car last night. I would've gotten it for you."

Mr. Pickens frowned. "I didn't go out to the car."

"Well, somebody did."

Chapter 19

"Here, honey," Hazel Marie said as she put a plate of toast and bacon in front of Lloyd. "Eat your breakfast." Cooking and serving breakfast hadn't been the way I'd planned it, but nothing would do but that Hazel Marie and Binkie turn themselves into short-order cooks.

I'd planned to hire a cook so that they, as well as I, wouldn't be stuck in the kitchen. I mean, what's a vacation if you have to do the same things you do at home? And even worse if you're into camping, doing those things in the open air on makeshift stoves, which was something I'd never understood. But both women insisted that they'd rather handle breakfast and lunch themselves, so I'd left it to them because I didn't do it either at home or on vacation.

Mr. Pickens pulled out a stool next to Lloyd and said, "Who?"

"I don't know," Lloyd said, shrugging. "I thought it was you. I got up sometime real late to go to the bathroom and when I started back to bed, I glanced out the back window. Our car door was open and the interior lights were on. Somebody was in the front seat, but from the angle—I was looking straight down—I couldn't see who it was. And, anyway, by the time I put my glasses on and got back to the window, everything was dark. So I just thought it was you."

"Hold on a minute," Mr. Pickens said. "Honey," he said, stopping Hazel Marie as she was leaving the kitchen, "did you lock the car when we got home last night?"

"No," she said, smiling. "I wasn't driving."

"Oh, dang. I was, wasn't I?" Mr. Pickens started toward the back door. "Coleman, come walk out to the car with me."

Lloyd grabbed his toast. "I'm coming, too."

And Sam put down his coffee cup and said, "I believe I'll tag along, as well."

I watched from the window over the sink as the men gathered around the Pickenses' vehicle. Mr. Pickens had the door open and was sitting behind the wheel. Even though I was watching from an angle not quite as acute as Lloyd's the night before, I could see his arm and hand reaching for the glove compartment, opening it, and rifling through the contents. Coleman, Sam, and Lloyd were leaning over to check out the interior.

Mr. Pickens turned on the engine and let the car run for a few minutes before switching it off. Sam and Lloyd walked around the car, kicking the tires, which for the life of me I couldn't see the purpose of. Coleman leaned on the open car door, talking with Mr. Pickens. Then he stepped back as Mr. Pickens exited the car. The four of them then stood around discussing the situation. I wished I could hear what they were saying and what conclusion they'd reached. The thought of someone wandering around the house and rummaging in the cars during the night was unsettling to say the least.

"What about the other cars?" I asked when they were back in the house, tempted to wring my hands. "Has anybody been in them?"

"They were all locked," Sam said, as he and Coleman suppressed grins that Mr. Pickens's car had been the only accessible one.

Lloyd, following Mr. Pickens in, asked, "Nothing was missing, was there? I mean, we hadn't left anything that anybody would want, had we?"

Mr. Pickens, looking grim, said, "No, everything was there, even the extra package of diapers in the back. The only thing of interest is still there. . . ." He stopped as Hazel Marie came into the living room with both twins ready for the beach.

Lowering my voice, because I knew that he never wanted to worry Hazel Marie, I asked, "What's the only thing?"

Lloyd edged in close to hear the answer.

"The car registration," Mr. Pickens said. "Which has Hazel Marie's name and our address. But," he went on more strongly, "what good would that do a local vandal? Which is who it probably was—just somebody going along the street, looking for something easy to steal." He grinned then. "They could've had the diapers if they were that hard up."

We made a ragtag line trooping across the dunes to the beach with towels dragging and little girls stumbling in the deep sand. But the beach was magnificent, and I was glad I'd decided to accompany them. No telling how many more sunny days we'd have with Marty unable to make up his or her mind which way to go.

We set up camp under the two large beach umbrellas that the homeowners had been thoughtful enough to make available to renters. We had two coolers filled with ice and drinks and snacks, innumerable towels, boxes of wipes, bottles of suntan lotion, sun hats, and toys that one child or another apparently couldn't go an hour or so without.

Etta Mae and Lloyd immediately splashed into the waves, diving into them and emerging beyond the breakers, which worried me no end. But Coleman and Mr. Pickens were close by, and soon Etta Mae had ventured out as far as she dared. She screamed and laughed, bobbing up and down with the rolling waves, calling to Lloyd, and enjoying herself immensely. She was like a child in giving herself totally to the delight of the moment.

After a while, she came out of the water, stooped down to talk to Latisha, then took her hand. Slowly and very gingerly, she and Latisha walked toward the water, Latisha cringing and yelling each time water foamed over her feet. Etta Mae kept encouraging her, and finally Latisha was in the ocean up to her waist. Clinging to Etta Mae, she experienced the up and down rocking motion of the waves for the first time.

By the time they came back to shore, Latisha had a glow of

accomplishment on her face. "I did it, Miss Lady!" she called as she ran up to me. "I been in the ocean and nothing got me!"

"I'm proud of you, Latisha," I said, shifting away from the spray. "You're a brave girl, but remember, you must not ever go in alone."

"Oh, I won't. Now that I got Etta Mae to take me, they's no need to go by myself. But now," she said, looking around, "I'm gonna get me a suntan like she's doin'." And, snatching up an errant towel, she spread it beside Etta Mae and stretched out on it.

Well, well, I thought, smiling to myself. It looked as if Etta Mae now had a new friend and possibly a little shadow, as well. My hope had been that Etta Mae would attract a nice, polite, and prosperous young man for a brief romance that could possibly blossom into something else, but the beach wasn't as crowded as usual, and no males meeting my criteria sauntered past. So maybe Latisha qualified as a temporarily acceptable substitute; at least she was somebody to talk to or, more likely, to listen to.

We had called Lillian the evening before, and she had sounded much more like herself, assuring me that she was well on the way to full recovery. She had then told me the latest Abbotsville news which I'd not yet recovered from.

"Miss Julia," she'd said, "you know that ole Mr. Thurlow Jones? Well, he fall off the roof an' break his leg on one side an' his hip on the other. They say he stove up good."

"The *roof*! What was he doing up there?"

"Fixin' the TV antenna 'cause his picture was flippin' past an' he couldn't watch it. He still in the hospital, an' nobody know when he get back home."

"Oh, my goodness, that foolish old man." I myself had had numerous run-ins with Thurlow Jones—he was the most aggravating man I'd ever known. He lived in a large two-story—three-story if you count the attic—brick house a few blocks from ours, and it was just like him to want to save money by fixing something himself. The fact of the matter, though, was that *every*thing needed fixing and, in spite of being as rich as Croesus, he and Ronnie, his huge Great Dane, lived in absolute squalor. And to think that at one time he'd presented himself as a suitor for my hand, having the gall to think that I would be flattered by his interest.

Wondering how in the world Thurlow would manage when he was released from the hospital, I had handed the phone to Latisha who had given Lillian a burst of information as to what she'd done during the day in great detail. Then with that done, she'd taken to responding with "Yes'm" and "No'm" several times before thrusting the phone back to me. After each phone call, I noticed that Latisha became quieter and quieter, and those quiet times were becoming longer as the week wore on. She was missing her great-granny and probably her own room and her own bed—home, in other words.

To forestall that aching feeling, after we'd returned from dinner that evening, I went out to the living room, holding up a deck of cards that I'd found in a drawer.

"Who wants to play Old Maid with me?" I sang out.

"I do!" Etta Mae said.

"Me, too," Lloyd chimed in.

I looked around. "We need one more. Four is the perfect number. Come on, Latisha, let's see who's the Old Maid."

"Well, it's not gonna be me," she said, frowning. "Besides, I don't know how to play."

"Oh, it's easy," Etta Mae said. "We'll teach you."

And so we did and had a good time doing it, although the first time Latisha was left with the Old Maid card, I thought she was going to cry. Etta Mae jollied her out of it, telling her that being an old maid had its compensations and that she ought to know because she was one for real.

The next round left Lloyd with the Old Maid, and Latisha thought it was so funny that she forgot all about missing her great-granny.

The next morning was Sunday, and as I dithered around thinking of going to church, then thinking of not going, and feeling badly about that, Thurlow Jones was still on my mind.

"Sam," I said, "I'm worried about Thurlow. How will he manage if he's as bad off as Lillian said."

"No need to worry about him, honey. He has enough money to buy all the help he needs."

"I know, but will he spend any of it? You know how tight he is." I sighed at the strangeness of some people, then asked, "You think we should go to church?"

"Well, it is Sunday," Sam said as if I didn't know it, "and that's what we usually do on the Lord's day. However," he went on in a deliberately ponderous way, "it is my considered opinion that the day promises to be a good one for swimming and sunning and maybe a little fishing. So, Julia, I think the Lord will forgive us if we take advantage of it, because that hurricane is beginning to edge up toward the coast of Georgia. This might be the last good beachified day we'll have."

"Then by all means," I said, smiling as my feeling of obligation melted away, "let's make the most of it."

Chapter 20

So we made our daily trek over the dunes to the beach, although to tell the truth, I was about to have had enough of it. Never a sun worshipper, I had nonetheless enjoyed being at water's edge while watching the children play, talking now and then with Hazel Marie and Binkie, and being astounded by the lack of sufficient clothing on other beachgoers. But enough is enough, especially since that Sunday morning was not bright and beautiful, but dull and hazy. Maybe we should've gone to church.

The overcast sky and ominously rolling waves, however, did not daunt our crew. Etta Mae slathered on suntan lotion and stretched out on a towel, convinced that the rays of the sun would do their work in spite of the cloud cover. The little girls continued to enjoy digging in the sand and splashing in the foam as the waves lapped at the shore. Latisha entertained herself by making what she called toad frog houses. She patted and smoothed wet sand over one foot, then carefully withdrew it to form a door and an empty interior. Using shells to outline a walkway to the door, she told me that during the night a toad frog would visit and leave his footprints at the entry. I didn't mention that the tide was coming in.

The men, including Lloyd, on whom I had kept my eye, went out much farther than I liked, but they didn't stay long.

Coleman was first out, striding up to the umbrellas and accepting a towel from Binkie. "Thanks, sweetie." Then to the rest of us, he said, "We're going over to Charleston. Anybody want to go with us?"

Binkie looked at Hazel Marie. "I'll watch the children, if you want to go."

Hazel Marie seemed tempted, but she said, "No, I don't think so. I'd like to do some shopping sometime, but not with three men standing around waiting for me to finish."

Mr. Pickens and Sam, with Lloyd trailing along, walked up in time to hear the last of that, and Mr. Pickens said, "Tell you what. This may be the last good beach day for a while. So if you girls want to wait and go shopping tomorrow when it might be raining, we'll go today and watch the children tomorrow. Lloyd," he said, turning to him, "why don't you come with us? Unless you want to wait and go with the ladies."

"I'll go with you," he said, a choice that didn't surprise me. He never lost a chance to spend time with Mr. Pickens.

Sam's eyebrows had gone up when he heard that he'd been so cavalierly volunteered to babysit, but he took it in stride. "That'll work."

And Coleman said, "Good deal. There're a couple of things I want to look at again."

Binkie stood up, brushed sand off her backside, and said, "We have all the camping gear we need, honey. But you need shirts. Why don't you look for a couple?"

"Yes, ma'am," Coleman said and gave her a quick kiss that missed its mark. They laughed together, then the men trudged over the dunes, Mr. Pickens's arm draped over Lloyd's shoulders.

That left us women, and little girls, to ourselves, and we continued doing what we'd been doing—lolling around and watching children.

When I was sure that the men had had time to change and leave the house, I bestirred myself to go inside for a little peace and quiet.

"Don't go," Hazel Marie said. "We're taking the children—wet suits, sand, and all—up to the hot dog stand. Stay and go with us."

"Thank you, but no. I'll fend for myself at the house." Gathering my things, I hurriedly made tracks over the dunes, hoping for a hour or so of solitude.

After a quick shower and change of clothing, I spent twenty minutes trying to do something with my hair, all the time appreciating the silence of the house. Just as I started toward the kitchen to fix a sandwich, the screen door slammed and LuAnne came in clutching a towel.

"I've had enough of ocean breezes," she said. "And I certainly don't want a hot dog. I should've come on back when you did. Oh, if you're fixing lunch, I'll just have a ham sandwich. If there's any ham left. I declare, Julia, I'd forgotten how quickly food can disappear in a house full of children. And grown men." Heading upstairs to her room, she said over her shoulder, "I won't be long."

And there went my quiet time, but I made the sandwiches and, leaving hers on the island, took mine to the big sofa in the living room.

She soon joined me, eating her sandwich beside me; then she curled up on the other end of the sofa, ready to talk.

"Julia," she announced, "I've just realized that I made a big mistake by coming here with all of you. I should've stayed home, and I've a good mind to pack up and leave this afternoon."

"Why, LuAnne, I thought you were having a good time. What's changed, and how would you leave? There's not an extra car."

"Oh, I could take a bus. I wouldn't mind that, but of course I don't know their schedule and, anyway, somebody would have to drive me to Charleston to catch it. So tomorrow will be better. Besides, I'm not packed yet."

"Well, I'm sorry you want to leave," I said, dismayed at her change of heart, although I knew that LuAnne was given to sudden and, often, rash decisions. "Has anything happened to make you want to go."

"No, not specifically," she said, looking off in the distance. "Well, actually, it's just everything. Oh, Julia." As the tears started, she jumped up to look for a Kleenex box, but came back to the sofa with a paper towel. Bounty, I think.

"Don't cry, LuAnne. Tell me what's wrong. Is it Leonard again? I mean, still?"

Her face covered with the paper towel, she nodded. "It's always Leonard. When I see Binkie and Coleman, and Hazel

Marie and J.D. being all lovey-dovey—and the men are so sweet—
it just cuts me to the bone."

"I know just what you mean. I used to feel the same way."

"Well, *see*," she said, glaring at me from tear-filled eyes. "You've
forgotten how it hurts to compare the way they treat their wives
and the way Leonard treats me. Julia, every time I hear J.D. Pickens call Hazel Marie *baby girl*, or see Coleman look at Binkie like
he could eat her up as he calls her *sweetheart*, well, it just tears me
up. It hurts so bad, I can hardly stand it."

"Well, my goodness," I murmured, stunned at the bitterness of
her words. "I'm sorry. I'm used to the way they carry on, so it
didn't occur to me—"

"Of course it wouldn't," LuAnne said accusingly. "You don't
have to just watch it, you have it, too."

"Have what?"

"A husband who acts like he loves you! Wake up, Julia, and
don't deny it. Sam treats you like you're the greatest thing since
sliced bread. And you don't know how much it hurts to see how
sweet and attentive he is to you when . . ." She stopped for a deep
breath. "When Leonard treats me like a piece of furniture. Or a
refrigerator because I feed him.

"And I'll tell you another thing. Sometimes when I go downtown and see those couples—especially the old ones—walk down
the sidewalk *holding hands*, it makes me so angry I can hardly
stand it. Leonard *never* holds hands with me, in *or* out of public.
In fact, he hardly ever even *walks* with me. He just shuffles along
two steps behind me like we're not even together."

I didn't know how to respond to this torrent of pain and vehe-
mence, so I said, "I guess I never thought about it."

"Well, why would you? But I can't stand having my face rubbed
in it all day long. I need to go home, Julia, and reconcile myself to
living without what you and Binkie and Hazel Marie have and
don't even appreciate. You just take it for granted."

"Oh, I don't think we take it for granted."

"Of course you do," LuAnne said with a flip of her hand. "Just think how you'd feel if Sam suddenly ignored you like Leonard ignores me. Think how you'd feel if you had to struggle into your coat while he just stood there watching you. Think how you'd feel if Sam said first crack out of the box every morning, 'What's for breakfast?' But of course you have Lillian, so I guess that doesn't apply. But, Julia, he has never, *ever*, called me a sweet name—not from day one of our marriage. And I remember one day I was in a shop and the elderly clerk said, 'What can I do for you, little darling?' Now, I know some women would've been mortally offended, but I wasn't. To have someone say something that sweet to me just tore me up, and I had to leave before I started crying."

"Oh, honey, that hurts me, too."

"But would Leonard ever say anything like that? No, he wouldn't. He makes me feel like I'm just an attachment, something he puts up with as long as I perform in the kitchen."

"Oh, LuAnne, I don't think that's true. He's quiet and withdrawn, and not very demonstrative, but a lot of men are like that."

She shot me an accusing look. "How would you know?"

That did it for me. "How would *I* know? I know because I was married to somebody who was worse than Leonard ever was for forty-something years, and I resent being made to feel bad now because I lucked out with Sam. And if you want to know the truth, I feel that I *deserve* him because of what I had to put up with for so long."

LuAnne wiped her eyes and sat up. "I think you do, too. And furthermore, I think *I* deserve somebody like Sam, too. And I'm going to start looking for him." She stopped and blew her nose on the paper towel. "Just as soon as I get home."

Chapter 21

Relieved that she wouldn't start looking that afternoon, I was happy to see the beach crew come straggling in, putting an end to our conversation. It did not, however, end my concern for LuAnne and her new plan. Where in the world would she find another Sam? He was one of a kind to my way of thinking. Good men don't grow on trees, you know.

I've said it before and I'll say it again—you never know what you're getting until you've married him. And to my—and LuAnne's—generation, that meant you were pretty well stuck with whatever you'd gotten. Everybody thought that I'd made a brilliant move when I entered into a marriage with Wesley Lloyd Springer. And I'd thought so, too, until I'd had to live in it. He'd been mature, wealthy, a town mover and shaker, and a churchgoer. And furthermore, he'd bathed frequently, dressed well, had good table manners—except for stirring his tea so long that I wanted to slap the spoon out of his hand—and didn't snore. What more could a woman want?

Well, take it from me, a lot more. A little kindness now and then, for one thing, instead of critical commentaries. Some thoughtfulness occasionally wouldn't have hurt, either. A few give-and-take conversations that didn't end with a lecture on how wrong I was, for another. And what about taking a little pleasure just by being in my company?

But LuAnne had been on the right track—what a husband calls you or how he refers to you in the company of others reveals his true feelings. Wesley Lloyd had spoken to me and of me in terms of pronouns—you, she, her, and occasionally simply Julia. Never, never had words like honey, darling, sweetheart, or anything of the kind issued from his mouth. At least addressed to me, they hadn't.

And don't tell me that those words can be used when they have no meaning behind them. I know that, but I also know that being called a sweet name can warm a cooling heart and erase a lot of bitter feelings. And a lack of loving words is quite likely to indicate a dearth of loving feelings.

I'm not wrong about that because right soon after Wesley Lloyd had been laid to rest, I'd learned exactly where his feelings had lain.

But enough of that. Suffice it to say that I understood LuAnne's longing for spontaneous indications of Leonard's love and commitment to her. But of course if he had another woman on the back burner, she wasn't going to get any. However, as much as I sympathized with her, I had heard about all I wanted to hear on the subject of Leonard Conover.

A sudden rain shower spattered against the windows and we both got up to look out. The ocean's edge was white with breakers and the sea oats were bent over by the wind.

"Oh, my," I said, thinking of the little ones getting sopping wet. "Everybody's out in this."

"They're probably at the hot dog stand," LuAnne said.

"There's no shelter at that thing. Let's hope they're in the hotel lobby, waiting out the rain."

"I hear somebody," LuAnne said, turning toward the back door.

And sure enough, in came Hazel Marie carrying one twin, Etta Mae with the other one, Binkie with Little Gracie, and Latisha loaded down with hats and towels—everything and everyone looking like a gaggle of drowned rats.

"Look, Miss Lady!" Latisha screamed as she swung a little red plastic pocketbook, as bright and shiny as patent leather, from its red strap. "Look what Miss Binkie got me in the hotel. We had to go in there to get out of the rain, an' they had a little store in there just full of all kinds of things. But this was the best of all. I been wantin' me a pocketbook, an' now I got one."

"Run dry off, Latisha," I said. "But your pocketbook is lovely and just perfect for Sunday school."

"Yes'm, but for more'n that."

Hurriedly bringing an armful of towels, I helped the mothers strip the little girls and dry them off, then reclothe them. And on top of that, entertain them while their mothers showered and dressed.

Latisha announced in her piercing voice that she was glad she'd gotten her hot dog eaten before the rain turned the bun to mush. "I never seen rain come down so hard," she said, "an' us out in it. I thought somebody was gonna get hit with lightnin', 'cause you know it come with hard rain."

"Well, you're safe now, Latisha," I assured her, although I'd not heard a clap of thunder in the first place. "But what're we going to do with your hair?"

"It jus' gonna dry by itself," she said. "A little rain won't hurt it, an' Great-Granny'll fix it when I get home."

"Well, if you're sure," I said, somewhat relieved because I wasn't sure that I remembered how to plait.

The men came in a little later, expressing surprise that we'd had rain. "It was clear as a bell in the city," Sam said.

"And hot as hell," Mr. Pickens said under his breath. "Well, ladies, who wants to go out to eat?"

We all looked at each other, torn between risking another near-drowning and having to cook a meal. Nobody said anything.

"Tell you what," Coleman said. "Why don't a couple of us go pick up some barbecue?"

Every face in the room brightened at the prospect, so Binkie set about making a list of who wanted what.

By the time we'd had our fill of barbecue and put the children to bed, the rain squalls had stopped and an almost full moon was lighting up the beach. Streaks of cloud, though, were hovering on the horizon with the occasional flash of lightning way off in the distance.

"Sam," I said, as we prepared for bed, "where is that hurricane? Was this rainy day a precursor?"

He grinned, then said, "Might've been, honey. I just checked the Weather Channel, and the eye's off the south coast of Georgia but it's not expected to turn inward. In fact, they said it's wobbling toward the east and out to sea. We'll just have to wait and see what tomorrow brings."

"Well, I don't want to be caught down here in a hurricane that's turned tricky on us. Maybe we should think about going on home."

"Still plenty of time, honey," he said as he crawled in beside me. "I bet Marty'll be hammering Bermuda tomorrow, and we'll have a beautiful day." He turned off the light, then turned to me. "If you'd like to take that bet, sweet girl, it's time to ante up."

With a brief sympathetic thought of LuAnne and what she was missing, I turned to my sweet-talking husband.

My eyes snapped open as a loud banging noise—*blam, blam, blam*—from the back of the house jerked me wide awake. Sam was already pulling on his pants, while the thump of feet hitting the floor resounded all over the house.

"What is it?" I asked, still sleep befuddled, although the room was bright with early morning sun.

"Somebody at the door." Sam left, pulling the bedroom door closed behind him.

The banging at the back door stopped, so Sam or Mr. Pickens or Coleman or maybe all three had gotten there to stop it.

What in the world was it? Maybe the vandal had returned and done some real damage to the cars this time. I threw back the covers, quickly put on a robe, and hurried out to meet whatever it was head on.

"Who is it?" Hazel Marie asked, peeking out from behind the door of her bedroom.

"What's going on?" Binkie looked over the railing from the second floor, while Little Gracie and Latisha huddled next to her.

"Somebody at the door, I think," I answered. "I just hope nothing's happened to the cars." By that time I was looking out the window over the kitchen sink, and my heart sank at what I saw. "Looks like island security or rent-a-cop or somebody official."

I turned around as Sam returned, trailed by Coleman and Mr. Pickens. "Are the cars all right?"

"They're fine, except for being close to empty," Coleman said. "Ladies, we're being evacuated. Get everybody packed while we go gas up."

Evacuated? That meant that time was running out, didn't it? It hadn't been a suggestion, but an order—get out and get out now.

"Sam?" I said, getting his attention. "Sam, is it the hurricane? Is it headed this way?"

"Sure is. It's roaring up the coast, headed for Charleston and the islands. Which means us."

"Well, what happened to Bermuda is what I want to know. Last night you said it was wobbling that way."

"Sounds like it stopped wobbling and worked up a head of steam. Get everybody ready to go, we'll be back in a few minutes."

Grabbing car keys, the three men didn't stop to dress, just headed out in short or long pants, T-shirts or pajama tops, sans belts and shirts. At the door, Sam pulled up short. "Julia, honey, run upstairs and get Etta Mae's keys. We need to get her car filled up, too."

I hurried up the stairs, realizing that there were three men and four cars, so I'd have to roust Etta Mae out of bed.

She met me at the door of her room, and when I explained the situation, she proved how a single woman looks after herself. I hoped LuAnne would take note.

"No problem," Etta Mae said. "I always fill up when I get where I'm going. I did it Friday night before coming here, and I haven't driven it since."

"Etta Mae, you are a wonder."

"No'm, just thinking ahead." She grinned. "I never want to be caught short."

I doubted she ever would.

Chapter 22

I quickly dressed, hands trembling with the need for speed—who knew when Marty would hit? If the island was being officially evacuated, then the storm had to be seriously headed toward us. The television was blaring warnings, showing overhead pictures of a huge cloud taken by idiots in an airplane, as well as pictures of people nailing plywood panels over windows and cleaning out grocery shelves.

Had we waited too long? How far inland would the storm rage? Would it follow us up through the whole state?

Emptying the closet and the dresser drawers, I stacked everything on the bed. Neither Sam nor I had bought anything since we'd been at the beach, yet I had the devil's own time getting our clothes back into suitcases and hanging bags. The pile seemed to have expanded since I'd packed them at home.

After checking and rechecking to confirm that I wasn't leaving anything, I dragged the luggage to the living room, leaving them there to be put in the car.

"Hazel Marie," I called as I headed toward her room. "You need any help?"

"I sure do," she said, spooning cereal into a little open mouth. She and the two toddlers, all three still in their nightclothes, were on the bed while she tried to get some breakfast into them. "I have to get them fed or there'll be no living with them. But if you'll get the suitcases out of that closet and start dumping things in, that would really help." Catching one little girl who was trying to crawl off the bed, she swiped a spoonful of cereal into her mouth. "Do you know how long we have? I still have to get these two dressed, and myself, too."

My word, I thought as I opened the closet and found four huge suitcases—she must've brought everything they owned. But I made no comment while I scooted them out and threw one on the bed. When I opened it, one little girl began crawling into it.

"I don't know," I answered. "Sam didn't say, just told me to get ready to go because they'd be right back."

That had been an optimistic prediction because the men were still gone. Actually, I wasn't all that aware of how time was passing because I kept busy hurrying everybody along and helping where I could.

Lloyd came clomping down from his third-floor penthouse, bringing his small suitcase.

"You sure you have everything?" I asked, meeting him on the stairs. "Once we're on the road, there'll be no turning back."

"Yes'm, everything but a wet bathing suit hanging on the back porch. I'm going to get it now."

"Oh, my, I'd forgotten about the porch. How about gathering all the suits hanging out there and putting them in plastic bags? We'll straighten out what belongs to whom when we get home."

He nodded and turned away to continue down the stairs. Then he stopped and said, "Can you believe that the sun's shining and the day looks perfect, yet they're saying a storm's on the way?" He shrugged. "Maybe beach weather is different from ours."

"I've not taken the time to think about it, Lloyd," I said, looking around to see how the sun filled the many-windowed house with bright light. "But you're right. It certainly doesn't look threatening. You don't think we were given wrong information, do you?"

He grinned. "No'm, because everybody else got the same information. I saw about six cars parked up and down the street with men in uniforms getting out to knock on doors."

"Well, we can only do as we're told. So be sure and get those bathing suits, then see if you can help your mother."

Walking past Binkie's door, I saw that Little Gracie was dressed in shorts and a T-shirt, while Binkie was forcing a suitcase closed. I waved and went on to see about Latisha.

She had already packed her little bag by herself, so I checked to be sure she hadn't left anything.

"You're sure you have everything, aren't you?" I asked, glancing back. "Nothing left in the living room or anywhere?" I picked up her suitcase because her hands were full.

"No'm, I got it all," she said, clutching two plastic grocery bags filled with shells.

Just as I started down the stairs, I heard a rolling clatter and Latisha yelled, "Oh, dangnation! My shells is everywhere!"

And sure enough, shells were scattered all over the upstairs hall and partway down the stairs.

"Well," I said with just a slight eye roll, "pile them up as best you can so nobody'll step on them. I'll bring you some more bags."

"Better be better'n these," she said as she got on her knees and began sweeping shells into piles. "Wish I'd already give some to Miss Hazel Marie, so I wouldn't have to pick up so many. I'm a good mind to just leave 'em."

"No, let's get them up. But hurry, Latisha, we have to be ready to go when the men get back."

Gradually we all gathered in the living room, our luggage stacked together near the back door. And still, the men had not returned. I was beginning to worry, wondering what was keeping them. It got worse when Binkie started the coffeepot and made toast—it was beginning to feel as if it were a normal day.

LuAnne paced around the house wringing her hands, looking out the windows, and wondering aloud if we were in the eye of the storm. After talking in a corner for a while with Etta Mae, LuAnne came up to me.

"Julia," she said, "there's no need all of us staying in the path of danger. So Etta Mae and I are going to go ahead and get out of here. At least she had the foresight to prepare for just such an emergency."

"Well, okay, LuAnne, if that's what you want to do. But I thought we might all try to stay together on the way back."

"We want to go on," LuAnne said, looking for confirmation from Etta Mae, who'd walked over to join us. "I need to get back, and besides, Etta Mae's been advising me about getting a divorce.

She's had two of them, you know, so she knows what she's talking about."

"Is it okay if we go on?" Etta Mae asked. "Ms. Conover is anxious to get started."

"Of course," I told her. "If it's all right with you, it's fine with me. But, Etta Mae, I'm so sorry your vacation is being cut short. I wouldn't have had it end like this for anything."

"Well, me, either. But I sure enjoyed every minute I've had of it." She smiled at me, hesitated a moment as if considering a hug, then picked up a suitcase. "We'd better get our stuff in the car if we're going. We'll stay in touch by cell phone. Let us know when you leave."

Cell phone, I thought, and went to the kitchen where Sam had both our phones plugged into a charger. I put everything—wires and all—in my purse. I often forgot my cell phone, but never my pocketbook. I wouldn't leave home without it.

As Etta Mae's little red car backed out of the yard and started down the street, Lloyd stood watching from the kitchen window. Binkie had walked out to the car with them, waved good-bye, and was now back in the living room, checking the local news on the television set.

"I kinda thought about going with 'em," Lloyd said, as he turned from the window, "but there's not much room in her backseat. Besides," he went on, grinning at me, "Latisha wants to ride with me, so guess we'll go back the way we came."

"Well," I said, "with Mrs. Conover gone and most of the diapers used up, Sam and I have a big, empty backseat."

"That," he said, "is a good thought. Let me go round up Latisha and see what she wants to do."

As he left, Binkie came into the kitchen, poured coffee, and handed me a cupful and a sweet roll. "We've rushed around so much that now we have to wait. And a good thing, I guess, because we need to clean out the refrigerator and the pantry. If there's anything you want to take, now's the time to get it. Plenty of snacks are left."

We set about cleaning out the kitchen, while our suitcases, plastic bags, toys, and all manner of this, that, and the other sat waiting to be packed into trunks and backseats—if we'd had trunks and backsets available, because the men still weren't back.

"What could be keeping them?" Hazel Marie asked, a frown of concern on her forehead. "I hope nothing's happened."

Binkie said, "Probably waiting in line to get gas. I don't know how many people are on the island, but if they're all being evacuated, there'll be mobs at the gas stations."

"Oh, my," I said, "you think they'll run out of gas? The stations have to be filled up, too, don't they?"

"Oh, I doubt they'll run out," Binkie said, trying for reassurance. "That hurricane's been on the news for days. The stations will be prepared."

"I hope you're right," I mumbled, looking out the window again at the empty yard. But I determined right then that I would pass along to Sam Etta Mae's habit of keeping a car ready for a fast getaway at all times.

Chapter 23

Lloyd came over for a sweet roll, saying, "Boy, people're leaving all over the place. It's a good thing Etta Mae left when she did. The street's full of cars."

Then, hearing something, he turned around and ran out on the back porch. "J.D.'s back!"

That set us all a-dither as we ran around collecting children, double-checking suitcases, going to the bathroom one last time, while I listened for Lloyd to sing out that Sam and Coleman had pulled in, too.

Instead I heard Mr. Pickens stomp in and Lloyd ask, "Where's Mr. Sam and Coleman?"

"Still in line, I guess," Mr. Pickens said, sounding tired and short tempered, "somewhere. The station we went to first ran out of gas one car behind me. Sam and Coleman had to pull out and look for another one."

Oh, my, I thought, tempted to wring my hands; how far would they have to go? What if they ran out of gas before finding gas?

"Hazel Marie," Mr. Pickens said, "let's get on the road, honey."

"We're leaving before the others?" she asked.

"That's the plan," he said, short and abrupt. Exhaustion lined his face, or maybe it was worry that was doing it—who knew with him? He was still in flip-flops and Bermuda shorts and the T-shirt which he'd undoubtedly slept in, and from his expression he had no intention of changing to anything else. Unshaven and uncombed, he was more than a little rough looking.

Of course, there wasn't a whole lot of difference in his rough looks when he was cleaned up and nicely dressed.

Before long, we had the Pickenses' large trucklike vehicle loaded with suitcases and odds and ends that always accompany children. The little girls were unhappily buckled into their car seats—one was crying because she wanted to go to the beach and the other was screaming because they were leaving Lloyd.

As they pulled out of the yard, Binkie said, "I'm feeling a little abandoned. How about you?"

"Well, at least it's quieter, which is the best I can say. But, Binkie, what if Sam and Coleman don't get back? What if the gas has run out and they're over in Charleston and can't get back?"

"They'd call us. In fact, I don't know why they haven't already called. I've tried to reach Coleman, but the phones are acting funny. But, listen, let's not worry about it. Maybe the storm will veer off again, and we'll have another whole week here. I wouldn't mind being abandoned if that happened."

"Well," I said, "you may be feeling abandoned, but I'm feeling stranded. We are on an island, you know."

Lloyd and Latisha were glued to the television, watching the progress of Marty.

"Hey!" Lloyd suddenly sang out. "Come look at this."

Binkie and I walked over to see a view of the hurricane—the eye of which was plainly visible—whirling right off the coast of Georgia.

"They're expecting it to make landfall between Savannah and Charleston by tomorrow morning," Lloyd said. "Both cities are being evacuated right now. Miss Julia," he said, turning wide eyes to me, "what if we don't get out?"

The wind rattled the front windows right about then, and we all thought about the possibility of weathering the storm where we were.

But Binkie was having none of it. "No way. The cops will get us off the island, and the worst that could happen is that we'd end up in a shelter somewhere." She stopped, bit her lip, then said, "I do wish Coleman and Sam would get back, though."

Feeling the need to move around, I walked out onto the front porch, and nearly got blown back inside. The wind—still in gusts—was fierce, but the closeness of the rolling gray clouds really set me back on my heels. They had covered the eastern horizon and were rising toward the zenith. We should've been on the road hours before this, yet here we were in late morning with the sun about to be covered and the wind about to reach gale force. And Binkie and I were stuck on an island with three children and no wheels. And husbands? Well, who knew where they were?

"Binkie," I said, after closing the front door behind me and drawing her close, "maybe we ought to call somebody."

"I've been calling Coleman for the past hour and can't get through." She looked as troubled as I was feeling.

"Maybe we should begin thinking of where we could hunker down in the house—if we have to, that is."

"Well, I've heard that a bathtub with a mattress on top is the place to be in a tornado if you can't get underground. But I don't know about a hurricane."

"Oh, my," I said, picturing the five of us riding out a hurricane in a bathtub.

"They're here!" Lloyd yelled, as he ran from the kitchen window to the door. "Both of 'em! They're here."

Latisha and Little Gracie ran after him, although Binkie grabbed Gracie to hold her back. "You need to go to the bathroom? Hurry, so we'll be ready to go home with Daddy."

The two men walked in looking tired and bedraggled, but both were grinning.

"Don't ask," Coleman said, as he swept Little Gracie up in his arms. "Man, what a morning. We've helped push two cars that ran out of gas, broken up a couple of fights, been in three lines, almost getting to the pumps twice before finally getting filled up."

"Daddy, Daddy," Little Gracie said, getting his attention. "We thought you'd gone home without us."

"Never in this world!" he said, hugging her tight. "I wouldn't leave my girls. No, ma'am, I wouldn't."

Latisha, who'd been clutching her bags of shells as she kept a watchful eye on the goings-on, said, "Well, I'm glad to hear it, 'cause Miss Binkie was talkin' 'bout puttin' us all in the bathtub."

"Here, honey," Binkie said, giving Latisha a reassuring pat with one hand and, with the other, handing Coleman a sweet roll that was cold and hard by this time. "How far did you have to go?"

Sam, still in his pajama top halfway tucked into his pants, and his beach sandals, said, "We ended up at the far end of Mount Pleasant. Everything from here to Sullivan's Island is jammed with cars, OUT-OF-GAS signs, and people with nasty tempers."

"Remind me," I said, putting my hand on Sam's arm just to touch him, "to tell you how Etta Mae avoids such entanglements."

"By thinking ahead, apparently," he said, smiling somewhat ruefully. "Where is she, anyway? I know she had a full tank. Has she already started back?"

"Yes, and LuAnne went with her. They've been gone at least an hour, maybe longer."

Sam's eyebrows went up. "LuAnne, too? That's interesting."

"More than you know. She intends to get firsthand instructions from Etta Mae on getting a divorce. She's probably taking notes."

"Good Lord," Sam said, shaking his head, then turning to a more pressing problem. "Look, honey, can you put your hand on a shirt for me? I don't want to wear pajamas all day."

Lloyd and Coleman had already begun taking the luggage downstairs and loading the cars, but I was able to hold them off long enough to locate a shirt.

Binkie, giving the kitchen counter a last wiping down, said, "Miss Julia, you want to take some of this food with you? Or shall I throw it out? There's bread, peanut butter, some cheese, and lots of Fritos and Doritos."

"Oh, let's don't throw it out. Just divide it up, and we'll both take some. We'll stop for lunch before long, but having a few snacks on hand couldn't hurt."

And what a fateful prediction that turned out to be.

Chapter 24

We drove away from the house with Coleman and Binkie behind us and Latisha looking back, mumbling, "So long, big, ole yellow house. See you later."

She and Lloyd were in our backseat along with his books, her plastic bags of shells, a tennis racket or two, and a big sack of Doritos, peanut butter, and two bananas. Latisha had carefully stashed her pocketbook between two hanging bags of clothes in the trunk, saying that she was about tired of having that thing bumping against her side all day long.

"Not a lot of traffic, is there?" I remarked as Sam drove toward the bridge connecting the islands and onto the road which would eventually take us to the interstate.

"I hate to tell you," Sam said, "but that's probably because we're the last ones to leave."

"Well, it's better than being embroiled in a traffic jam."

Sam glanced at me and grinned. "Hold on to that thought."

But before I had time to hold on to anything, cars began to converge from all sides—easing into lanes and making room for themselves where there was no room. It was a marvel to me that where there'd been almost no cars at all suddenly was filled with them.

"Oh, my goodness," Lloyd said, sitting up as far as his seat belt would let him. He was staring through the windshield. "Would you look at that!"

I was already looking, and as far as the eye could see, which was several blocks to the great bridge and up to the crest of it, there were cars, trucks, pickups, SUVs, vans, and every sort of vehicle known to man lined up bumper to bumper on both lanes. And not a one of them was moving.

"What's going on?" Lloyd asked.

"Could be an accident," Sam said, "but I'm afraid it's because everybody's trying to get on the interstate. I expect it's full."

I frowned at the thought. "How can an interstate be full?"

"They're evacuating Charleston, honey, as well as everybody all up and down the coast."

Latisha, realizing that we couldn't move until everybody else moved, said, "Look like we gonna be stuck here for*ever*."

"We just have to be patient, Latisha," Sam said. "We're just one of thousands of cars heading west on the interstate."

He wasn't wrong about that, because by the time we got to the ramp, some thirty minutes later, and some kind soul had let us ease into the westbound lane, we became just one more vehicle on the longest parking lot on the east coast. I didn't know when or how Coleman and Binkie got onto the interstate, but by that time they were far behind us even though our progress was measured by inches rather than miles.

I'd never seen anything like it, and it got worse, for in a mile or so, the four westbound lanes tapered down to two, and it was like watching a herd of cows trying to push through a narrow gate. A few drivers just gave up and pulled to the side of the road. Others gave and received a few dents, but, given the heat of the day and the anxiety engendered by Marty, most drivers were being patient and considerate.

And what's more, everybody and his brother must've been trying to use their cell phones. The lines or the satellites or whatever cell phones run on were completely jammed. We couldn't check on Binkie and Coleman, much less reach Hazel Marie and Mr. Pickens.

Lloyd said, "The road will clear out in a few minutes, won't it, Mr. Sam? I mean, some will turn off onto I-95, won't they?"

"I expect so—those heading north, anyway. I doubt many will be going south. They'd likely run right into the storm if it hits between Charleston and Savannah."

We finally passed under I-95, the main north-south artery, and from what we could see, it was as packed full as the one we were on. And still, we crept along a few feet at a time, then stopping for no discernible reason to wait various lengths of time before creeping along another few feet.

And to make it worse, there sat the two eastbound lanes—right across the median from us—as empty as a swath of prairie. Even worse than that, our tortuous progress was made more acute by the occasional highway patrol car streaking past on it, lights and sirens going full blast.

"Why in the world," Sam asked, "don't they open those two lanes for westbound traffic? *No*body will be driving *toward* Charleston today."

"I was just wondering the same thing," I said. "It would certainly relieve the congestion."

"Well," Sam sighed, braking to a stop, "speaking of congestion. Looks like we'll be sitting for awhile." He waved to the driver of the car next to us, then leaned forward to stare ahead. "Looks like a bunch of patrol cars pulled to the side up yonder. May've been an accident."

I leaned up to try to see. "In our lane, you think?"

"Doesn't matter. It'll be on this side of the highway, that's for sure. Look, an ambulance just pulled in."

"Oh, me, that's not good news," I said.

"Yeah," Lloyd said, "because now we'll probably have to wait for a wrecker to clear the highway."

"Right, so we're stuck for awhile. Tell you what," Sam said, turning off the ignition, "let's save a little gas. Everybody roll down the windows."

Well, they Lord, the heat rolled into the car like a living thing, heavy, sultry, and suffocating. But we weren't the only ones suffering heat exhaustion—all the drivers were turning off their motors as we sat waiting in the middle of a low-country interstate, the heat waves visibly rising from concrete and hot hoods. The most pressing concern now seemed to be the possibility of running out of gas. No one wanted to have to pull out of line, and even if they did, there were no gas stations in sight. Hardly any signs of life any-where, if you want to know the truth—just pine trees, barbed-wire fences, and black-water marshes on both sides.

Two young men walked from their cars to the grassy verge and began throwing a baseball back and forth. Mothers were out, walking children, hoping, I assumed, to tire them out enough to make a nap possible. And young people were zipping back and forth around and between cars on skateboards, making Lloyd be-moan the fact that he'd not brought his.

"That's all right, Lloyd," Latisha said. "I couldn't keep up with you if you'd brought it."

Lloyd opened his door. "I think I'll run back a little ways and see if Coleman's close to us."

"I'll go with you," Latisha said, tumbling out beside him.

"Don't go far," I said, unsure if wandering off along the side of the road was a good idea. "They may clear the road and we'll have to move." Then, softly to Sam, "Will they be all right?"

He nodded. "We aren't going anywhere anytime soon." And to Lloyd, he said, "Ten minutes, no longer."

That was a long ten minutes, and I fidgeted the whole length of it, not liking at all the thought of two children running along a major highway in hopes of seeing a familiar face.

"Sam," I said, fanning my face with a catalogue, "I hate to even bring this up, but I may soon have to use the bathroom."

Sam grinned. "Honey, you have two choices—keep waiting or walk out to the bushes. I'll go with you."

I looked at the row upon row of pine trees, separated from my open door by a grassy ditch, and took note that whoever had planted them had kept the undergrowth under control. Bushes were few and far between, and none large enough to shield a squat.

By then, many more drivers and passengers were wandering up and down the highway, pausing to chat awhile with each other, and seeming to take the stopover well in stride. Making the best of it, which was commendable in this situation, even if it was the only thing they could do.

I, on the other hand, had had enough of it. "Why don't the cars in the other lane cut across the median and drive west on the east lane? If that car next to us would do that, you could follow right along behind him."

"Honey, there're half a dozen highway patrol cars up ahead blocking the east lane. We wouldn't get far and we'd lose our place here."

"So I guess we're just going to sit here forever," I said, then half smiled for sounding so much like Latisha.

Before he could answer, Lloyd and Latisha, panting and sweating, tumbled into the backseat.

"We found 'em," Lloyd said, wiping his face with his shirttail.

"Yeah," Latisha said, "an' I went to the bathroom in the woods. Binkie went with me to watch for snakes."

"Snakes?" I said.

"An' ants. Binkie said to watch out for anthills. You don't want them things to get on you."

Oh, my, something else to worry about, because fairly soon I was going to have to do something about my increasing discomfort.

Lloyd swung his feet out of the car. "I'm going to run up ahead and see if I can find out what's holding us up."

"Me, too," Latisha said, following him.

"Don't go far," I said, but they paid me little mind. Everybody else was out of their cars, milling around, trying to pass the time and get their minds off the heat.

"Sam," I said, "I can't wait any longer. But, I declare, I can't just go right out in full public view."

"Hold on. I've got an idea." He got out of the car, went to the trunk, and came to my side of the car. Then he shook out a blanket and held it up. "Slide right down beside the car. Between the blanket and the door, you'll have all the privacy you need."

Bless his heart, it was a perfect solution until right in the middle of relieving myself, a khaki-colored bus filled with criminals from Charleston jails rolled past on the clear opposite lane, yells and whistles and catcalls filling the air because I may have been covered on all sides, but not from the top.

Mortified, I crawled back into the car and scrooched down out of sight. But others were in the same painful situation, because two men walked over to Sam and asked to use his blanket for their suffering wives.

One of them said, "We'll watch for any passing buses. But it's a dang shame they get them prisoners out while we're stuck out here stifling to death."

I was thinking the very same thing.

Chapter 25

"I wish they'd come on back," I said, briefly reveling in my private relief even though I'd had to give a public performance to get it. "They don't need to be running up and down the highway."

"Better than sweltering in here," Sam said, wiping sweat from his face. "When they get back, I'll turn the motor on for a few minutes and let the car cool off." He grinned. "Maybe they'll take a nap."

I leaned forward and finally spied Lloyd and Latisha on their way back to the car. They were walking—well, more like dragging—along the verge toward us. Completely sapped, I thought, and about time.

"Here they come," I said. "Go ahead and turn on the air-conditioning, Sam. They're worn out."

When the engine started, so did the radio, and Sam and I listened as a worried announcer told us that Marty had gained in strength after leaving heavy rains and mudslides in Puerto Rico. While tracking past the coast of Florida, the hurricane had left havoc in its wake, and was headed now for Georgia and South Carolina. The governors of both had declared states of emergency.

Still, we sweltered under lowering clouds without a drop of rain or a gust of wind. Who would've thought that such a raging storm was headed our way while we could do nothing but wait?

"Turn it off, please, Sam," I said. "No need for the children to hear that, especially since we're pretty much sitting ducks."

As the two children climbed into the car, we closed the doors and rolled up the windows. I'd never been so grateful for the cool air rushing from the vents and commenced fanning my tunic top to make the most of it.

"Man!" Lloyd said. "I've never been so hot in my life. You ought to see what's ahead, Mr. Sam. A huge wreck—about four or five cars. Somebody said that one of them was trying to pass and the others wouldn't let him. Anyway, it's gonna be awhile before they clear it out."

"Tell about the fight," Latisha urged.

I turned to look at them. "What fight?"

"Oh," Lloyd said, "it wasn't much—two men flailing at each other. The cops broke it up, but tempers were really flaring. Miss Julia, you should've seen this—on our way back, somebody cracked an egg on the hood of his Lexus. And it cooked! He had a mess on his car, though, because it stuck when he tried to flip it."

"I wouldn't eat that thing on a bet," Latisha said, shuddering. "He shoulda used some grease."

As I murmured, "My goodness," Latisha went on. "I sure am gettin' hungry though."

"Me, too," Lloyd said, as he began rummaging through the bags in the footwell. "We brought some snacks, didn't we?"

Well, yes, we did, thanks to Binkie, so Lloyd pulled out a jar of Jiffy peanut butter, a bag of Doritos, and two slightly overripe bananas.

"I suggest," Sam said, "that you eat the bananas and leave the rest."

"We'll share 'em," Lloyd said, and, carefully halving the bananas, passed our shares up to us. I hadn't realized how hungry I was, but it was closing in on two o'clock in the afternoon and it had been a long time since our skimpy breakfast.

"I'm still starvin'," Latisha said after consuming her banana half. "Open up that peanut butter, Lloyd, and pass them Doritos."

They began dipping and crunching, and after a few minutes Sam and I joined them, although we both knew it wasn't a good idea.

After Latisha and Lloyd cleaned the peanut butter jar with their fingers, Latisha swallowed hard a couple of times and said, "I think my tongue's stuck. I sure could use something to drink."

So could we all. Why hadn't I thought to bring bottles of water or cans of soda or anything wet? It would've been hot by this time but still drinkable, and, I declare, my throat was so coated with peanut butter, I could barely swallow.

"Hey, look!" Lloyd yelled as he opened his door and hopped out. "Come on, Mr. Sam!"

Sam was right behind him. They took off dodging between parked cars and careening across the median, joining a swarm of others who were leaping from cars and converging on a rusty pickup coming west on the clear eastbound lane.

"What is it?" I asked, craning my neck to see what the attraction was.

"Water!" Latisha yelled. She was looking out the side window at the scramble of thirsty people headed for the pickup. "I mean I think it is. Look, Miss Lady, they got that truck bed loaded down with crates full of bottles. And they just handin' 'em out. First come, first served."

"Oh, my goodness," I said. "Good Samaritans to the rescue. How thoughtful. I hope they don't run out before Sam gets some."

"Me, too," Latisha said. "My mouth is all cloggled up with that peanut butter."

Mine was "cloggled up," as well, and I would've given a pretty penny for a long, cold drink of water.

"Here they come," Latisha said, "an', hot dog, they got some."

She opened the door for Lloyd, who tumbled in, his arms full of bottles. Sam, laden with more bottles, got into the front seat and handed me a sweaty one.

I quickly uncapped it and took a long drink. It wasn't very cold, but it was wet, and I'm not sure I'd ever had anything for which I was more thankful.

For a few minutes, nothing was heard in the car but gurgles and sighs as the four of us assuaged our thirst.

Finally coming up for air, I asked, "Who were those kind, thoughtful people who knew how thirsty we were?"

Sam laughed. "I don't know. They probably live around here somewhere and realized an opportunity to make some money."

"You mean they were *selling* it?"

"Yep," Sam said, "but you have to give them credit—they saw a need and met it. It's called entrepreneurship, and, I'll tell you this, this water is worth every penny I paid for it."

Lloyd said, "They made out like bandits—ten dollars a bottle."

"Well," I said, going over numbers in my head, "that's probably not too bad. They had to buy it themselves, load up the crates, and use their truck to drive here. That's called overhead," I said, giving Sam a nudge with my elbow. "And," I went on firmly, "I was so thirsty, I would've paid twice that for one long drink."

"Yes'm, me, too," Lloyd said, "and it sure beats lemonade stands for making a little money. Wish I'd thought of it before we left the beach."

"Oh, look," Latisha said, pointing out the front window. "Here come the fuzz."

And, sure enough, a gray South Carolina State Patrol car with its distinctive blue stripe came speeding down the clear lane, lights flashing and siren wailing. It pulled up sideways in front of the pickup. The patrolman got out, looked up at the men handing out bottles of water from the truck bed, and, with hands on his hips, began talking with some authority. From his gestures, we could see that he was telling them to turn around and get off the highway. But the officer hadn't counted on the dozens of irate people crowding around, waiting to get their hands on something wet.

In light of the dire circumstances of long-stalled drivers, the trooper gave up. Clamping his broad-brimmed hat on his head, he climbed up onto the truck bed, and began handing down bottles to the scrambling crowd of outstretched arms. The quicker he could empty the truck, the quicker he could get it off the highway. Smart.

"Hope you've all cooled down," Sam said, switching off the ignition. "Better save gas."

But as soon as he did, the line of cars in front of us started easing forward and he turned it back on. "We're moving, folks. Let's see how far we get this time."

All along the two rows of cars in the westbound lanes, engines cranked, brake lights flashed, and slowly we began to creep along. We were moving at last.

"I hope Coleman got some water," I said. "Little Gracie surely needs it. Sam, did you see him at the truck?"

"No, I didn't. Try the cell phone again."

I did, but still no luck with that.

Then Lloyd said, "We're not going very fast. Why don't I jump out and take some bottles to them? We've still got a few extras."

But Sam vetoed that. "Since we're moving now, we might lose you, Lloyd. If we have to stop again, you can try it. But for now, we're going all of twenty in a seventy-mile-an-hour zone."

"We're just a-zoomin' along," Latisha said.

"It feels like it, doesn't it?" I said, as we all laughed. And after being stuck in ninety-five-degree heat on a concrete highway for hours, it did feel as if we were zooming right along.

After hours of stop-and-go travel, we neared Columbia, having bypassed a few small towns, and Sam said, "I'm going to have to take a chance and come off. We've got less than half a tank of gas, so if we get stuck again we could be in trouble."

"I hate to get out of line, Sam," I said, worriedly. "We might never get back in."

"I know, but surely a lot of people will be pulling off. We're far enough from the coast that the hurricane won't be a problem. Besides, if we can't get back in line, we'll just find a hotel and spend the night."

Easier said than done, as had been several other things during that interminable day. We ended up waiting in line at a gas station, because others had had the same idea as Sam, but we were lucky. Sam's big car required high-test gas, and that pump was the only one left with gas in it.

While Sam filled the tank, Latisha, Lloyd, and I roamed the aisles of the service station, stocking up on edibles and drinkables. We piled up plastic-wrapped sandwiches, apples, a few candy bars, and bottled water on the counter, determined not to ever go hungry or thirsty again.

When Sam got back in the car—after all of us had waited in line for the bathrooms—he said, "Well, we'll have to try our luck with the traffic. They told me inside that there're no hotel rooms available anywhere in the city. Charleston has moved to Columbia."

"Wait, wait," Latisha said. "I need me some chewing gum. Can I run back in and get some?"

Sam opened his door. "Come on, Latisha. I'll go with you."

As Lloyd and I watched them hurry back into the service station, I said, "Bless her little heart. She's been a good traveler, hasn't she? No complaints and no whining when we've all had plenty to complain and whine about. I hope Lillian's not worried about her, but with cell phones out of commission, I can't let her know anything."

Lloyd didn't say anything, just grunted in response, but then he said, "Miss Julia, I don't know if this means anything, but when Latisha and I walked back to see Coleman and Binkie, I saw those people again."

"What people?"

"Those three people we saw on the beach yesterday. You know, the ones looking for stray hundred-dollar bills."

"Well, they had to evacuate like everybody else."

"Yes'm, I guess. But they were in a big, black Suburban—that's an SUV, Miss Julia, like the Secret Service uses, and it had tinted windows. I wouldn't have seen them, but that woman rolled down her window just as we walked by. She looked right at me, or maybe at Latisha—I couldn't tell—then turned her head real quick and rolled her window up again."

"That sounds odd," I said, "but sitting out in the heat makes people do strange things. Did Latisha see her?"

"No'm, and I didn't tell her. She'd probably go up and talk to them. When we came back by, all the windows were up, but I felt like they were watching us."

"Hmm," I said, hearing the touch of concern in Lloyd's voice, which I trusted enough not to discount. "Well, we'll keep an eye out for them. I can't imagine, though, that they're interested in us. Likely as not, they're driving around looking for a place to spend the night.

"As for me," I went on, "I just hope we soon get home. My bed is calling me."

"Mine, too," Lloyd said, grinning.

Chapter 26

As we began the last leg of our journey home, the traffic thinned out somewhat, although there were still more cars on the road than usual. I could imagine beachgoers and Charleston residents filling motel and hotel rooms all across the upstate. And frankly, if we'd not been so close to home, I would've voted for a stopover at any Motel 6 that had a light on for us.

Full dark by this time, the temperature outside was noticeably cooler as we started up the mountain toward Abbotsville. It was taking us more than twelve hours to retrace the route that had taken barely five to get us to the beach in the first place.

Latisha and Lloyd were asleep in the backseat, and I was dozing off and on only because I felt the need to stay awake to keep Sam company.

"You know," I said to him, pitching my voice low for the sleepers' sake, "I've hardly given a thought to Etta Mae and LuAnne this entire day. Or to Hazel Marie and her family. I guess I've just assumed, since they left before we did, that they didn't get caught in the traffic."

He didn't respond, so I leaned closer and said, "Sam? You're not asleep, are you?"

He laughed. "Not yet, but I'll be glad to get home. As for the Pickenses and Etta Mae, I've kept an eye out for them—checking cars pulled to the side and those that had been abandoned. I expect they're all home by now. Coleman and Binkie should be the last ones in. Or us. But as soon as we get there, let's call around and make sure everybody made it."

"Yes, and I must call Lillian, too, regardless of how late it is. She's surely heard about the hurricane so she'll be worried."

He nodded, and after a little while, I said, "I wonder how Etta

Mae and LuAnne got along. I don't mean handling the traffic and the waiting and so on. I mean how the two of them managed together. If LuAnne talked the whole way, Etta Mae will be worn to the bone. She's not a chatterbox as LuAnne is, so it could've been a miserable drive for her. Oh, and here's another thing—I wonder where LuAnne wanted to be dropped off. I doubt she'd go to the condo, and she can't get into our house, and Etta Mae's single-wide isn't big enough for a guest."

"Maybe," Sam said, "she's at a local motel. That would be the logical place if she didn't want to go home."

"Well, who knows what she wants to do. She's gone back and forth so many times, I can't keep up with her."

When we reached Abbotsville a little after eleven that night, Sam turned onto the long, empty Main Street—not a creature nor a car, except ours, was stirring its entire length.

"What a relief," I said, "not to be hemmed in on all sides. Everybody's in bed where they're supposed to be."

"We really roll up the sidewalks at sundown, don't we?"

"Yes," I agreed with some smugness, "and we're certainly the better for it."

Sam turned onto Polk Street and, in the second block, into our driveway. Thank the Lord.

"LuAnne's car is still here," I noted. "Wonder where she is?"

Sam didn't respond, just carried Latisha, who was out like a light, into the house and up to the room that I kept for her and Lillian. I walked Lloyd in, guiding him into his room where he collapsed on the bed. Taking off his tennis shoes, I drew a sheet over him and left him to sleep in the clothes he was in.

By the time I'd checked on Latisha and gotten back downstairs, Sam had brought the suitcases and Latisha's two bags of shells into the kitchen. He was looking in the refrigerator for something to eat and finding it almost bare.

"Look in the pantry, Sam," I said. "There may be some crackers and peanut butter."

"No, thanks," he said, smiling as he surveyed the pantry shelves.

"I've had my fill of peanut butter. But here's a can of tomato soup. I'll heat it up."

"While you're doing that, I'll call around and be sure everybody's safely home. Just hope I don't wake anybody. It's already past midnight."

Hesitating for a moment, I decided to get the worst one over first. So, hoping that Hazel Marie would answer the phone and not her short-tempered husband, I punched in her number. And got a rough growl in response.

"Yeah?"

"Mr. Pickens? It's Julia Murdoch, and I'm calling to let you know we're home and Lloyd is spending the night with us. Good night. Go back to sleep." I hung up before he could say another word.

Sam, stirring soup on the stove, laughed. "Bet I can guess who that was."

"Yes, well, just giving him a taste of his own medicine." I punched in Lillian's number, worrying that I would wake her but not daring to wait till morning.

And it was a good thing I called because she was wide awake and praying for our safety. "We're all all right, Lillian. It's been a long, hard day, but Latisha is safe and sound and asleep in your room upstairs."

"Law, Miss Julia, I been worriet to death 'bout that big ole storm they talkin' about. I kept on tryin' to call you an' the phones wasn't workin', an' all I could do was keep prayin'.'"

"I know. We were trying to call out, too, but so was everybody else on the East Coast. But we're home now, so go on to sleep and I'll see you tomorrow. How're you feeling, anyway? Do you need anything?"

"I'm doin' fine, 'specially since y'all out from under that bad storm. I'm gonna sleep good tonight."

"You do that, Lillian, and thank you for your prayers."

I clicked off, then looked up Etta Mae's number, again hoping that I wouldn't wake her. She answered immediately.

"It's Julia Murdoch, Etta Mae," I said, "reporting in. We just got home, and I'm calling around to check on everybody. When did you get in?"

"We got to town a couple of hours ago, then stopped at Cracker Barrel and had some supper. Traffic was bad until we started up the mountain, but I heard that it was worse behind us."

"It certainly was—we were in it. But what did you do with LuAnne?"

"Oh, she's here. She's sleeping on the sofa."

"My goodness, Etta Mae. Didn't she have anywhere else to go? I'm sorry that you still have her. Did she talk you to death?"

Etta Mae laughed. "She can talk a lot, can't she? But it was all right. She's having a hard time."

"I know she is, but she has to make her own decisions and not burden everybody else. Oh, well, I'll come get her in the morning and you can have some peace."

"That's all right. I have to go out to the grocery store, so I'll drop her at your house. If that's where she wants to go."

Well, who knew where LuAnne would want to go, but it was unconscionable of her to stay any length of time with Etta Mae. I mean, there was barely room for one person in that single-wide, much less two, especially if one of the two was a restless, bustling woman like LuAnne Conover.

"Sam?" I said after hanging up with Etta Mae. "Do you think Binkie and Coleman are in yet? They were behind us all the way."

"Why don't you leave them a message to call us when they get in? I've poured you a bowl of soup, so come eat it."

And that's what I did right after leaving Binkie a message to call when they got home, no matter the time.

We were just crawling into bed forty-five minutes later when Binkie called.

"We stopped at a McDonald's halfway up the mountain," Binkie said. "Or we'd have been home earlier. Gracie was starving and so was I."

We commiserated for a few minutes over our arduous journeys, and I told her about the perils of peanut butter on a hot, waterless day. She'd laughed, because they'd had a similar problem with the saltine crackers and cheese they'd had.

"I'll tell you this," she said, "those men selling bottled water were lifesavers. I don't care what they charged, we would've paid it."

Agreeing, I hung up and slid into bed beside Sam. "Sam?"

"Hmm?"

"Thank you for a wonderful vacation, but if it's all the same to you, I'm glad it's over."

Chapter 27

"*Lillian!*" I stood stock still in the door to the kitchen the next morning, staring at her. "What are you doing here?"

"Fixin' breakfast, like I always do." She was clomping back and forth from the stove to the sink, unperturbed by my shocked demand.

"But you've had surgery! You aren't supposed to be on that foot. You should be home." After the day we'd had on the road, I'd slept later than usual and had awakened to find Sam already up and gone to have breakfast with a group of buddies downtown.

Now here was Lillian, with a large, clumsy-looking bootlike thing Velcroed onto her foot and halfway up her leg, stirring grits with one hand while checking on biscuits in the oven with the other.

"I got enough of me bein' home, doin' nothin' but listenin' to Miss Bessie talkin' all day long. Besides," she said, turning to me with a smile, "the doctor, he say I can do anything I feel like doin'. An' I feel like seein' Latisha, an' you, an' Lloyd, an' Mr. Sam, an' knowin' y'all back home where you belong. So set on down 'cause breakfast is ready."

"Well, they Lord," I said, giving up and sitting down at the table. "I'm glad to see you, too. But, Lillian, I don't want you to undo whatever the doctor's done. Please don't push yourself. You know we can get along just fine until you're back on your feet. So to speak."

"Yes'm, I know you can," she said, with a tiny roll of her eyes as she set a plate of grits and sausage in front of me.

"Have the children come down?" I asked, lifting a fork. "Have you eaten? Fix a plate and keep me company."

"Yes'm, they been down an' now they gone to Miss Hazel Marie's so Latisha can give her some of them shells she got. I ate with them, but I'll have some coffee with you. I'm ready to set a while anyhow."

She settled at the table with her cup while I concentrated on the first real breakfast I'd had in over a week. Sweet rolls and cereal are fine every now and then, but not every morning.

"You need to stay off that foot as much as you can," I warned her. "Don't be going up and down the stairs or running around the house."

"No'm, I won't be doin' no runnin'." She laughed at the thought of it. "But I can do the cookin' an' set here in the kitchen just as well as I can set at home. An' they won't be no Miss Bessie to get at me here. I tell you, Miss Julia, that woman pretty near wore me out."

"I hate to hear that, Lillian. The fact that she was around to look after you was the only reason I was willing to go to the beach. What did she do that bothered you so much?"

"She talk," Lillian said with a great sigh. "An' talk an' talk. Then she cry a little, then she moan an' groan 'cause she miss that ole devil."

"Who?"

"Why, Mr. Robert, that's who. If you can b'lieve it."

My eyebrows shot up. "Mr. Robert *Mobley*? She *misses* him? I thought he was awful to her."

"He was. But she forget about how he beat up on her, an' how he kick her out time an' time again, an' how he left that ole house of his to the church an' not to her, so she didn't have a roof over her head."

"But I thought. . . ."

"Yes'm," Lillian said, nodding her head, "it was the Reverend Mr. Abernathy what took a hand an' made the deacons hold off on takin' that house out from under her. He fix it so she can live there for the rest of her life or until she want to leave.

"But in spite of it all," Lillian went on, shrugging her shoulders, "that poor, pitiful woman don't do nothin' but go on an' on 'bout what a fine man Mr. Robert was even though ever'body know he the devil's own self. But she grievin' 'bout how she miss him an' what in the world she gonna do without him."

"Well, my word," I said, placing my napkin beside my plate. "Has she lost her memory or lost her mind? You'd think she'd thank her lucky stars that he's no longer around to mistreat her."

"Yes'm, you would. But all I hear this whole week long was how she got nobody now, an' how she wish he'd come walkin' in the door. I tell you, Miss Julia, it pretty much make me sick how she give anything to have him back. I tol' her one time that she better off without him, an' she got mad at me an' almost walk out. An' that was before I could get around by myself, so I had to 'pologize an' tell her how much we 'preciate all Mr. Robert do for the church. But I had to grit my teeth to do it 'cause Mr. Robert 'bout the meanest man ever lived.

"And, law, Miss Julia," Lillian went on, "if I never hear that man's name again, I be happy. I get so tired of her goin' on an' on 'bout him, an' what if she do this, an' what if she do that, an' what do I think, an' do I have any advice for her."

It was all beginning to sound strangely familiar, so I asked, "And did you have any?"

She nodded sagely. "Yes'm, I did, but she don't wanta hear it. So I keep it to myself best I can. With them kinda people, Miss Julia, they don't wanta hear what you got to say—they jus' want you to listen an' nod your head an' say 'That's right, yes, you right,' don't matter how crazy they sound."

Pushing off with one hand on the table, Lillian heaved herself to her feet. "So I'm glad you folks is home, so I have a place to get away from Miss Bessie ever' day."

"Why, Lillian, you could've come over here anytime you wanted to. I told you that."

"Yes'm, I know, but for a while I needed Miss Bessie's help, so I jus' let her talk while I tune her out."

Hmm, I thought, maybe I could tune LuAnne out when she starts in on Leonard—and I would, if I could figure out how to do it.

But speak of the devil—no, not Mr. Robert—LuAnne rang the front doorbell about that time, ending our conversation. For the first time I beat Lillian to the door, hampered as she was with an ungainly walking cast. LuAnne, looking about half pitiful, stood there amid several suitcases, assuming, it seemed, that a room awaited her.

Etta Mae waved to me from her little red car, then sped off down the street—thankful, I supposed, for being free of the guest who'd outstayed her welcome.

"I'll tell you what's a fact, Julia," LuAnne began as she shoved her luggage into the hall. "I am so tired of being cramped into tiny spaces I don't know what to do. If you'd spent nine hours doubled up in a little sports car, you'd know what I'm talking about. To say nothing of trying to dress and undress and get a bite to eat in a trailer that was made for midgets."

"Come in, LuAnne," I said—unnecessarily since she already was. "At least you spent only nine hours on the road, while we spent over twelve, and nearly perished of thirst. And, of course, you knew that Etta Mae had limited space. I was surprised that you spent the night with her."

"Well, what else was I to do? You weren't here, and I certainly wasn't going to go crawl in bed with Leonard. He gets the wrong idea often enough already."

There was nothing for it but to help her carry suitcases up the stairs and deposit them in the room so recently occupied by Latisha—evidenced by the unmade bed. LuAnne grimaced, but I brought in fresh linen and told her to get on the other side and help.

"Lillian's not able to climb stairs," I said as I stripped the bed. "So let's get this done, then go down and have some coffee."

Resigned to having a house guest with no end in sight, I carried the coffee tray that Lillian had prepared and led LuAnne into the library.

We settled on the sofa—one on each end—poured our coffees, and sat back as LuAnne began to talk and I began to listen.

"I called him first thing this morning," she said, assuming that I knew of whom she was speaking, and, unhappily, I did. "Thinking that he'd have heard about the hurricane and be worried. And do you know what he said? He said, 'Why're you back so soon?' He didn't even *know* that we'd been in danger of losing life and limb, either at the beach or on the road coming home. I mean, Julia, the television has been full of it! But it's not the news that he watches all day long." She leaned her head back against the sofa. "He just does me in."

"Uh-huh, I understand," I said, nodding but reluctant to add anything of substance, being unsure of what her mood was at the moment. Then, preparing myself for another round of Leonard this and Leonard that, I set my mind to letting her talk while I tried tuning her out. Mentally scanning for a suitable topic to tune in on while she talked, I found nothing that held my attention for more than a second or two. It was like trying to find a good music station on the car radio.

My attention suddenly swung back to LuAnne when she abruptly said, "When you go to the grocery store. . . ." Then she stopped and sat up straight. "Well, of course, you don't go to the grocery store, do you? Lillian does the shopping for you."

"I most certainly have been to the grocery store—not often, I admit, but plenty of times."

"Whatever," she said with a wave of her hand. "But when you've gone, have you ever noticed how some wives treat their husbands? They're always older couples—the ones I'm talking about—and obviously retired or he wouldn't be with her in the middle of the day. I mean, he has nothing to do but follow her around, and you can tell that she doesn't like it. All the years of their marriage, she's done the shopping and the errands and seen after the children, while he's been occupied with more important things. You know, like running a company or building a business, giving orders to underlings, and so forth. But now, when he's no longer in charge of anything, he tags along a few steps behind her just to have something to do. I bet he even goes to the hairdresser with her. And every time he makes a suggestion or asks a question, she just snaps his head off. I mean, I once saw a woman shove her husband with the cart when he wasn't fast enough to get out of her way. And the tone of voice! Telling him to keep up and stop dawdling, to stop putting things in the cart, and to watch out for other shoppers. I mean, Julia, if you weren't looking right at them, you'd think she was talking to a child."

"Now that you mention it," I said, recalling a few incidences, "I have seen something like that."

"Well, you know what I think? I think that that kind of husband has lorded it over his wife all the years of their marriage, maybe making her feel she wasn't important, criticizing and lecturing her about every little thing, and now that he's slowed down and no longer sits at a desk giving orders, she's getting back at him."

"You may be right, but it's a sad thing to see."

"I don't know," LuAnne said, musingly. "What it means to me is that he's reaping what he sowed. If he's treated his wife like hired help all those years, what can he expect? I think that after a lifetime of it, a wife has nothing left for her husband but just what he's taught her."

"Well," I said, smiling, "now that you're getting into psycho-babble, as Sam calls it, I'll have to reserve judgment."

"I don't blame you," LuAnne said, reaching for the coffeepot to refill her cup. "But what I'm saying is that it's an illustration of what's good for the goose is also good for the gander, and Leonard better take heed."

She had switched the genders, but even so, it came out as a threat to do as the gander was doing, and it startled me so much that coffee sloshed over into my saucer.

Chapter 28

"Oh, LuAnne," I said, "you don't mean that." She'd halfway threatened the same payback once before, but I'd discounted it as simply a means of saving face. But here she was, doing it again and much more seriously.

"Well, why not? If he can do it, so can I. And don't think I haven't had opportunities, because I certainly have." Then she added darkly, "And you'd be surprised to know who with. With whom, I mean."

"But at our age? Think about it, LuAnne, it would be so . . . *unseemly*."

"Oh, I'm not talking about falling in *love*, or anything so silly and romantic. That's for starry-eyed teenagers, anyway. No, what I'm saying is that if Leonard can get his solace outside of marriage, then there's no reason that the goose or the gander—whichever one I am—can't do the same."

That might depend, I thought but didn't say, on just how one defined solace.

Voices—Lloyd's and Lillian's—in the kitchen saved me from responding aloud to LuAnne's astonishing statement, and thank goodness, because she had rendered me speechless.

Lloyd walked across the hall, then stopped in the door of the library. "Oh, sorry, Miss Julia," he said, "I didn't know you had company. Morning, Mrs. Conover, nice to see you again."

"And you, too, Lloyd," LuAnne said, almost offhandedly. She didn't much like being interrupted while delivering another tirade against Leonard.

I, however, welcomed the interruption. "How's everything at your mother's house?"

He grinned. "Hectic. Mama said it'll take days to get the twins back in their routine. They were both crying because they didn't have a beach to go to this morning."

"Sometimes," I said, shaking my head, "it seems easier to forgo vacations than to have schedules disrupted. But is there something you want? Anything you need?"

"No'm, just wanted to talk a little, but it can wait. Nothing important. We can talk later."

That put me in a quandary. Lloyd didn't often come to me wanting a private conversation, so I deemed his request important. Besides, having had difficulty finding a topic with which to tune out LuAnne, I was open to an interruption.

LuAnne, however, made no effort to give us a few minutes alone, and since she didn't take the hint, I could hardly ask her to excuse us. So I excused myself.

"Excuse me, LuAnne," I said, standing. "I'll be back in a few minutes." Walking over to Lloyd, I put my hand on his shoulder and turned him around. "I have something upstairs for you. Walk up with me."

When we got to the upstairs hall, I said, "Now, honey, what's bothering you?"

"Well, I'm not sure, but I think I saw that car again."

I frowned. "What car?"

"That black Suburban I saw on the interstate—you know, the one with those people we saw on the beach. It was parked on the other side of the street about a block down, facing our house. Mama's house, I mean. Not this one." Lloyd had two homes—mine and Sam's, and his mother's and Mr. Pickens's.

"Well, that's strange. Are you sure?"

"Wel-l-l, no. Not positive, anyway, because with those dark windows, I couldn't see inside. But when I left the house, I walked up the block away from it, then circled around so I could come up behind it and check the license plate. But it was gone when I got back around."

"Would you have recognized the license plate if you'd seen it?

I mean, did you get the number when you saw the car on the interstate?"

"No," Lloyd said, grimacing. "There was a big truck up close to the back of the SUV, so I couldn't see the plate without being obvious about it. I sure would like to get that number, though, so I'll know if I see it again."

"Well, I don't know what to think, Lloyd," I said, not wanting to either discount or increase his concern. "I can't imagine what those people, if it was them, would be doing in Abbotsville. Clearly, they were not from here."

"No'm, you could tell by the way they talked. You know, kinda northern or something."

I nodded. "And by all the jewelry that man was wearing. You wouldn't normally find that around here." I thought for a second or so, then went on. "I think you should talk to your father, and see what he makes of it. Just to be on the safe side."

"Oh, man," Lloyd said, throwing out his arms. "I would if I could, but he left early this morning for Richmond—some insurance case, I guess." Mr. Pickens was on retainer to a large insurance company, so he was often called away to investigate cases of possible fraud.

"Then," I said, "again to be on the safe side, let's talk to Coleman and let him know what's going on. He can have deputies drive by your mother's house every now and then. He'll be interested because I think it might be against the law to have car windows blacked out."

"No good," Lloyd said, shaking his head. "Binkie called Mama this morning and told her they were leaving to go camping up in Pisgah Forest. They still have a few days off because we had to come home so early."

"Well, for goodness' sakes," I said, feeling slightly abandoned by the ones on whom I would normally rely. "I guess that means that you and I will just have to keep an eye out and watch for those people. *If* it's them in the first place. And if it is, we should tell Sam what's going on. By the way," I went on, "did Latisha see them? Where is she, anyway?"

"She stayed to play with the twins. Mama said it would give her a chance to get some things done. So, no, she didn't see them, either on the interstate or across the street."

"Good, let's keep it that way. And in the meantime you and I can be keeping our eyes open as we're out and about. But Latisha shouldn't be out walking by herself. Lillian wouldn't like it."

"No'm, she won't be. Mama wouldn't let her. In fact," he said, looking at his watch, "I need to go get her. It's lunchtime, and Lillian's fixing hot dogs."

"And, Lloyd," I said, putting my hand on his shoulder, "I wouldn't be too concerned about this. Black SUVs are a dime a dozen everywhere you look."

"I know," he said with a grin. "But I'm gonna be checking every one I see."

As he left to retrieve Latisha, I mulled over what he'd told me, and the more I mulled, the less credence I could give it. What would those flashy people we'd seen on the beach be doing in Abbotsville? And, as I'd mentioned to Lloyd, there were so many black SUVs on the streets, you couldn't stir them with a stick. On the other hand, new, expensive Suburbans with blackened-out windows were a different kettle of fish and tended to stand out from the crowd.

Putting off rejoining LuAnne in the library, I walked into the kitchen to see how Lillian was doing. Fine, it seemed, for she was sitting at the table reading the newspaper.

"I'm glad to see that you're resting," I said. "Why don't you elevate that foot while you're sitting there?"

"'Cause I got to get right back up soon as Latisha an' Lloyd get here," she said, folding the paper and putting it aside. "Now, Miss Julia, I know you don't much care for hot dogs even with chili, but the chil'ren do, an' they's more goin' on here than you know."

"More? Like what?"

"Like Miz Conover don't like 'em, either." Lillian smiled. "She say they give her gas."

"I see," I said, smiling back. "Well, don't offer to make anything else. You should stay off that foot as much as you can."

Lillian had a sixth sense about such matters as less-than-appreciative guests, and often did her part, pleasantly and unobtrusively, to hurry them on their way.

"Lillian," I went on, following her from the table to the sink, "I tried what you suggested about tuning out somebody who talks too much, but it didn't work too well. I couldn't keep my mind centered on a different station."

"Yes'm, they can us'ally tell when your mind wander off of what they sayin'. So then they all of a sudden come out with something right smart that get your 'tention back."

"Yes! That's exactly what happened. So," I said, leaning against the counter, "do you have any other suggestions? Was there anything that worked for you with Miss Bessie?"

"Well, here something that'll work ever' now and then, 'cept you got to choose something that give you lots to say 'cause you have to keep their 'tention on what you're sayin'. See, what you do is start talkin' 'bout something else—it don't matter what—jus' something that'll get them thinkin' on what *you* sayin' for a change. But you got to be ready to talk an' talk, an' keep on talkin' so they got to listen an' maybe wonder what you talkin' 'bout an' why you goin' on an' on 'bout it. But that don't matter, 'cause what you doin' is keepin' them from talkin' 'bout whatever it is they keep talkin' 'bout, so they have to let you get a word in edgewise for a change."

"Hmm, that would be a change, and a welcome one." I thought about Lillian's suggestion for a few minutes, wondering just how I could go about changing the subject whenever LuAnne started in on her favorite one. "You know, Lillian, I enjoy conversing with a friend as well as the next person, but when that friend begins to sound like a broken record, it gets to be downright tiresome. The hard part of it is that I care for this friend—she would do any-thing in the world for anybody in need. But I'm beginning to think that she really doesn't want help with her problem. I mean, I don't see her actually *doing* anything that might solve it. She just wants to talk about it."

"Yes'm, I know that kind, an' Miss Bessie one of 'em, too. 'Cause she can talk an' talk till the sun go down an' come back up again 'bout how she want Mr. Robert back, but she know good an' well he gone for good. She can talk all she want to—she know she safe."

Hmm, I thought, maybe LuAnne knows she's safe, as well. Leonard wasn't about to go anywhere—she made his life too easy even if he was seeking solace elsewhere.

Chapter 29

So, with a renewed plan of defense against LuAnne's bombardment of words, I returned to the library. Apologizing for leaving her alone, I took a seat and began to head her off by making a suggestion.

"Speaking of grocery stores," I said, "would you like to go shopping with me? Lillian can't very well go, and she shouldn't, but the pantry and refrigerator need to be restocked. It won't take long—Lillian will give us a list. And I thought there might be a few things you need."

"Well, I guess I could, but it's certainly been a relief to be free of that chore for a few days. You know, there're some things that Leonard can't eat—he gets indigestion real bad—so I have to plan his meals carefully. Of course, who knows what he's eating now. I hope he's suffering for it, too. Wonder if that woman would take care of him like I do? I bet she wouldn't, don't you?" LuAnne took a deep breath, then went on as I frantically searched for a change of subject. "And, you know, Julia, I don't even know who she is. That ought to be the first thing on my list—find out who she is. I should know my enemy, shouldn't I? Be thinking about how I can find out, if you will. I'll bet half the town knows, but would anyone tell me? No, they wouldn't. Do *you* know, Julia? I want you to tell me if you do."

"No, LuAnne, I don't have any idea, but—"

"Well, anyway, I keep thinking I ought to kick him out, or leave him, or something. I mean, who wants an unfaithful husband? But, Julia, at one time—and you may not believe this but it's true—Leonard was an absolute dreamboat. Every girl in school tried to get his attention, but he had eyes only for me." She leaned back against the sofa, a faraway look on her face. "He was the strong, silent type, don't you know." Then she sat straight up. "Of course I didn't know he'd stay that way the rest of his life." Which of course was a good thing because she'd had no competition.

But now, she was just beginning to warm to her subject again. So I sat there, wracking my brain for a change of subject—any subject. Any topic would do if it would replace the one that constantly monopolized our conversation.

"Have you ever noticed," I began, landing on something as far from Leonard as possible, "how everything seems to be abbreviated to initials these days?"

"What?"

"Why, you know, on television. They do it on practically every commercial, although I've noticed that it's mostly on commercials about medical disorders. It's as if all the commercial makers have gotten together and decided they should use a kind of shorthand."

"What're you talking about?" LuAnne was staring at me with a befuddled look on her face.

"Well, just listen to this—IBS, OIC, UTI, COPD, RA, OAB, BED, and AMD. Now, I can understand using initials for some disorders. After all, some of them stand for problems that one shouldn't discuss publicly, especially in mixed company. But why discuss them on television in the first place? They belong in the sanctity of a doctor's office, it seems to me. At least, that's where I'd discuss them if I had any."

"Julia . . . ?"

"But, see, LuAnne, here's what I think. I think that rather than being reticent about airing a personal problem, those afflicted are actually and deep down quite proud of it. So proud, in fact, that using initials indicates their membership in an exclusive group, and only other afflictees will recognize a fellow member. Sort of like a particular handshake which I've heard is used by Masons in order to recognize one another. Have you ever heard of that?"

LuAnne frowned even more. "Maybe, but—"

"Well, maybe not. I don't know, but I've heard that early

Christians had certain signs that enabled them to recognize each other, but which unbelievers wouldn't understand. But I don't think that would work with these commercials. After all, they're right out in public for anybody to see and understand if they listen carefully. Because they'll say—at least once—in each commercial the full name of the disorder so the uninitiated, if they're quick, can interpret the initials."

"Julia, I—"

"Oh," I said, quickly resuming, "I understand if you don't catch it the first time, but just wait. They'll run the thing a dozen times a day, and if you're suffering from chronic obstructive pulmonary disorder, or age-related macular degeneration, or binge-eating disorder, or rhematoid arthritis, you'll be able to place yourself in the right club because you'll know the password. Pass initials, I mean."

By this time, LuAnne had leaned far enough away from me that she was practically hanging off the arm of the sofa. The look on her face would've deterred a less determined woman than I. But I was on a roll now.

"But when it comes to urinary tract infections, overactive bladders, and irritable bowel syndrome, I can understand the need for initials. Oh, they still imply exclusiveness, but at least it takes a few minutes for the images of bowels and bladders to form in your mind, even as you sympathize with the poor afflicted actors who can't find a bathroom."

LuAnne sprang from the sofa and began gathering coffee cups and saucers. Stacking them on the tray, she said, "I'll just take these to Lillian, and, Julia, if you don't mind my saying so, I think you need to rest a while. I'll get a list from Lillian and go to the store for you."

"No, wait, I wanted to tell you what I overheard in a gift shop at the mall one day. It just illustrates what I've been talking about."

"Well, just for a minute," she said with a sigh as she sank again onto the sofa. "I have to get the groceries."

"This won't take long, but I was just wandering around the shop, looking at the pretty things, and all of a sudden I realized that two women were talking on the other side of a rack of note cards I was looking at. One of them whispered something like, 'My OAB is giving me fits. I can't get anything done for having to go to the bathroom.' And the other one whispered back, 'Honey, you don't know about an OAB until you have a UTI. You'd really have something to complain about then.' Now, see, LuAnne, I would've thought they were members of some secret society talking in code if I hadn't learned about such things from television ads.

"But listen," I went on, "I had to look up one on Lloyd's computer because I couldn't ask him to do it. Now, see, everybody by this time knows what ED means, which is shameful enough. I mean, they've been beaming ads about that into family homes for years, which I think is highly inappropriate. Don't you? But now they've added BPH to it, and at first I thought they were talking about a gas station, which I thought was strange. They don't explain or spell it out at all, and it's a good thing they don't because nobody would understand it, but it's not a gas station. Let me tell you, anybody with ED would not want BPH too. And, LuAnne, would you believe that there's something worse than IBS? You could have a D tacked onto it as well, and that really puts you in an exclusive group, especially if it's the explosive type, which it's likely to be."

LuAnne, looking around frantically, hopped up again. "Go lie down awhile, Julia. You could use a nice little rest. I'll look in on you when I get back from the store." Forgetting the coffee tray, she scurried off to the kitchen and, as the back door closed, on to the grocery store.

And I, having outflanked another repetitive discourse on LuAnne's marital options, sighed and leaned my head back, as the blessed sound of silence surrounded me. Maybe now that she had left the house to get away from my endless talking, she would better understand Leonard's search for solace—read that as peace and quiet.

Chapter 30

Right before Lloyd and Latisha came in for lunch, LuAnne called and told Lillian that she was having lunch downtown and would get the groceries afterward. Maybe she really didn't like hot dogs, or maybe she wanted to stay away from my rambling monologues as long as she could.

I felt slightly ashamed of myself, but not so much that I wouldn't try changing the subject again if need be.

Having gone in to help Lillian with lunch, but more often getting in her way, I had asked, "Mrs. Conover not back yet?"

"No'm, so good thing I had hot dogs in the freezer, else we be eatin' grits for lunch. I give her one of the household checks for the groceries. Was that all right?"

"Oh, of course. I wouldn't expect her to pay for all we need after being away so long." Although, I thought but didn't say, a thoughtful guest might've at least offered.

The children had come running into the kitchen then, letting the door bang shut behind them.

"Man!" Lloyd said, pushing his hair out of his face. "It's getting rough out there. That wind is blowing like sixty."

Latisha laughed. "Yeah, it nearly blowed me away."

Going to the window, I looked out at the row of Bradford pear trees bent over by the wind, noticed some debris in the air, and saw a spattering of rain from the dark clouds overhead.

"My goodness, what's going on? It was beautiful outside the last time I looked."

"Better turn on the Weather Channel, Miss Julia," Lloyd said as he sat at the table. "We're in for the edge of Marty. It made landfall between Charleston and Savannah as a category three storm, so we'll be getting high winds and heavy rain."

"Oh, no. I thought we'd gotten away from that thing. For goodness' sakes, we're two hundred miles from the coast. We aren't supposed to have hurricanes."

"It's following us, Miss Julia," Lloyd said, grinning as if gale force winds didn't bother him at all. "They say that the storm surge has flooded Charleston's streets. Water's coming up from the manholes, and the islands are taking a real beating."

"Well, I'm glad we got out when we did," I said, taking my seat at the table and giving a skeptical eye to the hot dog on my plate, "but you and Latisha should stay in this afternoon. That wind will be blowing things around and you could get hit with something."

"Yes'm, I know," he said. "But I was all set to play some tennis. No telling when the courts will be dry again, so that's the end of that."

Latisha, sounding much like her great-granny, said in a knowing way, "You don't wanta be hittin' no balls in this weather, Lloyd. They might come flyin' right back atcha."

He laughed. "They just might. But I hate to miss any more time on the courts. School starts next week, you know."

"Don't remind me!" Latisha put her hot dog down on her plate. "Puttin' that in my mind jus' about make me sick."

I was up in our bedroom unpacking suitcases and thinking vaguely of lying down when I heard LuAnne come in downstairs. Glancing at the clock, I wondered at the four hours it had taken her to get both lunch and groceries. But it had been four hours during which I hadn't been forced to think of Leonard Conover.

Hearing LuAnne's footsteps on the stairs, I picked up a stack of clean clothes and put them in a drawer.

"Julia?" LuAnne hesitantly said as she stood in the doorway. "How're you feeling? Did you get a nap?"

"Oh, I'm fine, LuAnne. Come in. I'm just trying to get unpacked."

"Well," she said, perching on my chintz-covered chair, "I just wanted to tell you that I think I've figured out who the woman is who's offering Leonard solace. And who knows what else, because you know that's not all she's offering."

That got my attention, so I sat on the edge of the bed and waited to hear. "Who?"

"Helen. Helen Stroud."

"Oh, LuAnne, no! Why in the world would you think that?"

"Because it makes sense. Helen's not married, for one thing. In fact, she's a divorcee, so she's probably looking for a man. And Helen can keep a secret. You know how closemouthed she is. And another thing is that one time Leonard helped her with her coat while I stood by struggling with mine. I think she's the obvious one."

"LuAnne," I said tiredly, as I prepared to refute her argument. "Listen, Helen's not married, that's true. But that doesn't matter because Leonard is and it hasn't stopped him from looking around."

"Doing more than looking," she interrupted darkly.

"And you're right," I went on, "Helen can keep a secret, but so can any number of other people, including me. And helping her with her coat one time in all the years we've known each other is a poor reason to suspect her. No, LuAnne, you should be looking elsewhere. I could never believe it's Helen. In fact, I'd say she'd be the last one to get involved with someone else's husband."

Not only could *I* not believe it of Helen, but she was beyond the belief of anyone. For one thing, Leonard was so far beneath Helen's level of interest that it was laughable to even consider. Helen would be attracted only to a successful, confident, and intellectual man, and Leonard was none of the above.

"Well," LuAnne said, "I wouldn't put it past her. But, Julia, if it's not her, who could it be? I've wracked my brain and I can't come up with anybody."

"Have you asked him? I mean, have you come straight out and asked who she is?"

"He won't tell me, and I don't know what to do. I can't stay here forever, and I can't go home. And sometimes I miss him, and other times I want to flay him alive, and I'm so mixed up I don't know what to do."

Here we go again, I thought, as the house creaked in a sudden gust of wind. Glancing out the window, I could see papers and twigs blowing across Polk Street as my poor boxwoods were getting soaked by a downpour. All I could think of was being trapped inside listening to LuAnne bemoaning her fate.

Change the subject, I thought, and proceeded to do so.

"Have you ever noticed," I began, "how television commercials lead our culture? Or maybe they follow the trends, I don't know. But we're back in the Me Generation, or maybe we never left it. There's this one in which several actors and actresses say, 'See *me*. See *me*.' And another in which a young woman, on the verge of tears, says, 'When I have an outbreak, I'm not *me* anymore.' And, LuAnne, there was one in which a young man is buying a hamburger, and he proudly says, 'I like this place because it lets me be *me*.' Now I ask you, who else *would* he be? And does a choice of hamburger toppings indicate whether he's himself or not? It beats all I've ever heard."

"Julia," LuAnne said, rising from the chair, "I've come to a decision. You need to rest, and I need to take hold of my problem. I'm going home and I'm going to dog every step Leonard makes. I'm going to devote every minute, day and night, to following him, listening in on the phone, whatever it takes until I find out everything I need to know. *Then* I'll know what to do."

"Why, LuAnne, I think that's an excellent idea. As it is now, you've given him a free hand to do whatever he wants, to go and come, and to have a guest if he wants to. Yes, I think you need to be in your home to protect your interests. But, I want you to know that you're welcome here for as long as you want to stay."

"Thank you, Julia, you've been a good friend." She stopped, bit her lip, then went on. "I don't mean to be critical, but do you think you might be watching a little too much television?"

"Why, no. I hardly watch it at all—just the news with Sam and some HGTV on occasion. Why do you say that?"

"Well . . . ," LuAnne said, a concerned frown on her forehead. "No reason, I guess. It just seems that you know an awful lot about what's on it—none of which is very edifying."

"You're certainly right about that, but," I said with a wave of my hand, "listen, I think you're doing the right thing by going back to Leonard. Maybe the two of you can talk things out. Just turn off the TV and hide the remote. Then sit there staring at him until he has to talk to you."

"Maybe, but I want you to know that even though I'm giving Leonard another chance, I won't be sleeping in the same bed with him."

"I wouldn't, either," I murmured, shuddering at the thought.

Chapter 31

Her mind firmly made up, LuAnne lost no time in gathering her things and getting them into her car during a brief respite in the downpours. Cautioning her to watch for fallen limbs as she drove up the mountain, I endured a hug, then stood on the porch waving good-bye.

"Well, Lillian," I said as I went back to the kitchen, "I wonder how long that'll last. I do wish her well, though. It's no fun thinking that you've been betrayed for years all unbeknownst to you. And I know what I'm talking about."

"Yes'm, I know you do. But you had it easier 'cause Mr. Springer already passed by the time you find out. Miz Conover, now, she got to keep on livin' with it 'cause Mr. Conover keep on livin'."

"Law, Lillian, don't make a point of that. When she gets in one of her rages, she might try to remedy the situation."

Lillian laughed. "No'm, she won't do that." Then she stopped, gave me a sidewise look as if she were testing the waters, and went on. "I tell you what she want me to do, though. Miz Conover, she come an' tell me I oughta keep my eyes open. She think you got something bad wrong with you."

Surprised, then stung, I said, "Why in the world would she say such a thing? Just what's supposed to be wrong with me, I'd like to know."

"Well, she say you jus' been talkin' up a storm 'bout nothing that nobody want to know. She say she can't get a word in edgewise, no matter how hard she try."

I stared at her, then laughed. "*Exactly!* It worked, Lillian; what you said I should do worked!"

Then the lights flickered and the room dimmed. Lillian whirled around and said, "What . . . ?"

"We've lost power," I said, "but hold on. The generator will come on in a few seconds."

But not before we heard footsteps on the stairs as Lloyd and Latisha came running down. "The power's off, Miss Julia!" Lloyd called, as if I hadn't noticed.

Latisha ran to her granny and hid her face in Lillian's apron. "That big, ole storm's comin' here!"

Just then the generator started up, the lights came on, the ceiling fans whirred, and everything looked a great deal brighter.

"Well, Lillian," I said, relieved that something worked the way it was supposed to, "I was going to tell you to go home early, but the way that wind's blowing, there'll be more outages. I think you and Latisha should stay the night here."

"I think so, too," Latisha said, back to her confident self again. "That ole house of ours sure do creak an' carry on when the wind blows."

"This one does, too, Latisha," I said, "but I think we're safe. I do wish, though, that Sam would come on home."

"Oh, me!" Lillian cried, throwing up her hands. "I forget to tell you. Mr. Sam, he call and say to tell you he goin' to look at some property with Mr. Burnside. He be home by suppertime."

Len Burnside was a real estate broker and longtime friend who knew Sam's propensity for buying far-flung land that nobody else wanted. Every once in a while, Sam got a bee in his bonnet about owning undeveloped tracts of land, usually those that involved long treks through brush and over hill and dale to get to. But if it had water on it, even a little creek, he would snap it up, telling me that land was valuable because they weren't making any more of it.

"My word, that means he's out in this storm!" I looked out the window and saw the same thing I'd seen the last time I'd looked. And Sam was out in it.

It was bad enough to worry about him caught somewhere in a thicket, but now I began thinking of Hazel Marie alone with those babies. Turning to Lloyd, I said, "Call your mother, honey, and see if they've lost power. I expect a tree is down somewhere, so it could be hours before power comes back on. Use your cell phone—it should be working—and tell her to come over here if she wants to."

In a few minutes Lloyd came back into the kitchen, saying, "Mama's still got power. Guess she's on a different grid from us, but she said that all the stoplights and streetlights on Main Street are off."

"That means," I said, "they'll get the power back on before we know it." I jumped as something—a limb, a trash can, something—crashed against the house. Latisha screamed, and Lillian called on the Lord. Lloyd's eyes got big, and my nerves were jumping all over the place.

"Quick," I said, "Lloyd, let's you and me and Latisha run through the house and draw the curtains—just in case a window gets broken."

By the time we'd gathered back in the kitchen, which for some reason seemed the safest place, I'd had enough of the storm we couldn't get away from. Vaguely worried about LuAnne getting up the mountain safely, and deeply worried about Sam out somewhere braving the elements, I put my mind to keeping the children calm and occupied with something other than the remnants of Marty that were raging outside. It's a fact that when the weather is really bad, people tend to huddle together, lower their voices, and hope that if they don't call attention to themselves, they can ride it out.

"I guess," I said, "if we had the cards, we could play Old Maid. But we don't, so somebody think of something else."

"I know something we can do!" Latisha sprang up, her face bright with a sudden idea. "Let's go get Lloyd's mama an' her glue gun. Then we can bring my shells downstairs and dump 'em out so we can find the best ones, 'cause Miss Hazel Marie said she'd show me how to decorate picture frames an' mirrors an' things. That'd be fun, wouldn't it?"

Not really, I thought, picturing my kitchen table strewn with sandy, salt-water-leaking shells, but I said, "Let's save that for another day, Latisha. It's too risky to be driving in this weather."

Lillian, looking skeptically at Latisha, said, "I don't know as I want you usin' no glue gun. No tellin' what you get stuck to."

"Well," Latisha said, her hands on her hips, "I aim to make me some pretty things so I can sell 'em an' make me some money." Then almost under her breath, she said, "I might want me a scooter or something."

"How about a puzzle?" Lloyd said, and dashed upstairs for one that he'd had since the fifth grade. He spread the pieces out on the kitchen table, and we all sat around putting together a picture of a sailing ship.

The back door suddenly swung open, scaring me half to death, as Sam, thoroughly drenched, came running in.

"Oh, thank goodness!" I said, going to him. "Where've you been? I've been worried sick. Oh, Sam, you are soaked!"

"I'm fine, honey. I'm fine," he said, shrugging off the raincoat that had not repelled water. "Just picked a poor day to look at property. I tell you," he went on, smiling, as I handed him a towel, "this was no time for man or beast to be out. But, beautiful land, Julia, as much of it as I could see. Lots of mist and fog, then we got caught in a downpour, but it has acres of hardwood, lots of rhodo-dendron patches, and a fast-running stream. Well," he ended with a laugh, "I guess any stream would be fast-running today."

"Go put on some dry clothes, Sam," I said, "before you catch your death. Take a warm shower, too. Did you have lunch?"

"No, but we had a big breakfast. We sat around the back table at the Bluebird until close to eleven, just talking. Then Len told me about this tract he wanted me to see, and off we went." Then, ruefully, he added, "I'll check the weather the next time we head for the hills."

Preparing for bed later that evening, I went over in my mind the welfare of those I cared about. Although Marty had calmed down considerably in our area, there were still the occasional gusts of wind that rattled windows and made us all look up at each other.

But Hazel Marie and her babies were safe and dry in her house, and every bed in my house was filled with Lloyd, Latisha, and Lillian. Well, and Sam and me, too, and all I could do was hope that the storm was doing no damage.

Deciding that no news was good news except in the case of Etta Mae, I tried not to picture her inside that single-wide trailer bouncing around in high winds like a tin can. In which case, she wouldn't be in any condition to let us know, anyway.

So, hopefully, we all were reasonably safe and snug in dry beds and under strong roofs. I crawled into bed beside Sam and prepared to sleep the sleep of the just.

Just as I was on the verge of slipping over the edge, Sam turned onto his back and said, "Julia?"

"Hmm?"

"You asleep?"

My eyes opened. "Not now."

He laughed. "I heard at breakfast this morning who Leonard's involved with."

That woke me up. "Who?"

"Somebody who works in the County Inspections office in the basement of the courthouse, who's worked there for years, apparently, and Leonard's job—whatever it was—would've taken him there every day or so. At least, that's what they say."

I sat straight up in bed. *"Who is she?"*

"Well, nobody was sure of her last name. She's just known as Totsie."

"Totsie!" I shrieked. "What kind of name is that?"

"Lie down, honey," Sam said. "It's a nickname, I guess, but Hank Childers said that's what's on her nameplate. He knows her fairly well—he's a contractor, you know."

"Oh, my word," I said, collapsing back onto my pillow. "Leonard Conover and a woman named Totsie? What else did they say?" I said, sitting up again. "What does she look like? Some little flirty thing in short skirts and tight sweaters? Somebody who'd wear *black* underwear? That's what a Totsie sounds like to me."

"Just the opposite, they said."

I absorbed that for a few seconds, then asked, "Are you going to buy that property you looked at today?"

"I'm thinking about it."

"Good. You'll have reason to go see about zoning and permits, and I want a full description when you do."

He laughed and drew me back down. After a few minutes of silence, I said, "That breakfast group of yours really knows what's going on in town. Which means that I don't ever want to hear another word about how women gossip."

We had a quiet laugh together, then I tried to sleep while visions of a woman named Totsie danced in my head.

Chapter 32

And those visions were still there when I got up the next morning. Sam was about to go downstairs as I continued to stand in front of the mirror, trying to do something with my hair.

"Wait a minute, Sam," I said, laying aside the hairbrush and turning to him. "Do you think I should tell LuAnne?"

"Tell her what?" Which meant that Totsie wasn't occupying his mind the way she was mine.

"Why, you know—who the woman is."

"Good gracious, Julia, I wouldn't tell her for the world. No telling what it could lead to. No, honey, let's keep it to ourselves. She'll learn who it is soon enough, but she'll never forgive you for knowing it before she does."

That didn't exactly make sense, because why would she hold Leonard's gallivanting against *me*? But after thinking about it, I knew that Sam was right. I shouldn't be the one to reveal all the squalid details to LuAnne, even though, I admit, I was dying to tell her.

By the time I got to the kitchen, Sam had already left to meet Len Burnside for another look at that mountain property—this time, more adequately dressed and shod for inclement weather. I found Lloyd and Latisha at the table eating breakfast, while Lillian leaned on the counter, talking to them as she eased the weight on her cast-bound foot.

Looking sharply at her, I said, "Is that foot bothering you this morning?"

"No more'n usual." She straightened up and began spooning scrambled eggs onto my plate.

"You did too much yesterday. Let me have that plate, and you sit down. Elevate that foot, too. I want you to stay out of this kitchen today and take care of yourself."

"Yes'm, I will. I might even set out in the yard and let the sun shine on it."

I went to the window to look out at the drenched yard—mud puddles and raindrops on grass and leaves sparkling in the bright sunlight. Thready clouds against a bright blue sky scudded in the high-altitude wind, but the promise of a fine August day was in the offing.

"Lloyd," I said, sitting at the table as he took his plate to the sink, "I know you want to play tennis today, but the courts will take awhile to dry. Why don't you and Latisha pick up some of the debris in the yard this morning?"

I had to smile at my use of the typically Southern way of giving a command by way of a question. But how much more pleasant and courteous it was to ask for cooperation rather than issuing abrupt orders. Besides, it was easier to get things done if everyone was agreeable.

"Sure, we can do that," Lloyd said. "The courts might be dry by lunchtime. Come on, Latisha, let's get to work."

"Oh-h, me," she said, dragging herself upright. "All I do is work, work, work from sunup to sundown."

Lillian and I laughed at the absurdity of Latisha's heavy workday. "Don't try to move any large limbs," I cautioned. "You could get hurt. Leave them where they are, and Sam will get them later. Just pick up what you can and pile it all by the curb on the street. The city'll send a truck by in a day or so."

After insisting that Lillian sit in the living room with her feet resting on a footstool, I took myself in hand and called LuAnne. Not that I particularly wanted to, mind you, but because she would expect me to check on her well-being, especially after the first night of her return home.

"LuAnne?" I said when she answered. "How—"

"I'm fine, Julia, but I'll tell you right now that I don't have time to listen to any more television commercials."

"Why, LuAnne, I just wanted to see how you and Leonard are getting along. Television commercials have nothing to do with it." Although if she had launched into another diatribe about her pitiful circumstances, I had intended to point out how frequently constipation was openly discussed on the air—no initials or euphemisms ever disguised that uncomfortable condition. Frankly, discussing it publicly struck me not only as shameful, but as an indication of how poorly some people had been raised.

"Believe me, I know it, and I hope you're off that subject for good. But, Julia, I'm glad you called. You wouldn't believe how happy Leonard is to have me home. I made blueberry pancakes for him this morning, and he just beamed. Maybe the secret is to cater to his needs more than I've been doing."

"Umm, maybe. Although it seems to me that that's what you've always done."

"I don't need any negative thoughts, Julia," she admonished me, while those pressing negative thoughts of *Totsie, Totsie, Totsie* ran through my head. I mentally clamped my mouth shut.

"Well," I said, "I just wanted to check on you and remind you that what it really comes down to is this: What is best for *you?* What do *you* want?"

"Oh, Julia," LuAnne said, her voice choking, "I know what I want. I want a happy—or, at least, a halfway happy—marriage, and I'm not sure I'll ever have it. I can't make blueberry pancakes every morning for the rest of my life. And he just keeps saying that nothing's wrong, that he's happy with the way things are— *still* are."

"Well," I said again, at a loss as to how to respond. "I'll support you in whatever you decide to do. But, LuAnne, I don't think you'll ever regret making this one last—*possibly* last—effort to improve your marriage. You know, though, that there are some couples who're just plain mismatched, and no matter how much one of them tries, the basic personality of the other can never be changed. That may sound like some of Sam's psychobabble, but it's the truth."

"I know it," she mumbled, then blew her nose. "He's in there now watching a game show, and refuses—absolutely refuses—to talk about *her*."

"Well . . . well," I said, wracking my brain for something to console her. "I guess a lot of people stay in unhappy marriages for fear of the alternative, and I understand that." And I did, for I was wondering, as I had often wondered before, what I would've done if I'd discovered Wesley Lloyd Springer's perfidy while he was still engaged in it. Jumping out of a safe, though miserable, marriage without a parachute would make most women pause.

"Miss Julia!" Lloyd called as the back door slammed shut.

"Oh," I said, my heart lurching at the urgency in Lloyd's voice, "I have to go, LuAnne. One of the children may be hurt. Talk to you later."

Hanging up the phone, I hurried to the hall. "In here, Lloyd. What's happened? Is Latisha hurt?"

"Uh, no'm," he said calmly enough, as he shook his soaked sleeve loose from his arm. "We're okay. Why?"

"Well, for goodness' sakes, I thought . . . well, it doesn't matter. Why were you calling me?"

"I'm pretty sure I saw that car again."

"Here? On this street?"

"Yes, ma'am. See, we were picking up the front yard, and I stood up with an armload, and there was that black Suburban just sitting . . . well, just slowing down in the street. It was like it was passing our house until somebody saw me, and it stopped. I stared at it, and I know they were staring at me. They had to be—nobody else but Latisha was around, but then it sped up and went on by."

"My word, Lloyd," I said as a chill ran down my spine. "Are you sure it was the same car?"

"Well, gosh, it *felt* like the same one—blacked-out windows and all. I ran to the sidewalk to try to read the license plate, but it was too far away. I'm pretty sure it was a Florida tag, though. I couldn't see the numbers—didn't have my glasses on, dang it."

"Well, Lloyd, I don't know what to think." But that wasn't true. I knew what I was thinking, and I was thinking that those shady people we'd met on the beach were taking an inordinate interest in the boy standing right in front of me. First at his mother's house—the one whose address they could've found in a glove compartment—and now at my house, perhaps by chance as they tooled around? It was as if they were mapping his locations, and my skin began to crawl at the thought.

Chapter 33

"Where's Latisha?" I asked.

"Sitting on the back steps cleaning her shoe." Lloyd grinned. "She stepped in something."

"Well, tell her to leave them outside, and both of you come on in the house." I wasn't sure what we should do, indeed if anything, seeing that both Mr. Pickens and Coleman were out of reach, and Sam was out in the woods somewhere. I could, however, keep Lloyd—seemingly the object of interest—out of sight until Sam got home.

"We're not finished picking up the yard. I mean I'm not, because Latisha spent the time laying her shells out in rows on the front steps and counting them. Looks like she has about a hundred."

"Don't worry about the yard," I said. "Lloyd, listen, I don't want to scare you, but we should be cautious until we find out who's in that car. And, of course, until we're sure it's the same car you've been seeing. So I'll tell Lillian to keep Latisha occupied in the kitchen—no need to upset her—and you and I can sit by the window in the living room and see if it comes back around."

"Well, I was gonna meet some friends at the tennis courts this afternoon. . . ."

"Oh, I think keeping watch for about an hour will do it," I assured him. "If the people in that car are interested in us, they'll be back around soon enough."

"Maybe I can read and watch at the same time. I've still got some summer reading to finish before school starts."

I smiled—neither book nor street would get much attention if he tried to do both. "After we've watched a while, I'll drive you to the courts. I don't think you should be walking alone until we find out more. For now, though, I'll sit and watch with you."

And that's what we did, sitting across from each other in my matching Victorian chairs in front of the double window that faced the street. I paged absently through a magazine, looking up and out every second or so, while Lloyd was soon absorbed in his book.

Then an article on how to clear out clutter caught my attention, and I let a few extra seconds pass without looking up.

"*There it is!*" Lloyd jumped up, his book falling to the floor as he ran to the door. "They're back! I'm going after 'em!"

I sprang from my chair and followed as fast as I could. "Wait, Lloyd! Don't go out!"

I caught his shoulder just as he opened the door. "We can't catch them, honey. All we'll do is let them know we're on to them."

He looked through the sidelight by the door, then slumped back. "It's gone. I wish I'd had a rock or something."

"Listen now, we still don't know if it's the same car. You've only seen it from the front and from the side, with just that quick glance at a Florida tag." Even as I was trying to deter him, I was feeling the same urge to do something—almost anything would be better than sitting around watching while somebody else was watching us.

"Go get your racket," I said. "I'll meet you at the car, and we'll drive around and see if the car's in the vicinity. Then I'll take you to the courts."

"Well," I said as I pulled into a parking space beside the tennis house at the country club, "it seems to have disappeared. No sign of it anywhere."

"Maybe we should've made a wider circuit," Lloyd said. "But I doubt they'd linger around after making two passes. They probably figured that somebody would notice them."

"I don't know, Lloyd. I keep thinking that we could be making one car out of half a dozen similar ones. On the other hand, we did have a break-in at the beach, and they have their windows blacked out, which is a little unusual. The only reason for doing that is so no one will know who's in a car. That alone is worrisome enough."

"And don't forget," Lloyd added, "how that woman rolled up her window so quick on the interstate. I mean, Miss Julia, she looked right at me, and I was walking by not three feet from her, and that window zipped up like nobody's business."

"Still, it's all supposition at this point," I said, yet fretting inside that it might not be. "Now, listen, Lloyd, I want you to stay right here on the courts—there're plenty of people around, and those people in the car aren't going to come walking in." There was a certain privilege—namely, exclusiveness—that went along with country club membership, and I paid enough in dues and fees to be assured that no unknown persons would threaten Lloyd's safety.

"If I'm not back," I went on, "call me when you're ready to come home. I do not want you walking home by yourself, okay?"

"Yes'm, I'll call you." He got out of the car, waved at me, and hurried into the tennis house. Several people were on the courts already, and I waited until I saw Lloyd walk out and join three boys who had been batting balls around while they waited for him.

Before going home, I drove up and down the street in front of Hazel Marie's house, checking things out. There wasn't one black car parked on either side of the street, so I pulled into her driveway and walked up to the door.

Knowing that I considered drop-in company rude and disruptive to one's daily routine, Hazel Marie's eyes widened in surprise when she saw who was ringing her doorbell.

"Miss Julia!" she exclaimed. "How are you? Come in, come in. I just put the babies down for a nap." Which, I assumed, meant that she'd been thinking of taking one, too.

"I can't stay long, Hazel Marie," I said, stepping into the wide hall of the house that had once belonged to Sam. "I know you have a dozen things to do, but I need to talk to you for a minute."

After being shown to a seat in the living room and turning down offers of coffee, tea, lemonade, orange juice, or water, I said, "Hazel Marie, I don't want to worry you, but . . ." And I went on to tell her about the lurking vehicle which appeared to be tracking Lloyd's movements and keeping tabs on his whereabouts.

"But, *why* . . . ?" Hazel Marie was stunned, fearful, and outraged— her face changing as each emotion reached it. She jumped up, ran to the door, and locked it. Returning to the living room, she demanded, "Why *Lloyd*, Miss Julia? Why're they after him? Did he do anything to them? Say anything? I don't understand it."

"I don't, either, but keep in mind that we don't know who they are, or if they're the same people we saw on the beach, or even if it's Lloyd that they're actually interested in. It's incomprehensible to me. But I thought you should know, so if any strange person comes to the door—"

She whirled around. "I'm calling J.D. He needs to come home, and come home right now." Then she whirled back to me. "He's at the tennis courts? I'm going to get him."

"No, wait, Hazel Marie. He's perfectly safe there—he's with a dozen people who know him, and he's under strict orders to wait for me to pick him up. See, I thought it best for him to be busy over there, rather than sitting around at home worrying. Actually, I didn't want to alarm him by showing *my* concern. I mean, he's aware of the car—obviously. He's the only one who's seen it. The fact of the matter is, though, we don't know if it's the same car."

"Well," she said, sitting on the edge of a chair, "J.D. will be home in a couple of days, so I guess we can just be real careful until then. But, Miss Julia, I think Lloyd ought to stay with you till then, if that's all right. I mean, you'll have a man in the house, and all I'll have is Granny Wiggins." Granny Wiggins was Etta Mae's grandmother who helped with the twins and occasionally wielded a dust cloth around the house.

Hazel Marie smiled, although somewhat wanly, and went on. "Well, James, too, but nobody'd want to tangle with Granny."

James, who had worked for Sam before we married, lived in the apartment over the Pickenses' garage. He was a wonderful cook, but, being afraid of his own shadow, couldn't be depended on for much of anything else.

Instead of going home, I backed out of Hazel Marie's driveway and headed back to the tennis courts. No need sitting at home, worrying about Lloyd's safety, when I could sit over there and know he was safe.

By the time I parked and went into the air-conditioned tennis house, the sky seemed to have become hazy and low hanging. Heat bore down as heavy and sultry as it had when we'd been parked on Interstate 26. Marty, according to the Weather Channel, had calmed considerably after barreling inland, but was still wreaking minor havoc to the east and north of us.

But, I declare, the muggy air felt as if Marty were making a U-turn and heading toward us again. Actually, though, the forecast, according to Lillian, had predicted a storm front coming up from the Gulf, bringing torrents of rain, local flooding, downed trees, and power outages. I sighed, thinking that if it wasn't one thing, it was another. But that's the dog days of August for you.

I sat in the cool tennis house, glancing occasionally out the window at Lloyd and his three friends playing a ferocious game, while children in shorts, women in shorts, and men in shorts came and went in and through the little building. When Lloyd and his friends finished and came inside, they were all drenched with perspiration. Red faced and panting from the strenuous game, the boys downed cold drinks, spoke pleasantly but casually to me, and made plans to play again the following day—if it didn't rain.

Lots of luck with that, I thought, hearing a low rumble of thunder as Lloyd and I headed for the car.

"Lloyd," I said, turning the ignition, "you're certainly capable of getting home by yourself, as your friends are doing. So I hope I didn't embarrass you by waiting for you."

"Shoot, no," he said. "I was glad to see you already here. I didn't have to wait around—the tennis pro would've put me to work picking up balls if he'd seen me."

"Well, good. Now, listen, your mother and I have decided that it would be best if you stay with us until your father gets back. Is that all right with you?"

"Sure, I guess so. But what about Mama? I might ought to stay with her. I mean, if that car really is staking out our house."

"She thinks it's better for you to be with Sam—you know, to have a man around. Besides, she'll have Granny Wiggins."

"In that case," Lloyd said with a grin, "no need to worry, is there?"

By the time we got home, rain was coming down in buckets. We ran for the house, sped on by flashes of lightning and cracks of thunder. Latisha was setting the table for dinner as we came running in, while Lillian stirred something on the stove.

"We gettin' us another storm," Latisha said, as if we hadn't noticed. "We pro'bly have to spend the night again."

"Oh, no, we won't," Lillian said. "I gotta get home an' see 'bout that ole house. We be settin' out pans all over the place if it start leakin'. Now, you folks," she said, turning to Lloyd and me, "better get dried off quick, 'cause this 'bout to go on the table."

"Well," Latisha said, mumbling to avoid seeming to talk back. "I don't know how we gonna get home, seein' our ole car on its last legs. It jus' grind away 'fore it ever get started, then it go buckety-buck all down the street."

"Well," Lillian said right back at her, "you can walk if you want to." Which put an end to that.

While waiting dinner for Sam, I mentally took up another subject mainly to get my mind off the stormy conditions outside. I'm never at ease when the elements are acting up, but Latisha had brought to mind the need for Lillian to have a dependable car.

At that point, a bright idea lit me up. Better that Sam be wandering around used car lots than slogging all over creation looking at far-flung mountain property. One stone for two birds was the way to solve two problems—finding a new used car for Lillian and keeping Sam, with Lloyd in tow, close to home until our in-house deputy and private detective could take over.

Chapter 34

After dinner that evening, as Lillian was preparing to leave, I was still going back and forth about sharing my concerns with everybody around the table. I'd been hesitant about overreacting, thereby worrying everybody needlessly, but then again, forewarned is forearmed. Latisha was sitting right there, listening to everything. Although I'd heretofore refrained from saying anything within her hearing, I finally decided that we all needed to know what was going on—maybe, especially, she did. She'd seen those people up close and personal on the beach, so she'd recognize them as quickly as Lloyd and I would. And if they were here in town and if she did see them, without knowing any better, it would be just like her to walk right up to them and start a conversation. And who knew where that would lead, especially if they were here on sneaky business.

So, getting their attention in spite of Lillian's apple pie, I reported what was happening and, with Lloyd's help, recounted each sighting of the black Suburban. Or suspected sighting, as the case might've been. I did, however, downplay the apparent focus on Lloyd, putting it as more of an interest in all of us who'd rented the big yellow house at the beach.

"But," Latisha broke in, "they didn't know we come from that house. We went back on the sidewalk, 'member?"

"But," Lloyd countered, "they could've seen us come over the dunes on our way to the beach—at least seen our footprints. There was nobody on the beach except us. And them."

I nodded. "That's true."

Sam frowned throughout the telling, then said, "Well, it all sounds unusual, I'll give you that. And it was odd that somebody went through the Pickenses' car at the beach, but, even if it's the same trio who's showing up here, they could be on legitimate business. A lot of Floridians are looking for mountain property, you know."

I know, I thought, *and so are certain Abbotsvillans.* I smiled and patted his knee. Sam had mountain property on the brain.

"Yes, sir," Lillian said, nodding, "you right about that. Lotsa people want to move here. But I don't see no FOR SALE sign on this house or on Miss Hazel Marie's, either. So what they doin' drivin' 'round lookin' at *them* an' nobody else's?"

Nobody had an answer, until Latisha's face lit up with a sudden inspiration and, in that shrill, piercing voice of hers, announced, "I know why they here, and I know what they want. They think we got us a pile of hunderd-dollar bills on the beach, an' they want some. But all we got to do is put a big sign on both houses that say WE DON'T GOT ANY, an' they go back where they come from."

If only it were that easy. After going to bed, Sam and I continued to talk far into the night—maybe for a full hour before falling asleep.

"One thing, Julia," Sam said for about the third time, "if you see that car again, I do not want you approaching it for any reason whatsoever. Get the tag number if you can so Coleman can run it, but get it only from a distance. Otherwise, let it go. When he and Pickens get back, they'll handle it. There's no need for you to be doing anything." After a few minutes of silence, he pulled me closer and said, "Are you listening to me?"

"Yes, of course I am. I'm just thinking, wondering what they could want. I mean, Latisha was right—undoubtedly, they think we came away with enough money to choke a horse or, anyway, to be worth stealing or scamming from us, but I can't figure out why they'd come to such a conclusion. I've gone over that brief meeting on the beach a dozen times, Sam, and there's no way we gave even an inkling that we'd found any of that washed-up money." I sighed and turned over. "I just don't understand it."

"I'll stay close tomorrow in case they show up again," he said.

"Thank you, but here's another thing," I said, flipping onto my back. "Lillian needs a new car, and from the sound of it, a new roof, as well. You and Lloyd can do something about both tomorrow, and you can leave that Suburban alone, too."

"I'm a little ahead of you," Sam said, seriously enough, "I've been thinking about a car for Lillian, but I didn't know her roof was leaking."

"I didn't, either. But she never complains—just think about that bunion of hers. I had no idea it was bad enough to need surgery. And if we hadn't gone to the beach, I'm not sure she'd have had it removed at all." I let the silence stretch out for a few seconds. "Which makes me appear to take her for granted, and that makes me feel bad."

"We'll make it up to her, honey." Sam turned and put his arm around me. "Lloyd can go with me, and we'll get on both, first thing tomorrow. Today, I mean."

As rain thundered against the roof, and the room lit up with a flash of lightning, I hoped that Lillian's house was withstanding the storm. I couldn't help but picture her setting pans around the rooms to catch rainwater. I nestled against Sam and determined that we would make sure that she and Latisha were as safe and dry as we were. And that they'd have a decent car that wouldn't go buckety-buck down the street. It was the least I could do for the most faithful—except for Sam—friend that I had. Besides, I would sleep better, too.

"Sam?"

"Hmm?"

"Tomorrow—well, today, I guess—after you call a roofing contractor, and after you find a car for Lillian, I think you should have some business to conduct at the County Inspections office. Then come straight home and tell me what that Totsie woman looks like."

"Julia?"

"Hmm?"

"Go to sleep, honey."

———————

Sam was up and gone before I could drag myself out of bed the next morning, and by the time I was dressed and downstairs, Lillian and Latisha had come flying in, drenched from the heavy rain and loaded down with sacks and suitcases.

"We 'bout got drownded last night, Miss Lady!" Latisha yelled. "Mr. Sam, he come an' tell us to get outta that house fast as we can. And here we are, an' I got my shells with me, too. An'," she went on, "Great-Granny let me stop at Miss Hazel Marie's on our way home last night, an' she showed me a surefire way to stick my shells on, but I'm gonna do it my way first 'cause I think I got it licked."

"Law, Miss Julia," Lillian said, ignoring Latisha as she wheezed from her run to the house, "you shoulda seen it. That ole roof jus' give way and rain come pourin' in." She grabbed a roll of Bounty towels and commenced to dry off Latisha, then herself. "If Mr. Sam hadn't showed up 'bout that time, I don't know what we woulda done."

"You'd have come here," I said. "Just as you have. But what happened to the roof?"

"It jus' ole, I guess. It been leakin' a long time, but nothin' like it done last night. Not even my big cannin' pot would hold it. I jus' thank my Jesus for Mr. Sam. He take one look, an' next thing I know he got a roofin' man out there. That man say he can't do a thing, though, till it stop rainin', 'cept put some tarpaper over the holes, an' Mr. Sam say for us to come over here. I hope that's all right, Miss Julia."

"And I hope to goodness," I said somewhat sharply, "that you know you and Latisha are welcome at any time, but most especially when you've been washed out of your own home."

Rain continued off and on for the rest of the day, sometimes in dribbles and other times in torrents, along with gusts of wind, lightning, and thunder. It was no time for man or beast to be outside, but Sam deemed it perfect for kicking tires and checking odometers.

With Sam and Lloyd heading to the used car lots, Latisha, relegated to entertaining herself, stood with her hands on her hips as she studied the card table that Lloyd had brought up from the basement for her. With a sigh, she spread out the contents of two plastic bags of shells and began to pick out the broken and chipped ones to throw away.

Then she looked up and said, "I'm thinkin' this card table might be too little. How 'bout I pour 'em out on the big table?"

"No, ma'am, you're not," Lillian said. "That's where ever'body eat, an' nobody want to eat with shells strewed all around."

"Well, *I* would, but, okay, I'll use this little dinky table." With intense concentration, she continued to move shells from one pile to another until she had them arranged to her satisfaction. Then she slid off the chair, announcing, "Now I got to go to the bathroom." And off she went.

I smiled as Lillian shook her head with a slight roll of her eyes. "That chile," she said.

"At least she's entertaining herself," I said, "and on a day like this, that's a big plus. In fact, I think I'll try to find something to do myself."

Chapter 35

An hour or so later, with the rain seeming to have set in for a long stay, the front doorbell rang. Hurrying to answer it before Lillian tried to hobble from the kitchen, I opened the door.

"Etta Mae! How nice to see you," I said, unable to hide my surprise at her visit. "What in the world are you doing out on a day like this? Come in, come in."

"I can't stay," she said, her raincoat dripping on the hall floor. "I'm on my way to the drugstore. But I wanted to drop this off for Latisha." She held out a small wooden frame—no picture, no glass, just a plain wooden frame.

"For Latisha? Why?"

"I told her at the beach that I had an old one she could have. She called a little while ago and said she sure could use it, so here it is."

"Well, for goodness' sakes," I said, thinking to myself, as Lillian had said out loud, *"That child."*

Then, as Etta Mae turned to leave, the fortuity of her visit struck me. "Wait, Etta Mae. I've been meaning to call you, so your timing is perfect. Let's go in here. I won't keep you long."

Looking a little apprehensive, she followed me into the living room. "Is anything wrong? How's Mrs. Conover?"

"She's all right—still talking about doing something, but never actually doing anything. And as far as something being wrong, we just don't know. That's what I want to talk to you about."

Her face dropped. "Oh, Miss Julia, I'm so sorry. What have I done?"

My heart dropped as well as she so quickly assumed that she was in the wrong.

"Not one thing, Etta Mae," I said firmly and, I hope, convincingly. "No, I just wanted to ask if you've seen a black Suburban—that's one of those big trucklike vehicles, only the beds are closed in with nicely appointed interiors. It could've been parked somewhere or maybe looking as if it's following you on your patient rounds."

She frowned. "A Suburban?"

"Yes, and the one I'm talking about has its windows blacked out so you can't see who's in it."

"Yes'm, I know what they're like, but I don't think I've noticed one. But then, I haven't been looking. Why?"

"I think you would've noticed, Etta Mae, if it had been after you."

"*After* me?"

"Yes. Come sit down. I need to tell you about it."

"Maybe I'd better," she said, easing onto the edge of my Victorian sofa. "What's going on, Miss Julia?"

"Well," I said, sitting across from her and preparing to report on the sightings, "it started at the beach. At least, we think it did."

And I went on to describe how Lloyd, Latisha, and I had met that money-hunting trio on the beach, and how I'd dismissed them but Lloyd hadn't, and the fact that that very night somebody had searched Hazel Marie's car. Which was strange in itself because there was nothing in it worth stealing.

"The next sighting was when we were parked on the interstate," I went on. "Lloyd saw them—or at least, he saw the woman—practically face-to-face, and her reaction to seeing *him* was as guilty looking as it could be. Then Lloyd saw the Suburban parked on his mother's street near her house. And after that, he saw it driving very slowly past this house. Now, if that's not suspicious, I don't know what is."

Etta Mae looked warily over her shoulder toward the hall, as if expecting that huge vehicle to come barreling in. "That gives me the shivers," she said.

"Me, too. Especially after listing the sightings that way. It sounds so planned and deliberate, but we don't know what they could want."

"Maybe they think we got some of those hundred-dollar bills."

"That's what Latisha thinks, but you know we didn't. And I made that plain when we spoke to them on the beach that day."

"And you're sure it's the same Suburban that you keep seeing?"

"Well, no. And that leaves us questioning everything else. So we don't know if we have an actual problem or if the Chevrolet company has flooded the market with a sale on Suburbans." I stopped, bit my lip, then went on. "Actually, Etta Mae, I'm deathly afraid that they're interested in Lloyd—you probably know that he and I share a sizable estate left by Mr. Springer, so he could be a person of interest to them. I've not mentioned that possibility to Lloyd, but that car shows up wherever he happens to be—they seem to be watching this house and Hazel Marie's. It makes me sick to my stomach to think of what they might be planning. And both Mr. Pickens and Coleman are gone until the weekend."

"Yet it doesn't sound like they've actually *done* anything. I mean, so you could report them to the sheriff."

"That's it in a nutshell," I said, marveling again at the quickness of her mind. "We can't do anything until they make a move. Anyway," I went on, standing up because I was too antsy to sit still, "I thought you needed to know so you can watch out for them."

"Oh, my goodness," Etta Mae said, jumping up. "I'll be watching my back all the time, you can count on that. And you better believe I'll let you know if I see them." She shivered again and tightened the belt of her raincoat. "I have to go, Miss Julia. I'm picking up a prescription for one of my patients."

"I thought you'd be off the rest of the week." I smiled somewhat ruefully and added, "I mean, you're still supposed to be on vacation at the beach."

"I'd just as soon be working," she said, heading toward the door, "and save my vacation days for better weather."

After watching Etta Mae splash along my front walk to her car at the curb, I turned back to the living room and sat by myself for a moment or two. I hoped I hadn't frightened her unnecessarily, but nothing is worse than for somebody who says nothing, then to say, "I knew it all along," after something has happened.

Besides, I happened to know that Etta Mae had some strong connections to a few sheriff's deputies—maybe one in particular. She wouldn't hesitate to call on them—or him—if she needed to.

I momentarily considered whether I should tell LuAnne about the black car, but it wasn't as if she was in any shape to handle another cause for concern. It was highly likely that adding another problem to the one she already had would throw her into a frenzy, and I wasn't sure that she—or I—could handle any more agitation.

I stood there for a minute, turning Etta Mae's small wooden frame around in my hands, smiling at the thought of her driving out of her way and in the midst of her busy day to bring it to Latisha. It didn't surprise me, though, for Etta Mae would no more disappoint a child than she would ignore one of her ailing patients, even if she got soaked in the process.

Bestirring myself and putting aside my wandering thoughts, I went to the kitchen and presented the frame to Latisha. She was delighted to get it—at first. But after turning it over and around several times, she announced, "I thought it'd be bigger."

"Five by seven is a good size, Latisha," I said, "depending, I guess, on what you want it for. Are you planning to put shells on it?"

She looked up in surprise. "How did you know?"

"Oh, just a lucky guess."

"Well, don't tell anybody 'cause it's gonna be a surprise." She picked up a shell and examined it carefully, looking for flaws. "If I ever figure out how to do it."

Chapter 36

Leaving her to it, I went to the desk in the library and began writing checks for the few household bills that had come in—anything to stay busy on such a dreary day. After putting stamps on the envelopes, I sat for a while, thinking of Sam and Lloyd and what they might be doing.

Totsie, I thought, and hoped to goodness that Sam would get a good look at her. What kind of woman would attract the attention of a man who had no interests other than the television schedule? And what kind of woman would be attracted, in turn, to such a dull and boring man? I'd known Leonard for forty years or so, and I couldn't call to mind one decent conversation I'd ever had with him. He'd just always been around. Wherever LuAnne was, so was Leonard—quiet, retiring Leonard, who, unbeknownst to anyone, was finding solace in the Abbot County Inspections office.

But solace from what? As far as I could see, Leonard's life was one long, unwavering line of dullness, unbroken by any effort on his part. Except he *had* broken it—if, that is, a twenty-year-long affair was any indication.

But to have found comfort with a woman called *Totsie*! Unbelievable.

"Miss Julia?" Lillian, breaking my reverie, stood in the doorway. "Is it all right if Latisha uses some of this?" She held up a tube of Elmer's glue.

"Of course it is. I should've thought to give it to her. But, Lillian, I'm not sure it'll stick to shells."

"It don't matter," Lillian said, "'long as it keep her busy."

Just as I was leaving the library to eat lunch, the phone rang.

"Julia? It's me, LuAnne. I can't talk long. I'm in the car on my cell—"

"Pull over, LuAnne. You shouldn't be driving and calling at the same time."

"I *am* pulled over! Don't interrupt. I want to tell you what's happening, but he may leave any minute and I'll have to hang up."

"Go ahead then."

"Well, it's like this," she said, gasping a little as if she were out of breath, "I decided to dog every step he makes, and, Julia, do you know what?"

"Uh, no."

"He doesn't watch television all day! Not by a long shot. He's in and out all day long. I've just been too busy with circle meetings and Garden Club meetings and Beautification Council meetings and grocery shopping and hair appointments and I-don't-know-what-all that I didn't know what he was doing. He would be watching television when I left, and he'd be watching when I got home, so I just assumed." She stopped to take a rasping breath. "But not any longer. I am making it my business to know where he goes and what he does."

"Well," I said, hardly knowing what to say, "well, I guess that would be good to know."

"Yes, but so far it's been as boring as he is—haircut, cup of coffee at the Bluebird, an Asheville paper at the newsstand, a stop at the shoe repair shop, and now he's in the basement of the courthouse."

I almost gasped into the phone. "The courthouse?"

"Yes, and you'd think he'd have had enough of it after working there for forty years. But they say it's hard for retirees to turn . . . Oh, Julia, he's coming out! I have to go." And she clicked off.

Oh, my word, I thought as I stood there with phone in hand. LuAnne had discovered Leonard's source of solace, but so far at least, she didn't know it.

By the time I got to the kitchen, I was so jittery with nerves that I doubted I could eat. Should I tell her? Or wait till she found out for herself? She was so close to the truth that if she just thought about it, she'd recognize that it's usually a fellow worker—or in this case, a female worker—who is the guilty partner.

Lillian put a plate on the table, then stood with her hands on her hips, glaring at Latisha. "Would you jus' look at that?"

I looked over at Latisha, busy at her little newspaper-covered table in the corner. Shells were fairly neatly placed into two piles, the frame was flat on the table, and Latisha was carefully squeezing Elmer's glue on a shell, the frame, and her fingers. Scraps of newspaper were stuck to her hands and arms. A streak of glue glistened on her cheek, as she carefully placed a shell on the frame, then pressed on it.

With a look of intense concentration on her face, she slowly lifted her hand. And the shell came with it. "Oh, dangnation!"

"Latisha," Lillian cautioned.

"Well, these things won't stick. This Elmer stuff don't glue anything but my fingers, an' I'm tired of messin' with it." And she wiggled her hand to show that several fingers were stuck together. Then, sliding off her chair, she mumbled, "I got to go to the bathroom."

"Wash your hands good," Lillian said as Latisha headed for the hall bathroom. "An' get that glue off so you can eat something."

I was halfway through my sandwich before she got back. By the time she picked up her own sandwich, a serene look was on her face as if she'd decided that shells that wouldn't stick no longer presented a problem.

And, indeed, she was in no hurry to go back to her piles of shells. She sat and chatted with me, talking about what a good time she'd had at the beach—collecting shells, going in the ocean with Etta Mae, and on and on.

"An' Miss Hazel Marie," Latisha went on, "she say that big ole black-haired man she's married to calls her a crafty woman." She looked at me with guileless eyes. "That's 'cause she makes things outta scraps an' plastic flowers an' such like." Latisha sighed. "I sure wish I had something that'd make my shells stay on. Don't do no good to have a frame if you can't dress it up."

"What about your sand dollars?" I asked. "Will you put them on your frame? They'd make a very pretty design."

She looked at me as if I'd lost my mind. "No, ma'am, that frame is a surprise for somebody, but them sand dollars is mine to keep. Lloyd said they're my beach treasure, an' that's why I'm keepin' 'em."

"Oh, well, I would, too. I just asked because I didn't see them with your shells."

"No'm, I got 'em put up real good. An' that reminds me," she said, sitting straight up with a sudden thought, "I left my pocket-book at Lloyd's mama's house. I got to go get it." And she started sliding off her chair.

"You not goin' anywhere," Lillian said, sliding her back on the chair. "That pocketbook be all right where it is. Eat your lunch."

"Well," Latisha mumbled, "I jus' hope them babies don't get into it. That'd be a ruination if there ever was one."

As Lillian and I reassured her that Hazel Marie would take care of it, Sam and Lloyd came walking in, and we all scrambled around getting lunch for them.

"Miss Lillian," Lloyd said, as he sat at the table, "you won't believe what kind of car we got for you. You'll love it!"

"Jus' so it run. That's all I want."

"What kind?" Latisha demanded. "What kind is it, Lloyd?"

"Wel-l-l," Lloyd said, a sparkle of delight in his eyes. "It's the perfect car for you and Miss Lillian. It's a red Mazda convertible. And it has a squirrel's tail on the hood ornament and a pair of fuzzy dice hanging from the rearview mirror. And, Miss Lillian, if you want racing stripes or flames of fire on it, Mr. Sam said he'd have 'em put on."

"Oh, my sweet Jesus, don't tell me nothin' like that!" Lillian was aghast at the thought.

"You'll love it," Lloyd said as we all laughed. "They're washing and waxing it for you right now. You're gonna be queen of the road in it."

"I hope to goodness," Lillian said, frowning as she looked from Lloyd to Sam, "you got something a decent woman would be drivin' 'round in."

"We did, Lillian," Sam said, smiling as he reassured her. "Lloyd is teasing you, but we were awfully tempted by that sporty little Mazda."

"I don't need nothin' sporty, an' nothin' little, neither."

"Aw, Miss Lillian," Lloyd said, "don't worry. We found you a really good car—it's a nice blue minivan, and it'll hold a ton of stuff. I can't wait for you to see it. Mr. Sam says it drives like a dream."

"That'd sure be a change," Lillian said with some relief. "Thank you, Mr. Sam. Me an' Latisha'll take real good care of it."

"You are most welcome," Sam said. Then, turning to the rest of us, he went on. "Now, folks, here's something else. On our way back, we stopped at Lloyd's mother's house to pick up a book he needed. When we left, as we walked out onto the porch, a black Suburban was passing by very slowly. Then, as if they saw us, they sped off—too quick to get the license number."

"I think," Lloyd said, "there was a nine at the end, but I'm not sure. It was raining again."

"Oh, my goodness," I said, uncertain, but fearful, of the purpose of the people in that roving car. "But at least you've seen it, Sam, so you know how strangely it acts."

"Yes, but we don't know if it's the same people." He stopped then, as we all thought of just who would be so interested in Lloyd's whereabouts if not the beachcombers.

"Oh, Latisha," Sam suddenly said, as he jumped up from the table. "I almost forgot. Hazel Marie sent you something." He reached into a pocket of his raincoat and pulled out her little red pocketbook.

Latisha's face lit up. "My pocketbook! Thank you, Mr. Sam. And you, too, Jesus." She carefully hung the pocketbook by its strap on the back of the chair at her table, then spoke directly to it. "Now you stay right there. I don't wanta forget you again."

Reaching into another of his raincoat pockets, Sam handed her a fairly heavy sack. "That's not all Hazel Marie sent."

"Oh, boy!" Latisha said. "I been waitin' for that thing!" She clutched the sack close and hurried to her little table in the corner.

"What is it?" Lillian said, eyeing the sack suspiciously.

"A hot-glue gun," Sam said, raising his eyebrows. "Apparently Latisha called earlier and said that she sure could use it if Hazel Marie could get it to her. We came by at just the right time. Or maybe," Sam said, casting a skeptical look at Latisha, who had lined up several waxy sticks on the table and was now unwinding an electrical cord from around a plastic gun, "at just the wrong time. I hope she knows how to use it."

"Law, Mr. Sam, you not the onliest one!" Lillian threw up her hands, then rushed to the little table. "Latisha, don't you plug that thing in!"

Chapter 37

Lillian snatched the glue gun out of Latisha's hands, wrapped the electrical cord around it, and stuck it back in the sack. Then she reached up and put the sack on top of the refrigerator.

"It's goin' right back where it come from," she said. Then, glaring at Latisha, she went on. "What you tell Miss Hazel Marie so she send you such a thing?"

Latisha's face puckered up in a scowl as she wailed, "I know how to use it! She showed me real good, an' she let me glue some flowers on her frame, so I can do it, Granny!"

"You better cut that out, little girl," Lillian said, "an' start behavin' yourself. That thing burn you up, an' no way in the world you gonna be playin' with it."

"Well," Latisha said, sniffing loudly. "Well, can I use it if somebody helps me? I'm outta luck if you don't, 'cause nothin' else'll make my shells stick."

Lillian thought about it, then gave in. "Well, I reckon so, if it's somebody knows what they doin'."

Latisha's face brightened as she glanced around. "Lloyd?"

"Uh-uh," he said, backing away. "Don't look at me. I don't know how."

Latisha pouted about that, then said, "Then I'll jus' have to pack all this stuff up an' go over to Miss Hazel Marie's again. She the onliest one that knows anything."

Lillian leaned over her and said, "Latisha, you 'bout to get too big for your britches, so you better find yourself something else to do. Now clean up the mess on this table 'fore you do anything."

Sam had quietly taken himself out of the kitchen while this was going on, and I was just about to follow him. Latisha was usually amenable to whatever was suggested, but she was dead set on creating some kind of surprise for somebody with her shells. It was unlike her to pitch a fit when thwarted, but she slowly began to mind her great-grandmother, putting the shells in a bag and wadding up the Elmer's glue—splotched newspaper.

"I guess," Latisha said, heaving a mournful sigh, "I'll jus' have to go watch television, but it won't do me no good like makin' something would."

Lillian just shook her head, murmuring, "Lord, give me strength," as Latisha stomped off.

"Maybe," I said to encourage Lillian, "when the rain stops, they'll find something to do outside. And, think of this, Lillian, school starts next week."

"Yes'm," Lillian said, "an' it can't come soon enough." Then she laughed. "That chile gonna be the death of me."

"Better by her, I guess, than by that bunion you had. How's your foot doing, anyway?"

"It doin' good. The doctor, he say I got to crip along on this cask for a little while longer, then it be cured. I sure am gettin' tired of it, though."

I poured a cup of coffee and leaned against the counter to drink it. "What's the latest on Thurlow Jones? Have you heard anything?"

"Well, it been a week since he got operated on, an' the hospital want rid of him. They say they gonna send him to some place that keep him longer, an' he don't wanta go." Lillian scrubbed a pot, then, without looking at me, she said, "He call me las' night."

"Thurlow called you? Why?"

"He want me to come work for him so he can come home. He say he match what you pay, an' go up a little."

Outraged, I said, "Why, that sneaky, underhanded old man! What a nerve! The very idea!" Then, the thought of Lillian leaving us brought me up short. "What did you say?"

"Well, I didn't say what I was thinkin', 'cause I wouldn't work for that ole man for all the tea in China. So what I say was I already got a good job, but I try to find somebody to help him out.

But, Miss Julia," Lillian said, turning to me, "won't nobody come work for him no matter how much he pay. Nobody can put up with him. I jus' don't know what he'll do, 'cause he too crazy an' everybody know it."

"That's a real relief. Oh, I don't mean because nobody will work for him, but that you won't. But by the way, what's happened to that old dog of his? What was his name? Ronnie?"

"Yes'm, they say he out in a kennel somewhere, an' he pinin' for that ole man. So you know that dog be the first thing he bring home when he get home hisself. An' that mean whoever work for him gotta work for that dog, too."

"Well, I guess I ought to go visit him wherever they put him. Thurlow, I mean, not Ronnie. But, I'll tell you this, it'll be all I can do not to knock him out of the bed with my pocketbook. The very idea of going behind my back to try to hire you! And I'll tell you another thing, Lillian, if you're ever tempted to take another job, tell me first. I don't know what I'd do without you."

"You don't need to worry 'bout that, Miss Julia. I'm not goin' anywhere. Won't nobody else put up with Latisha like you do."

We laughed together, I with a great lessening of anxiety over the thought of losing Lillian, and she with the rueful patience needed to raise a grandchild.

Sam walked in then, smiling at our laughter. "Lillian, if you're at a stopping place with dinner, let's go get your car. They should have it ready by now, and I want to ride around with you a little to be sure you're comfortable with it."

"Yessir, Mr. Sam," Lillian said, folding a dish cloth, "I can put everything on low an' it be all right. Lemme go get Latisha. She'll wanta ride in that new car."

"Well, call Lloyd, too, if you will. He helped pick it out." Then, turning to me, Sam said, "Come go with us, honey."

"No, I think I'll stay here. You'll have a full car without me. And I sure don't want to distract Lillian from learning where the light switch is or the windshield wiper."

Lloyd and Latisha, boisterous and excited about the new car, ran through the kitchen on their way to Sam's car. Sam would drive to the dealership where they'd transfer to Lillian's car for her test drive.

Just as I thought I'd have a few minutes of quiet, Latisha bounced back inside. Snatching her little red purse off the back of a chair where she'd hung it, she slung it on her shoulder. "Got to take my pocketbook," she sang out, then let the door slam behind her.

Welcoming again a few quiet minutes, I walked into the library and looked out the back window at the soaked yard. As much rain as we'd had the last few days, everything was drenched—tree limbs dripping, water puddling in low spots, and flowering plants looking stripped. But no rain was falling at the moment, though the sky was still gray and foreboding.

"Maybe," I said to myself as I left the window, "we'll have a beautiful Indian summer to make up for this."

Just as I got comfortable on the sofa, the phone rang.

"Julia?" LuAnne said as soon as I answered. Breathing heavily, she hurried on. "Julia, I've narrowed it down, but I need your help to confirm it."

I hesitated. "Confirm what?"

"Why, who it is, of course. I told you, I've been following him every day, and he's so oblivious he doesn't even know it. But I'll tell you this, he is not the homebody I thought he was. This is the second day—second this *week*, Julia—that he's been here, so I know this is where he meets *her*. And I'm going to catch him in the act if it's the last thing I do."

Wondering where *here* was, I mumbled, "Well, I'm not sure. . . ."

"Don't back out on me now, because I have everything worked out, and all you have to do is exactly what I tell you."

"Like what?"

"I'll tell you later. I'll call you tomorrow, probably about mid-morning, so you be ready to go. I'll pick you up and we'll follow him. Then I'll tell you what to do."

No longer hesitant, I was now alarmed. "LuAnne, I don't think—"

"Just be ready." And she hung up, leaving me holding a dead phone and probably the bag, as well.

What in the world was she going to do? And why did she need me to help her do it? I jumped up and began to pace from one side of the library to the other. It was a fact that LuAnne had a one-track mind. When she took on a project, she pursued it to the bitter end.

One thing was sure, though, I did not want to be involved in whatever that end was. Who knew what would ensue? Creating a scene or causing a spectacle could be the least of it. Maybe I should be somewhere else tomorrow when she called. But even as I considered absenting myself, I knew I wouldn't fail her. I would answer when she called and try my best to keep her from ruining her life. As for Leonard's life? Well, he was on his own. The old goat.

Hearing the clamour of Lillian, Sam, and the children returning from their joyride, I hurried to the kitchen to hear all about it.

"You oughtta see that car!" Latisha's voice had edged up to the deafening level. "Miss Lady, it's the best car in the world!"

"Well, I'm glad you like it, Latisha." Then, turning to Lillian, I asked, "How about you, Lillian? Do you like it?"

She was beaming. "I never thought I'd see the day I'd get a new car an' a new roof in the same week. Yes, ma'am, I like it. It crank right up when you turn the key, an' it stop when you want it to. Thank you, Miss Julia, an' you, too, Mr. Sam. You real good at pickin' out cars."

Lloyd was standing around, grinning at the delight of Lillian and Latisha. Sam touched my elbow and nodded toward the library. Leaving the others to recount the features of the new car—Latisha yelling about a radio with push buttons—I followed Sam out of the kitchen.

"Everything all right?" I asked when I reached him.

"I'm not sure," Sam said, a note of concern in his voice. "We left my car at the dealership and transferred to the minivan. I had Lillian drive in traffic out on the boulevard, then on the interstate to the first off-ramp, then back into town to the dealership. She did well, but the minivan is a little longer than her old car, so it'll take some getting used to. We sat for a few minutes when we got back while I made sure she knew where everything was."

"So how did she do? Are you saying you're worried about her driving?"

"No, no," Sam said, waving his hand. "She did fine. No, what I'm worried about is the black Suburban that seemed to pick us up on the boulevard and followed us onto the interstate. It didn't follow us off, but it was pretty obvious that we were heading back to town."

"Could you tell if it was the one we've been seeing?"

He shook his head. "No, there was no way to be sure. It was the same make with tinted windows that Lloyd has seen, but that's not enough for a definite identification. I'll admit, though, that seeing what looked like the same one apparently following us spooked me a little."

"Oh, my goodness, Sam, don't tell me that. If you're spooked, then I'm scared to death."

Chapter 38

I turned away and stomped across the room. "Why don't they just ring the doorbell and tell us what they want? All this sneaking around—or *stalking* around—has me so on edge I can hardly stand it. I've a good mind to call the sheriff."

"No use, honey," Sam said in his most soothing way. "Simply driving past our houses is not an arrestable offense. Let's just hold on until Pickens and Coleman get back. They'll get it straightened out."

Hold on was about all I was able to do, especially because in addition to watching others watching us, I had to worry about what LuAnne had up her sleeve for me to do.

It was late morning before LuAnne called and after I'd spent a few anxious hours. I had arranged for Latisha to take her shells, glue gun, and frame over to Hazel Marie's to work under her supervision, and Lloyd was at the tennis courts, both safely escorted by Sam at my insistence. Frankly, I hated having either of them out of my sight, but life had to go on.

And life picked up its pace when the phone rang. With neither a greeting nor a by-your-leave, LuAnne said, "When I blow the horn, you come running out. I don't want to lose him."

So I ran to her car when it slid to the curb, and LuAnne took off before I got the door closed. "I know where he's going," she said, "but I don't want to take a chance that he'll change his mind."

"Where's he going?"

LuAnne was hunched over the steering wheel, her eyes peering over it like lasers. "For the third time this week, the courthouse."

Uh-oh, I thought, and clasped the armrest.

LuAnne turned into the huge parking lot beside the new court-house, then began trolling the pear tree–lined aisles of parked cars.

"There it is," she said, pointing to a tan Camry or something similar. "That's his car. Perfect, he's here."

It didn't feel perfect to me, but then I still didn't know what we were doing.

LuAnne wheeled her car on past, then turned into a lane a couple of aisles over and parked beside a paneled truck.

"He won't see us here," LuAnne said. "He won't even look, he's so sure of himself. Or maybe of *me*. Now, Julia, here's the plan. I want you to go in that side door to the basement—see it? See where those people're going in? Go in there, and you'll see a large board right beside the door that tells where all the offices are. Be prepared to say what you're looking for, because somebody may ask you."

"What am I looking for?"

"Anything. Whatever. You own property all over the county, so surely there's something you need to see about. Maybe you want to check the water level on a plot of land. Or maybe you need an easement of some kind, or an inspection of a new building, or you could want to double-check a deed of Wesley Lloyd's. I don't care, just come up with something that'll let you wander around search-ing for an office. Only don't find it, because what you'll really be doing is looking for Leonard. Find out where he is and who he came to see."

"LuAnne," I wailed, "I can't do that! What if he sees me?"

"That's the beauty part, Julia. It won't matter a hill of beans if you run into him. You have legitimate business in the courthouse, and he doesn't. He's the one who'll avoid you, not the other way around."

Well, that made sense from her viewpoint, but not from mine. If he saw me, he'd know something was up—I don't hide guilt very easily. But, unhappily and reluctantly, I moaned, "Oh-h, me," and climbed out of the car.

Walking across the parking lot in the heavy heat was a trial in itself, but I trudged on, looking back occasionally to see LuAnne waving me onward. I pushed through the heavy door into the air-conditioned basement floor of the courthouse, which was full of twisting corridors and one office after another. Studying the board that listed the various departments, I stood for a moment gathering myself. Unbeknownst to LuAnne, I knew what I was looking for—the County Building Inspections office. That is, if the word from Sam's breakfast buddies at the Bluebird was on the money. I just didn't know what to do about it when I found it.

Should I walk right in and say I needed something inspected? Should I ask for Totsie? And what would I say if I ran into Leonard? I studied the board awhile longer as busy people came and went behind me. But it was either face LuAnne with nothing to report or go ahead and do it, so I began wandering the halls, reading the names on the office doors and glancing through the narrow windows as I went. Pretending, pretending, and hoping that Leonard had left by another door.

Hopefully imagining Leonard tooling home in his Camry as I scanned one door plaque after another, I turned a sharp corner and ran smack into him. It startled me so badly that I dropped my pocketbook. Befuddled by being face-to-face with LuAnne's solace-seeking husband, all I could think to do was hightail it out of there as quickly as I could. Mumbling, "Sorry, sorry," I bent over to snatch up my purse—and so did Leonard. Our heads cracked together—*hard*.

Stunned by the collision, I leaned against the wall while Leonard, holding my pocketbook and reeling a little himself, said, "Julia? Are you all right? What're you doing here?"

"I'm not sure," I said, holding my head and trying to focus around the flashing lights, wishing not to see who I was seeing. But there he was, tall and round shouldered, his bland face creased by a slight frown of concern. "I mean, getting inspected. My word, Leonard, I think I just got knocked a little goofy."

"Maybe you'd better sit down. My head's pretty hard, so you got quite a lick. Come on in here." He pushed open a partially ajar office door and guided me to a chair in front of a desk.

I leaned back, closed my eyes to stop the spinning, and heard a woman's voice asking Leonard if he'd forgotten anything. There was a little mumbling, but I wasn't hearing too well and didn't care to hear. Then Leonard said, "Maybe some water?" And in a few seconds a paper cup of water was put into my hand.

After sipping from it, I began to feel better, so I straightened up in the chair and decided that I'd had all the run-ins with Leonard that I could stand. "Thank you," I mumbled, beginning to rise as I put the cup on the desk. "I think I'll go home and come back another day."

"Are you sure you're all right?" I heard somebody ask that question, but Leonard's mouth was closed. I looked around, saw a short, plump woman with a head of bushy hair that needed a control product, sporting a pair of spectacles on a cord around her neck, gazing worriedly at me from behind the desk. A sizable badge on her sizable bosom read TOTSIE.

"Fine," I said, springing to my feet. "I'm fine. Thank you both so much. I must be going, thank you again." I snatched my pocketbook from Leonard's hand, noting—why, I don't know—as I did so that he was wearing pleated trousers which I thought had gone out of style years before. But Leonard had never been a fashion plate to start with, nor was his lady friend, who was clad—as I saw when she walked around the desk—in a granny-style gingham dress that reached the top of her rubber-soled Earth Shoes.

Feeling that I had perhaps been knocked back a few decades by the blow to my head, I careened out of the office and sped out of the building.

The heat hit me as I reached the parking lot, but, after staggering for a minute, I finally got myself headed in the general direction of LuAnne's car.

"Did you see her?" LuAnne demanded as soon as I collapsed

inside. "What does she look like? You didn't run into Leonard, did you? Talk to me, Julia. I've been going crazy waiting for you."

"LuAnne, get us out of here. It's hot as Hades, and my head is spinning. I'll tell you as soon as I catch my breath, but I'll thank you not to mention running into anybody ever again."

She wouldn't let me out of the car. Parked by the curb in front of my house, she kept the car running for the air-conditioning, but every time I reached for the door handle she held me back.

"Tell me again," LuAnne pleaded. "Tell me just how she looked—in detail. She had on a *gingham* dress? In a professional office? How tacky. You think she's the one he's seeing? Start at the beginning and tell me everything."

Feeling the throb of a low-grade headache, I nonetheless started to retell it. "Well, I rounded a corner—not looking where I was going, you know, because I was reading the plaques on the doors. Then all of a sudden, there he was. LuAnne, I nearly passed out. And that was before he nearly knocked me out."

"Oh, you've already told all that." And this from my friend with the one-track mind. "Tell me about *her*. Are you sure you were in the right office?"

"He'd just come out of it, LuAnne, so I'm sure," I said, although I didn't tell her how and why I was sure. But it had been Totsie I'd been looking for and it was Totsie—*with Leonard*—that I'd found, and I knew I'd never doubt any word coming from the Bluebird again.

"Well, how old is she?" LuAnne persisted. "What color are her eyes? Her hair? Is she thin, fat, tall, short, or what? And her name is *Totsie*? What kind of name is *that*?"

I closed my eyes trying to bring up Totsie's image in my mind. Which was no problem—I could see her as plainly as I'd seen her in the flesh. The problem was this: how to describe her in terms that LuAnne wouldn't recognize. Because the fact of the matter was that, excepting for her style, Totsie was almost a dead ringer for LuAnne herself.

Hand Totsie over to one of the stylists in Velma's Cut 'n' Curl, put an Ann Taylor suit on her with a nice brooch on the lapel, put her in a pair of medium-heeled Ferragamos, stop by the Estee Lauder counter, give her a cell phone with a prayer list to call, and you'd have the spitting image of LuAnne Conover. They could've been twins.

Chapter 39

"It s'posed to storm again today," Lillian said as she walked into the library where I was nursing a tall glass of lemonade and a headache.

"I don't think it's ever stopped," I said, leaning my head against the sofa. "Let me give this aspirin fifteen more minutes, and I'll go get the children."

"I don't know what you doin' with a headache. You don't hardly ever get such a thing. Mrs. Conover worryin' you to death?"

"You could say that. Lillian—" I said, then stopped, wondering how much to reveal to anybody. Then decided, not much. "What's the word from Thurlow? Have you heard how he's doing?"

"Drivin' ever'body crazy out at that long-term place where they put him. I seen Miss Edna who work out there, an' she say he pretty bad off, an' his temper even worse. Somethin' gonna have to be done, one way or 'nother, but nobody know what it is."

"Well," I said, "he can just loosen his purse strings and pay whatever it takes. Even if he has to bring somebody in from out of town who doesn't know him."

"Um," Lillian said, which was either agreement or not, depending. "Well, Miss Edna say he been havin' a visitor who come in an' stay a few minutes, then come stompin' out like she mad as fire. But she keep on comin' back."

I perked up at that. "*She?*"

"Yes'm, she. An' I hate to carry tales, but ever'body workin' out there know who it is, so I guess it don't matter if ever'body in town know it, too."

"Well, for goodness' sakes, who is it?"

"Miss Helen. Miss Helen Stroud."

Of course, it was *Mrs.* Helen Stroud, although she'd discarded her lying husband years before, but why strain at a gnat when you're asked to swallow a hornet?

"*Helen!*" I popped right up—LuAnne, Leonard, Totsie, and headache all forgotten. "What is she doing visiting *him*? I thought that was over and done with, though I never understood it in the first place."

Some years back, and as strange as it had seemed to everybody, Helen and Thurlow had taken an unlikely interest in each other. It was only after the first shock of it had worn off that most of us thought that Helen had lost her mind, but that Thurlow had hit the jackpot. Helen had put that shambles of a house of his in decent order, made him shave every day, put some decent clothes on him, and had even gotten him to church. Then it had all fallen apart, and I, for one, had been relieved, even though Thurlow had quickly fallen back into his old, trifling ways. It is truly hard to teach old dogs new tricks, and neither Thurlow nor Ronnie were suitable subjects for a total makeover. But, I'll tell you this: neat, self-contained, and fastidious Helen and that skinny, foul-mouthed tightwad would've been the most incompatible and unimaginable match on the face of the earth.

"Well," I said, "I guess stranger things have happened, but she probably just wants to see that he's taken care of. Helen has a strong do-gooder streak in her. That's why she's been president of every club, committee, and council she's ever served on. If there's any help anywhere for Thurlow, she'll find it, and I hope he has enough sense to appreciate it."

Lillian and I both looked around as a low rumble of thunder rattled the windows. "It startin' again," she said.

"Yes, and I'd better get over to the tennis courts," I said, dragging myself up. "Call Hazel Marie, if you will, and tell her I'll be by for Latisha in a few minutes."

"No'm, you don't have to. Mr. Sam call an' say he gettin' her an' Lloyd, too, 'cause he already out. They be here in a few minutes."

"Well, good. Oh, Lillian, I've been meaning to ask. How's the new roof coming along?"

"Real slow. Ev'ry time the roofers come, it start in stormin' again. I know you ready for us to be out from underfoot, but they say soon as the sun shine for more'n two minutes they'll get it done."

I smiled. "Neither you nor Latisha is underfoot. I like having you around, especially when you have such interesting gossip to share." And, right then, I decided that at an opportune time I would share with her the latest chapter in the ongoing Leonard Conover saga.

An opportune time didn't come until I was preparing for bed that evening, and it wasn't Lillian but Sam with whom I shared it.

"And Sam," I said, summing up my courthouse experience, "I'll tell you the truth, as much as I'd been knocked for a loop by Leonard's hard head, seeing Totsie pushed me over the edge. It was such a shock that I couldn't get out of there fast enough. I mean, I know I was a little addled, but I almost asked if Velma hadn't been able to take her this week. See, for a split second, I thought Totsie *was* LuAnne, and all I could think of was what a mess her hair was in."

"Julia, Julia," Sam said, shaking his head, but smiling even so, "why do you get yourself so tangled up in other people's problems?"

"Wel-l-l, LuAnne wanted me to. And it really did make sense for me to go in. I could've come up with a legitimate reason for being there—if I'd been able to think after being whacked so hard—while she'd have been hard pressed for a reason. But, Sam, the thing about it was that I couldn't tell her how much she and Totsie look alike. I mean, it was downright eerie, and I'm surprised that nobody at the Bluebird has remarked on it."

"Oh, we're not that observant."

"Maybe not," I said. "And I will admit that all that earth-mother look she has going on, including the bushy head of hair, would distract from the resemblance."

"Who's the earth mother? Totsie or LuAnne?"

"Why, Totsie, of course. Sam, you're not paying attention. LuAnne is always dressed and coifed to a T, and you know it."

"Coifed?" Sam's eyebrows went up as his eyes sparkled with amusement.

"Oh, you," I said, then more seriously, "Do you think Leonard realizes how much they resemble each other? If he's unhappy with LuAnne, why would he go after somebody just like her?"

"Different personalities, I guess," Sam said, stepping out of his pants. "Remember he said he was looking for solace, and I think men—maybe women, too—are attracted to specific types. Some people keep marrying essentially the same person time and again."

"Not always—you couldn't be more different from Wesley Lloyd—thank the Lord." The less said about my unlamented first husband the better, but I couldn't imagine any two types of men so unlike in looks, attitudes, personalities, and character than my first and second husbands. But then, maybe what Sam said was true, because I really hadn't been all that attracted to my first one to begin with.

"Uh, Julia," Sam said, as he pulled back the covers on the bed, "sorry to change the subject to a less entertaining one, but when I picked up Latisha, Hazel Marie told me that a big, black car had been parked across the street for most of the morning. She wasn't sure what make it was, but it worried her so she kept an eye on it from a window. She never saw anybody near it, but she's about ready to call Pickens to come home."

"Oh, my word," I said, stopping halfway on my crawl across the bed. "Sam, maybe it's time we do something."

"Well, it's worrisome, I admit, but we still don't know if it's the same car. Hazel Marie said she couldn't tell a Ford from a Jaguar. Which isn't all that surprising, I guess. But," Sam said, punching up his pillow, "I've a good mind to sit over at the courts tomorrow as long as Lloyd is there. That is, if it's not raining and he plays. And if any black cars show up, I'm going to find out who they are and what their business is."

"Good. I hope you will. But, listen, I've had a thought. We've been worried about the children, but what if it's Mr. Pickens they have business with? He runs into all kinds of strange people when he investigates criminal activity, so it stands to reason that some of them could be looking for him. And it was the Pickens car that was broken into at the beach, and the car's been seen most often around the Pickens house."

"That's crossed my mind, too. When is he getting back?"

"Sometime this weekend, Hazel Marie said. She's not sure exactly."

"Let's hope sooner rather than later," Sam said. "We ought to get together as soon as he gets in, either here or over there. Have Hazel Marie warn him, though, so he doesn't walk into something at his house."

"Sam, you're worrying me." And I rolled over close to him for the comfort. Or the solace.

"Just thinking ahead, honey, that's all. And getting mighty tired of black cars." Sam turned off the lamp and slid down in the bed.

After a few minutes, I said, "You have a black car, and so do I."

"Well," he said, stifling a laugh, "I guess there're black cars, and then there're black cars." And we laughed together.

Chapter 40

~❧~

"Julia," Sam said as I walked into the kitchen the next morning and found him having breakfast at home for a change. "Have you seen this?" He held up the morning paper.

"No," I said, smiling in spite of my usual pre-coffee reserve. "I just got up."

"Well, come look at it. It doesn't give a lot of details, but it's about the Great Money Windfall at the beach."

Craving a much-needed cup of coffee, I glanced at the small article, datelined Charleston, SC, which had been belatedly picked up by the local paper. "Why, Sam, it hardly says anything—nothing more than what we heard the morning it happened."

"I know, but look at the last sentence mentioning that the Coast Guard patrols that stretch of the coast on the lookout for smugglers. It doesn't *say* that the boat was involved in smuggling, but it sure implies it was. Those on board were questioned and released, so, obviously, no evidence was found."

"Right," I said, heading for the coffeepot, "maybe because they'd thrown their ill-gotten gains overboard. We'd already figured that out."

"Wait, honey," Sam said, holding out the newspaper, "look at this. It says that they questioned and released *two men and a woman. And,*" he went on, holding up a finger as if he were summing up before a jury, "who did you meet when you and the children took a walk that morning? Two men and a woman!"

"*Yes!*" I agreed, stopping short as a shiver ran down my back. "*And* they followed us in the evacuation where Lloyd saw the woman roll down her window!"

For a minute there, it seemed that we had reached a sudden understanding of what was going on. But that quickly faded, because we knew little more than we had before the paper had been delivered. Except that we'd possibly linked the three beach scavengers to the incapacitated boat from which the money had come.

Which meant, it suddenly seemed to me, that they'd been the very ones who'd thrown the money overboard. No wonder Lloyd had felt uneasy with them, and no wonder I could tell in an instant that they weren't from the South. The only time that people from around here throw money away is when they're having a good time doing it.

"But the question remains," Sam said, "why us? Or Lloyd? Or Pickens, or whomever they're interested in? I saw people clutching handfuls of hundred-dollar bills. None of us got a single one. So-o," Sam went on in a musing way, "that has to mean that they're after something besides the money, something more valuable to them than that. I mean, why else risk breaking into Pickens's car and finding nothing but his address? Which, I'm thinking, may have been all they'd wanted. I tell you, Julia, I'm liking this less and less."

"And to think that we actually had a pleasant chat with *smugglers*, and didn't know it. Well, with only one of them—his name was Rob—because the other two weren't very friendly. Even at the time, it seemed to me that at least those two were the results of poor raising. Breeding, too, for all I know."

I could easily have gone off on a digression about family genes, proper child instruction, and good manners, all in an effort not to think of what I was thinking. But it would've done no good.

I was thinking it, so I said it. "What on earth could we have that they want so badly?"

"Or," Sam said, "what do they *think* we have?"

There was no answer to that in our current state of ignorance, so there was nothing for it but to carry on with our normal activities. Lillian had been unusually quiet while Sam and I had discussed the situation, but she hadn't missed much of the conversation.

As Sam excused himself and left to go upstairs, she said, "Miss Julia, you think the chil'ren be all right?"

"I do, Lillian, I really do. We're watching them like hawks, and they're never on their own anywhere. Mr. Pickens will soon be home, and Coleman will be on duty Monday morning. We just need to hold on till then, and they'll put a stop to whatever's going on."

"Yes'm, I guess, but Latisha, she countin' on goin' back to Miss Hazel Marie's today. I don't want Latisha worryin' her to death day in and day out, so maybe I ought to let her use that hot gun over here."

"Whatever you think, Lillian, but Hazel Marie is aware of our concern, and you know she'll take care of her."

"Yes'm, I know she will, an' I tell you, I get more work done when Latisha somewhere else—like in school, which I wish would hurry up and start."

I smiled at that, listening to the early morning stir emanating from upstairs as Sam and the children readied themselves for the day. Then, clomping down the stairs like a herd of cattle, Latisha and Lloyd came into the kitchen, both dressed for the day—Lloyd in tennis attire and Latisha in a sundress with her red pocketbook draped over her shoulders—crossbody, I think it's called. She was carrying those plastic sacks of shells that went everywhere she did.

"Tennis all day today, Miss Julia," Lloyd announced, zipping the cover around his racket. "We're playing over at that private club with the indoor courts. So if it rains, we'll still be ready for the team tryouts next week."

"You'll have no trouble making the team, I'm sure," I said, although I knew he was preparing for the challenges that would be coming.

"Well," Latisha confidently announced, "I'm gonna finish my surprise today. That glue gun is the best thing I ever had. I'm gonna get me one for Christmas. If not before."

"Uh-huh," Lillian said with a roll of her eyes.

"Okay, kids," Sam said, putting his raincoat over his arm, "ready to go?" He leaned over to give me a kiss, then said, "You don't mind picking them up? Since Lloyd will be playing indoors, I'll give that mountain property another look, though we'll probably get rained on again."

Lillian said, "They say more rain on the way, an' I b'lieve it. My foot justa achin' this morning."

I looked at her with concern. "Well, sit down, Lillian, and elevate it. And, yes, Sam," I said, turning to him, "I'll be right here all day so I can get the children whenever they're ready to come home. Please don't drown on that mountainside."

I watched from the door as the children and Sam squished across a waterlogged yard to the car, glanced up at the clouds threatening to unleash more rain, and sighed.

"Lillian," I said, closing the door and relishing the quiet in the kitchen, "I am so tired of this weather. It's been one storm after another this whole month, but only one official enough to have a name. Now I want you to take something for that aching foot, then sit down and rest."

"Yes'm, let me get this last pan in the dishwasher, an' I think I'll do jus' that."

I went across the back hall to the library, my favorite room in the house, shivering a little in the dampness even though it was August, and debated turning on the gas fire in the fireplace. I resisted, though, and instead slipped on a cotton cardigan, sat down to read the newspaper, and adamantly refused to dwell on what I could do nothing about. Namely, three strangers with an uncommon interest in us.

I'd barely gotten to page three of the paper when the phone rang.

"Julia," LuAnne demanded almost before I got "Hello" out of my mouth, "you're not busy, are you? I need to talk to you. I want you to be the first to know."

"Well, no, I'm not busy. When—"

"Good, because I'm at the front door. Come let me in."

Thinking *What in the world has she done,* I hurried to the door through which LuAnne immediately marched, stiff and resolute. I followed her, murmuring a greeting, as she went directly to the library and took a seat on the sofa.

"Julia, you're the first one I'm telling, and I want you to know that I have no regrets and no second thoughts. I'm leaving Leonard."

"Oh, LuAnne, are you sure?"

"Of course I'm sure. I'm here, aren't I? And I've already told him, so the die is cast. I mean, after what I've learned, thanks to you, how could I stay with him? And when what he's just done gets around, nobody will blame me."

"I'm almost afraid to ask, but what else has he done?"

"He picked her up after work yesterday, walked out of the courthouse together as big as you please. He's gone *public* with her, and I am not going to put up with it. I got a good look at her and she was just as you described—ankle-length dress and all. But, Julia, you didn't notice enough details, because I cannot believe what she looks like. I'm surprised you didn't mention it."

Oh, me, I mentally moaned, thinking that LuAnne had seen her own resemblance to Totsie. *How hurt she must be that Leonard prefers a frowzier, though slightly younger, version of herself.*

"Maybe," I said, temporizing before committing myself, "being knocked on the head affected my vision."

"Don't worry. You'll get an eyeful soon enough, because she'll probably move in as soon as I move out. Which won't be long. I'm on my way now to look at Miss Mattie's apartment. If she could afford it, I probably can too."

"I hope you've thought this through, LuAnne. Are you sure you want to burn your bridges? It's a big step to make."

"I should've made it long before now." LuAnne stood up, standing as stiff and tall as her short stature would allow. "No woman worth anything would put up with a man who would choose her *exact opposite* to take her place. Julia," she said, whirling on me, "that woman, that Totsie, is the most *unlikely* replacement for me that I've ever seen. The least he could've done was to find somebody who outdid me in some way—I mean, in looks or class or *something.* Then I could understand it, but, no. He goes out and finds somebody so unkempt, so overweight, and so *dowdy* that it makes my skin crawl. I thought he'd have better taste than that, but if that's what he wants, he can have her. I have her beat, hands down!" Then she whirled around and headed for the door. "I've got to go before that apartment's gone."

And off she went, leaving me breathless and agitated because she had not seen the resemblance at all.

But on second thought, maybe deep down she had, which would make even worse Leonard's choice of a copy instead of the real thing.

Chapter 41

I fiddled around all morning—checking on Lillian, paying a few bills, thinking about LuAnne—on edge as I wondered if she had rented Miss Mattie's apartment and how she would do living alone. LuAnne wasn't cut out for the solitary life. She liked to talk and needed someone to talk to. Or at, as the case usually was.

And still it rained. In sprinkles, then in thundering torrents, the rain kept pouring down.

"Will it never stop?" I asked as Lillian and I sat at the kitchen table for a late morning cup of coffee.

"No'm, don't look like it," Lillian said, reaching for the sugar bowl. "Maybe we oughta start thinkin' 'bout buildin' us a ark."

I laughed, although it wouldn't have been funny to those living near creeks and rivers. They might well be already trying to convert cubits into feet and inches.

"Your foot feeling better?" I asked.

"Yes'm, that medicine set me right, an' a good thing, too, 'cause it about lunchtime. Lloyd say he eatin' at that indoor place, but Latisha need to come home. She been bothering Miss Hazel Marie long enough."

"I'll go get her. You don't need to be out in the rain with that foot." And to that end, I rose to get the car keys and my pocket-book, then to call Hazel Marie to tell her that I was on my way. "I won't get out, Hazel Marie. Just watch for me, if you will, and send Latisha out. I'll pull up right in front of your walk."

I declare, driving the four blocks to the Pickenses' house was a trial—rain coming steadily down, mist settling in and around the trees, and windshield wipers flapping back and forth like a high-speed metronome. I could hardly see a thing, although I knew the streets like the back of my hand.

Pulling to the curb at Hazel Marie's house, I lowered the passenger window a tiny bit and saw Hazel Marie in her doorway. She raised one finger, indicating that Latisha wasn't quite ready, so I rolled the window up, put the car in park, and disengaged the door locks so she could jump in before drowning. But almost immediately Latisha dashed across the porch and down the walk. Wearing a yellow raincoat with her little red pocketbook safely underneath, and her arms full of bags of who-knew-what, she flung open the car door and dove headfirst onto the backseat, spraying rainwater as she came. Then she pulled the door closed.

"Hey, Miss Lady!" she yelled as if I were a mile away instead of in the front seat. "It's rainin' cats an' dogs out there!"

"It sure is," I agreed, turning to greet her. "Buckle up now, so we can get home before it gets worse." She pulled the seat belt out and around as I waited to hear it click. Arranging one sack close beside her on the seat, she kept the larger one on her lap.

Then, as if the floodgates had failed, rain commenced drumming hard on the roof. "My word," I said, looking up, "it's really coming down now. We'd better wait till it slacks off a little."

Peering through the windshield, I could barely make out the hood ornament through the pouring rain and the tiny hailstones bouncing on the hood. The windows began to fog up from our breath, so Latisha and I just sat, waiting it out and, speaking for myself, wishing we'd gotten home before the skies opened.

"You know what?" Latisha said, apparently unruffled by the deluge.

"No. What?"

"I'm almost through with my surprise, an' I still got enough shells to make another one. All I got left to do is fill in a few bare spots on that frame, but Miss Hazel Marie said I oughta let it set awhile to be sure that glue's gonna hold. So I left it there, an' I hope to goodness them little girls don't get ahold of it."

"Oh, I'm sure Hazel Marie will take care of it. She won't let the babies . . . *what*?" I jerked around as I heard rapping on the window by my head.

Looking in at me through the rain, mist, fog, and a large, floppy hood was a watery face and a hand making a rolling motion. Without thinking, except to give aid to a stranded motorist, I rolled my window down a couple of inches, getting rain-splashed for my trouble. "Yes? What is it?"

With my attention focused on the hooded face next to mine, I was just aware enough to register that one of the back doors was suddenly snatched open as Latisha screamed bloody murder. I twisted around, but, held fast by the seat belt, all I could do was glimpse for a split second a dark figure leaning over Latisha. Then, just as quickly, the face beside mine disappeared and the figure in the backseat sprang away, slamming the door behind him. In and out before I knew it.

"Latisha, *are you hurt? Are you hurt!*" Scrambling to unbuckle my seat belt, my heart pounding and the rain spewing through my window, I leaned over the front seat to get to her. Still strapped in, Latisha had her head thrown back, wailing as if her heart was broken.

"What is it?" I screamed, though I could hardly hear myself through the racket she was making. "What happened? Did he hurt you? Latisha, talk to me. Are you all right?"

She stopped on a dime and closed her mouth, as tears streamed down her face. "My shells," she sobbed. "He took my shells."

"Your *shells*?" I couldn't believe it. We'd just been accosted in a rainstorm, invaded by two dark figures, and scared half to death, and all that had been taken was a plastic grocery sack of shells? What in the world would anybody want with a bag of seashells, available to anybody who walked on a beach?

Finally catching my breath enough to think halfway clearly, I engaged the door locks, rolled up my window, and shifted the gear into drive.

"We're getting out of here," I mumbled, not knowing whether the shell thieves were still around or not, but wanting to get safely home. Squinting through the rain and trembling as I drove, I saw a black vehicle streak past on a cross street, but in the sheets of water pouring down, it could've been anything from a pickup to a hearse. One thing was for sure, though, if it had been the same black Suburban we'd been seeing, its occupants had finally made a move. But for what? A sack of shells? We'd have given it to them if they'd asked.

"You all right back there, Latisha?" I dared not take my eyes off the street to check on her, the visibility being so bad. Hunched over the steering wheel, I eased the car along, straining to see the yellow line in the downpour and trembling from having been the victim of criminal intent on the part of someone with no sense whatsoever.

"Yes'm, I guess," Latisha said, sniffing wetly. "One good thing, though, that ole thief didn't get Miss Hazel Marie's glue gun. I still got it, so he's outta luck if he tries to make something with them shells."

"She let you bring it with you?"

"Yes'm, I begged her an' promised I wouldn't use it 'less somebody watches me."

"Well, I'm glad he didn't get it." But I was concentrating so hard on getting home that I failed to fully appreciate our good fortune in having been robbed by moronic thieves. I mean, my pocketbook was still on the seat beside me, and Latisha's was still across her shoulders.

So intent was I to stay in the right lane that it wasn't until I turned into my drive that I realized I'd driven four blocks without buckling my seat belt. "So sue me," I mumbled. "I don't care."

I jumped out, ran around the car to Latisha's door, unbuckled her, and, grabbing her arm, sprinted for the house.

"Lock the doors, Lillian!" I yelled as we, sopping wet, pushed through into the kitchen. "Hurry, lock the doors!"

Latisha ran to her, burying her face in Lillian's arms, so it was left to me to run around locking the doors.

"What in the world goin' on?" Lillian demanded as she took Latisha onto her lap. "What happen to my baby?"

"Oh, Lillian," I said, collapsing onto a chair beside her, my soaked dress dripping on the floor. "You won't believe it. I can't believe it! Latisha, honey, did he hurt you?"

Nestled in Lillian's arms, she shook her head. "He jus' get my shells, an' I'm not even finished with my surprise."

Lillian hugged her close and said, "But you still got another sackful at home, 'member?"

"Not many," Latisha said, tears welling up. "An' they all half broke. My best ones is gone." Then, straightening up to look at Lillian, she said, "Great-Granny, they's only one thing to do. We got to go to the beach an' get some more."

"Well, not today," Lillian said, hugging her. Then to me, "What happened to y'all?"

"I'll tell you the truth, Lillian, I don't know. It was the strangest thing, and I'm still shaking." But between us, Latisha and I told her what had happened, and she didn't understand it any more than we did. "Sam," I said, springing up, my wet dress clinging to places it shouldn't have. "I've got to get him home. And Lloyd. And warn Hazel Marie."

"Mr. Sam on his way," Lillian said. "He called a few minutes ago."

"Good, he can pick up Lloyd. I'll feel better with us all safely together." Then I called Hazel Marie and told her what had occurred right outside her front door.

"So keep your doors locked," I said, then reassured her that Latisha had not been harmed. "She's just upset over losing her shells."

"Oh, bless her little heart," Hazel Marie said, her voice filled with sympathy. "It took her a whole week to collect so many. I am just so sorry."

They Lord, I thought, we'd just been the subjects of a well-planned, perfectly coordinated attack by two muggers dumb enough to have snatched something absolutely worthless, and Hazel Marie was mourning the loss.

Chapter 42

~

"And you're sure," Sam said, leaning over to look directly at Latisha, "there was nothing else in the sack?"

It was early that Friday afternoon, and all I could hold on to was the anticipated arrival of Mr. Pickens and Coleman over the weekend. I was convinced that the thieving scoundrels had been the very people who'd been stalking us in the black car, which I was also convinced I'd seen passing in the rainy vicinity of the crime, and I was ready for some professional help in putting a stop to them. Meanwhile Sam was trying to get the full story between my telling it and Latisha's version.

"No, sir. I mean, yes, sir, I'm sure." Latisha nodded solemnly at Sam, then went on. "Except maybe for some sand in the bottom, 'cause you can't hardly ever get rid of all the sand in them shells."

"Well, I don't imagine they were after that." Sam smiled as he straightened up, then said, "You were very brave, Latisha. I'm proud of you."

After listening and adding to Latisha's account of the frightening event, I said, "Should we call the sheriff, Sam?"

He heaved a deep sigh and said, "I declare, I don't know. They're unlikely to give much credence to a report that somebody snatched a sack of sandy seashells. And," he went on, with a wry smile, "if I have to say that again, my tongue'll get so twisted, it'll come out wrong. But I'll call and report it, anyway. It could've been an attempted carjacking."

Putting a comforting hand on my arm, he said, "We'll know more when Pickens gets in tomorrow."

On his way home, Sam had picked up Lloyd, then dropped him off at his mother's house. I missed having him around, but Lloyd had wanted to see his little sisters, and he'd probably had enough of Latisha making every step he made at our house.

"Did you tell him what happened?" I asked, as Sam and I sat in the library later that afternoon. The house was inordinately quiet because Latisha, worn to a frazzle by the loss she'd suffered, was taking a highly unusual nap. Lillian had petted and coddled her until she'd finally fallen asleep in her lap.

Sam nodded. "Yes. Bare bones, but yes, so he'd know to be careful. That may've been why he wanted to go to his mother's—to watch out for her and his sisters. He's growing up, Julia. He didn't say much, but I got a real sense of how protective he feels toward them."

I agreed, though I had mixed feelings about Lloyd's growing up. Pride, of course, in watching him mature into a good and decent man, but a little sadness, too, in that he would soon no longer be our little boy.

I didn't want to think those bittersweet thoughts, so I brought Sam up to date on the LuAnne saga—anything to stop replaying the snatch and grab incident of the morning. "I think she's really going to leave him this time. She's threatened to do it off and on for years, and nobody's believed her. But if she signs a lease on Miss Mattie's apartment, that'll mean she means business. LuAnne doesn't spend money lightly. Oh, and, Sam, I don't think I've told you, but Lillian heard that Helen Stroud goes to visit Thurlow every day. I can't imagine what that means. They are the exact opposites in temperament and in . . . well, in everything, which is interesting because Leonard chose Totsie who is a carbon copy of LuAnne, although LuAnne thinks they're diametric opposites. What attracts people to each other is all so strange, isn't it?"

"All in the eye of the beholder, I guess," Sam said, less interested in the pairing off of our friends than in figuring out why thieves had wanted a sack of shells.

When the phone rang, he answered it, listened, then, glancing at me, said, "That'll be fine, Hazel Marie—just what we should do. You know, though, that we have Lillian and Latisha with us." A pause, then Sam smiled and said, "Good. We'll be there."

He hung up, and, smiling, turned to me. "I just accepted a dinner invitation for all of us tomorrow night. Pickens is on his way home, and Hazel Marie wants us to be there, too."

"Well, good. I am more than ready to shift strange black cars and idiotic thieves over to him." And just with the news of Mr. Pickens's imminent arrival, my spirits lifted considerably.

When the phone rang again, Sam answered it, spoke a few minutes, then handed it to me. "LuAnne," he said, and left the room for a more conducive place to read.

"Julia," she started as soon as I answered, "Miss Mattie's apartment's already rented. I'm just done in, because it would've been perfect for me. I mean, the owner, that nice Mr. Wheeler, has remodeled it, put in new appliances, and everything. Of course, he raised the rent, too, so I'm trying not to be too disappointed. But now I don't know what I'm going to do."

"I'm sorry to hear that, but keep looking, LuAnne. You'll find something, and it's not as if there's a time limit on moving out."

"Well, there certainly is! I'm already packed and everything. Boxes are everywhere, so there's hardly any room to move around. I just have to find a place and get out of here."

"What's Leonard saying about your packing up?"

"Oh, he still doesn't believe I'll actually move. Why, last night while I was cooking—"

"You *cooked* for him?"

"Well, yes. I mean, I had to eat, so I fixed enough for him, too. You don't stop a forty-five-year habit all at once, you know. Anyway, he's the same-old same-old, nothing disturbs or upsets him. At least, *I* don't. We'll see how he gets along when I'm not around."

The more interesting question to me was how *she* would get along when he wasn't around. More and more, I had come to realize that Leonard had been LuAnne's main topic of conversation over the years—what he had done or, more often, not done, how exasperated she was with him, and on and on with one complaint after another. What would she have to talk about if she actually left him?

Promising to listen for other rental possibilities, I lightly mentioned that Lillian and Latisha were with us until their house had a new, leakproof roof—just in case LuAnne thought that my guest room might be available.

It wasn't that I didn't want her moving in with us, although on second thought, I guess it was. I felt bad about that, because I knew that LuAnne would do anything in the world for me. Still, making such a drastic move as she was contemplating meant that she would sooner or later have to be on her own, and the sooner she realized that, the better off she'd be. Or so it seemed to me.

"Now, Julia," LuAnne went on, "I do not want to be the number one topic of gossip around town, so I'm keeping a low profile. I want to move out and get myself settled before everybody knows about it. I'd rather that the word gets out gradually after all is said and done. So don't tell anybody that I'm even *thinking* of moving out."

But even as I promised not to tell, I was thinking of all those who already knew—Sam, Lillian, Hazel Marie, Etta Mae, Binkie—and those were just the ones that I knew that she herself had told.

I didn't sleep well that night—visions of that dark figure leaning over Latisha kept running through my mind. And, as usually happens after any kind of shocking event, images of what I should've done and wished I'd done went right along with them. I pictured myself swinging my pocketbook over the seat and swatting whoever it was to kingdom come. Then I pictured myself smoothly unsnapping my seat belt, reaching back and snatching the intruder bald headed.

The fact of the matter, though, was that it had all happened so fast that I hadn't known what was occurring until it had already occurred and was over with. My only consolation was that there'd really been no time for any kind of reaction. That, however, didn't keep me from thinking of what I would've done if there had been.

Saturday morning dawned gray and threatening, but with windy conditions that gave hope to us waterlogged humans that the clouds might soon be swept away. Along with the hope of seeing the sun again, my spirits were further lifted by the thought of Mr. Pickens taking control of the nagging problem of a black car with black windows and its thieving occupants. Even better, Coleman would be back from his camping trip Sunday night, which meant that we'd have the full weight of official law enforcement working for us. Between the two of them, something would get done, although in the current situation, I'd put my money on Mr. Pickens. As a private investigator, he wasn't hampered by probable causes, warrants, and court orders, or by a sheriff who could fire him, as Coleman was.

"Sam," I said as we finished breakfast, "I think I'll go see Thurlow this morning. Take him some fruit or something. Anything to stay busy, instead of sitting around here wondering if something else will happen. And, besides," I went on as if expecting an argument, "we shouldn't let a bunch of heathens dictate our lives. And if they try to steal anything else . . . well, just let them try."

Lillian hobbled over to the table with the coffeepot. "What you think you gonna do if they do?"

"Don't worry. I've gone over it so many times in my head that I'm prepared for all contingencies. I'm keeping the car doors locked, for one thing. And for another, it's not raining so they won't surprise me again. Sam, you want to go with me? I'm sure Thurlow would rather see you than me, anyway."

"No, I'm meeting roofers at Lillian's house this morning," Sam said, smiling at her. "They've lost so many workdays that they're willing to work on a Saturday. You may have a roof over your head by tonight, Lillian." Then, turning to me, he said, "So I'll pass on Thurlow unless you'd feel better with me along."

"When it comes to Thurlow, I always feel better with someone else along." I smiled and patted Sam's arm—he knew that Thurlow had made amorous advances to me during my widowhood. To no avail, I quickly add, for I wouldn't have had him if he'd been the last man on earth. "But no," I went on, "I'll just look in on him as a neighborly gesture and figure it's my good deed for the day."

"Okay, then," Sam said, getting to his feet. "I have a few things I need to tend to here. But if you see that car, I don't want you following it. Just turn around and come home. I'll be around all day."

It wasn't until I'd driven through town and halfway to Thurlow's long-term care facility that it struck me what Sam was up to. It wasn't like him to stay around the house all day—he liked to be up and doing, seeing people, mixing and mingling. Oh, he could spend hours working on that legal history of his, but he'd still make time to be out and about.

So why not today as well? Because—it suddenly hit me like a bolt out of the blue—because he'd seen that it hadn't been shells the thieves had been after, but possibly Latisha. They'd gotten only a sack of sandy shells, but what if the dark figure had been intent on getting *her*? Maybe the seat belt had saved her. Maybe my reaction had been quicker than he'd expected or than I had thought.

When it dawned on me that Latisha could've been the object of the car invasion, I almost slammed on the brakes in the middle of the boulevard. Snatching her certainly made more sense than stealing seashells.

But did it? I declare, I didn't know, but the very thought of losing that little girl put me in a state of agitation, and I almost turned around for home. Why in the world would they want Latisha? She was precious to us, but what did she mean to a bunch of strangers who apparently spent their time dropping piles of hundred-dollar bills up and down the coastline? But then again, none of it made any sense at all.

Chapter 43

By the time I'd turned in under the Pine Grove Rehabilitation Center sign, the sprinkles of rain had stopped but not the drips from the trees. Getting out of the car and struggling with an umbrella, my purse, and the fruit basket, I decided that Thurlow didn't need a visit from me, and that I could certainly do without one with him. I would leave my fruit basket at the reception desk and get back home to discuss with Sam my sudden understanding of what we could be facing.

Having to park some little distance from the low brick building with its extended wings, I trudged toward the entrance, carrying the heavy basket and hoping that Thurlow would appreciate my efforts. He probably wouldn't, but I didn't plan to stay long enough to hear what he thought.

Just as I approached the double doors, they swung open and out stepped Helen Stroud and Mr. Ernest Sitton, Esquire, the steely-eyed lawyer from Delmont, deep in conversation. Helen looked up, saw me, and stopped short, a flash of consternation crossing her face as she tucked a manilla folder under her arm. Cool, calm, and collected, Helen seemed at a sudden loss by coming face-to-face with me.

Quickly reverting, though, to her usual calm expression, she said, "Julia. How nice to see you. Are you visiting Thurlow? I'm sure he'll be glad to see you."

"No, just dropping this basket off for him. And it's nice to see you, too, Helen." Then, turning to Mr. Sitton, who had been a very present help to me in executing Miss Mattie Freeman's will, I said, "And to see you, too, Mr. Sitton. I hope you're well."

"Well, indeed, Mrs. Murdoch." The short, paunchy lawyer would've lifted his hat if he'd worn one. "I hope you, too, are well.

But my business is done here, so if you ladies will excuse me, I'll be on my way." And off he went, carrying a bulky leather brief-case at his side. That left Helen and me standing together, awkwardly avoiding the other's eyes.

"Well," I said, sidestepping toward the door, "I'll just leave this and be on my way, too."

Without a word, Helen turned away and I, feeling slightly snubbed, went inside, wrote a quick note to Thurlow, and left the basket to be delivered whenever someone got around to doing it. Then I sailed back outside, determined not to let Helen's slight deter me from what was important. Which was to get home and make sure that Latisha was safe and that Sam and I were on the same page where she was concerned.

As I approached my car, I saw Helen waiting beside it. Before I could speak, she said, "Julia, I owe you an apology. Forgive me, but I was unprepared to see anybody I knew quite so soon." She looked away, then down at the folder in her hands. Taking a deep breath, she said, "I'd just completed negotiating a complicated contract, and, well, I was not expecting to see you. Or anyone."

"It's perfectly all right, Helen," I said, although it really hadn't been. "You don't owe me an apology at all. I completely understand."

"No. No, you don't, but maybe you will." Helen drew in her breath again, then, straightening her shoulders as if she'd decided to tell all, she said, "Everybody will know sooner or later, so I might as well tell you now. I'm moving into Thurlow's house to take care of him." She paused, glanced away, then back at me. "There'll be talk, I know, but it is entirely a business arrangement. He needs somebody, and I need the job."

She looked directly into my eyes as if to stare me down if I expressed shock or dismay. I did neither, although I felt both. "Well, Helen," I managed to say without stumbling, "that sounds like a beneficial arrangement for you both. Thurlow is fortunate that you're willing to take him on. I hope that it will be so for you, as well."

The twitch of a smile appeared at the corner of her mouth, even though Helen rarely gave any outward expression of her feelings. With a quick nod of her head, she said, "That's exactly why Ernest Sitton was here."

Then with a wave of her hand, she turned and headed for her car, leaving me somewhat stunned at the implication. Had she *married* Thurlow? No, surely lawyers didn't have that authority. Had she legally committed herself in some way? That's the way it had sounded.

But, no, if Helen was smart—and she was—it would be the other way around. It would've been Thurlow who'd been legally committed. I laughed, then, as I realized the double meaning of the term, because not a few of us had long thought that Thurlow was a mental case.

But then, as I slid under the wheel and closed the car door, I realized that Helen's last remark had been in response to my comment that Thurlow, in having her help, would be fortunate. And *her* remark about Mr. Sitton told me that he had been there to ensure that *she* would be equally so.

Hmm, now *that* was an interesting thought.

I drove home with a jumble of thoughts running through my head. What had Helen gotten herself into? And was it any of my business what she was doing? No, of course not, but I couldn't help but wonder. Thurlow Jones was the most disreputable and deliberately infuriating man in Abbotsville, as well as possibly the most wealthy. As was highly likely since he rarely spent a cent. Just look at that house of his—a large, two-storied brick edifice along classical lines centered on a weed-covered city block. Shutters falling off, peeling paint from dry rot on the trim, and overgrown trees blocking the sunlight. And I should know from my few visits over the years how dark, dank, and unkempt the interior was.

I couldn't imagine meticulous Helen living in such squalor,

and I haven't even mentioned Thurlow himself. If his house was in bad shape, he was in worse, and proud of it. He enjoyed scandalizing the locals with the way he looked and with what came out of his mouth. The man knew no bounds.

Well, I thought with a grim smile, with both legs broken he'd know a few bounds now. All Helen would have to do would be to stay out of arm's reach—Thurlow was known to pinch unsuspecting females.

With a jolt, the thought of Latisha flashed through my mind, and I switched from fretting about Helen to worrying about Lillian's great-grandchild. I'd read and heard about stolen children, so the thought of that little girl in the hands of strangers made my stomach turn over.

"Lillian," I said as I came through the kitchen door, "you won't believe . . ." Taking in the newspaper-covered card table, laden with a pile of shells and the glue gun, and an empty chair in the corner, my heart skipped a beat. "Where's Latisha?"

Lillian turned from the sink. "She in the liberry. Mr. Sam took her to see how the roofers comin' along, an' look like we can sleep in our own beds tonight. Right now, he teachin' her how to play checkers."

"Oh," I said, my adrenaline level dropping considerably. I pulled out a chair from the kitchen table, and sat down to recover. "Well, good."

"Yes'm, an' she jus' got crowned or kinged or something. You mighta heard her 'way down the street. But what won't I believe?"

"Well," I said, leaning forward, "you know you told me about Helen visiting Thurlow so often? Well, I just found out that she was doing more than visiting." And, with a sense of excitement and wonder, I went on to tell her what I'd learned in the parking lot of the Pine Grove Rehabilitation Center.

"That don't surprise me," Lillian said, so complacently that I had to tamp down my own response to the news.

"It doesn't?"

"No'm, lotsa people do that."

"But do *what*? That's what I don't understand. I mean, why would she need a lawyer if she's just taking a job?"

"Miss Julia," Lillian said, coming to the table to sit beside me and instruct me in the niceties of long-term care of the elderly and the bedridden, "it us'ally happen inside a fam'ly when somebody's a widow-lady or never married. She the one that take over the ole person—sellin' her own house if she got one, an' movin' in lock, stock, an' barrel with the ole person, an' promisin' to stay till death do them part. At which time, the widow-lady or ole maid, she get ev'rything the ole person have. Tit for tat, don't you know? An' the rest of the fam'ly, they know she deserve it 'cause they didn't have to put up with bedpans, an' doctors, an' givin' medicines, an' cookin', an' feedin', an' all a ole person have to complain about."

Lillian paused, then she said, "But it don't have to be fam'ly. It can be anybody that need more'n Social Security. So Miss Helen, she a smart lady. I 'spect she know what she gettin' into, an' I 'spect she fix it so it be worth it in the end."

"Well, they Lord," I said, sprawling back against my chair at the enormity of what Helen had committed herself to, as well as at the enormity of what Thurlow had promised to her. And not just promised, apparently, because who would trust him to honor a promise?

That's what lawyer Ernest Sitton had been doing—legally holding Thurlow, dead or alive, to his promise. My guess was that Thurlow had made a new will that favored Helen, and if so, I hoped it was air tight. As far as I knew, Thurlow had no living relatives, but in other cases one or two had been known to pop out of the woodwork when a death occurred.

"Well," I said to Lillian, "I can understand that, but how in the world will Helen manage until the end—*his* end, that is? I mean, Thurlow is just mean enough to live another twenty years out of spite. Even outlive her, for that matter."

"I 'spect Miss Helen already think of that." Lillian smiled. "He gonna have to dig real deep in his pockets if he want to go home. Miss Helen not gonna put up with slipshod livin' like he do."

Lillian was right about that, because one thing was for sure—there were no flies on Helen Stroud. But, my word, she would earn every penny. Knowing, though, as we all did, what she'd have to put up with, not one soul would begrudge her a cent.

But, poor Helen; what dire straits she must've been in to tie herself to Thurlow Jones for as long as he lived—if that's what she'd done. Even though he was apparently in poor physical condition now, he wouldn't be easy to live with even if he improved enough to dance a few jigs. In fact, he'd be worse.

"Well," I said again, this time with a shudder, "I guess there's no telling what one will do when one's back is against the wall. But, I'll tell you, Lillian, I would have to be at the very end of my rope to move in with the likes of Thurlow Jones. Think of living with him!"

"Uh-huh, an' think of livin' with that Ronnie, too."

Chapter 44

About midafternoon of that fairly dry Saturday I heard the phone ring, but it must've been for Lillian, or perhaps Sam, since I wasn't called to answer it. That suited me fine since it would most likely have been LuAnne, and I had other, more pressing, matters on my mind.

I'd not been able to talk privately with Sam even though he'd been home all day, spending the time with Latisha, entertaining her, taking her with him to check on the roof, or simply staying in the same room with her, wherever that happened to be. I understood what he was doing, but it was extremely worrisome to know that he felt he should keep such a close eye on her. Did he think it was even possible that those stalkers would attempt an invasion of our home?

But why not? They'd not only attempted, they'd carried out an invasion of my car. To even consider that they might come storming inside our home made me check the locks on every door. And as that possibility raised its ugly head in my imagination, I put aside the thought of shopping or visiting or anything else and decided to stay fairly close myself.

Wondering if Lillian had noticed the watchful eye Sam was keeping on Latisha, I went to the kitchen, only to meet her coming to find me.

"Miss Julia, that James jus' called, an' he say he got a pot of green beans cookin' an' a salat already made in the Frigidaire, an' corn already shucked, an' chicken ready to fry, but Mr. Pickens put him to work on something else, an' he can't cook supper. So he want me to come over and finish up."

"What's going on over there? Hazel Marie invited us to *eat* dinner, not to cook it."

"It don't matter. I tole him I was bringin' banana puddin' for dessert, an' I already got that made."

"I still don't understand," I said. "What does Mr. Pickens have him doing that's more important than making dinner? Especially since they invited four extra people to eat it. I know Mr. Pickens can be the contrariest man alive, but this is above and beyond."

"Well, James, he say Mr. Pickens get home 'bout a hour ago, an' Miss Hazel Marie set him down an' tole him 'bout that black car an' 'bout how they almost get Latisha outta your car, an' Mr. Pickens, he get out his shotgun, an' set James down on a chair out on the front porch right in front of the front door. He tell him to lay that gun 'cross his lap an' set there so anybody passin' by jus' keep on goin' even if they had a mind to stop."

"My Lord," I said, throwing up my hands. "Has Mr. Pickens lost his mind? I would no more put a shotgun in James's hands than I'd fly."

"No'm," Lillian said with a noticeable lack of concern, "he can't shoot nobody. That gun's not loaded. Mr. Pickens, he say James jus' settin' out there like a warnin' sign, 'cause if anybody need shootin', he gonna do it hisself."

As Lillian began to gather the things she'd need to cook in a strange kitchen, I stewed over the nerve of James in expecting her to do it. Or, rather, the nerve of Mr. Pickens for assigning James to the porch, while assuming that somehow or another his own dinner would magically appear.

Just as I was struck with an idea to relieve Lillian, the phone rang.

"Miss Julia?" Hazel Marie said. "I just got a call from Binkie and they're home. So they're coming to dinner tonight, too. And—"

"Oh, I'm so glad that Coleman is back, but, Hazel Marie, Lillian has been on her feet all day. That's too many to ask her to cook for, so I'm wondering if—"

"I'm way ahead of you," Hazel Marie said. "I couldn't believe that J.D. would give a gun to James in the first place, and not even think of what it would do to our dinner plans. So I'm picking up two or three buckets from Kentucky Fried Chicken. Unless," she went on, "you think that'd be cheating."

"*Cheating!* Hazel Marie, that's just what I was going to suggest. It's a fact that some people," I said without mentioning Mr. Pickens, "think that food cooks itself. Kentucky Fried Chicken will be perfect, and if anybody complains, we'll point them to the kitchen."

Lillian was much relieved not to be facing two or three skillets of popping grease while frying enough chicken to feed a dozen people. So after watching her put the large bowl of banana pudding in a cardboard box, then stuff newspaper around the bowl to keep it from sliding around, I followed her outside with a bag of tomatoes and cucumbers. Moving aside a suitcase and a couple of full paper sacks, she carefully set the box in the footwell of the backseat of her new used minivan, then turned to me.

"We goin' back to our house after supper," she said, "an' I was meanin' to take Latisha with me now to get her out of y'all's way. But she have a fit, wantin' to stay with Mr. Sam. He 'bout to spoil her, Miss Julia, but I sure do 'preciate him lookin' after her. I jus' hope he don't get enough of it, 'cause Latisha can wear on you real quick."

"He's doing exactly what he wants to do, but I expect that as soon as Mr. Pickens—and now Coleman, too—get on the case we'll all be going back to normal living again. Don't worry about her, Lillian. We'll bring her with us around five-thirty or so."

But I knew she would worry, as, indeed, all of us would. As I slogged back across the soggy yard to the house, I realized how eagerly I was waiting for an end to the constant uneasiness that had hung over our heads for the entire week.

A little later as I was getting myself ready to go out to dinner, even though it was only four blocks away, it occurred to me that exactly two weeks before on another Saturday night, I had been packing for our beach trip. Thinking over the week we'd had at the beach, I decided that it had been a success. No one had gotten cranky, or had their feelings hurt. Everybody seemed to have enjoyed the house as well as those who had filled it.

It was just our bad luck that Marty had chosen our beach time to make landfall, and just our bad luck that we'd had to evacuate and return home so early. But what a return it had been, and I'm not talking about that interminable drive on the interstate. I'm talking about the constant concern for the entire week that we had been under the scrutiny of unscrupulous smugglers who'd apparently thought so little of money that they'd thrown a pile of it overboard. Thinking back over the week that had just concluded, who would've thought that someone—or, most likely, *three* someones—would be overshadowing everything we did?

Going out to the upstairs hall, I leaned over the bannister and called to Latisha. "Do you need to do anything to get ready? It's about time to go."

"No, ma'am," she yelled from the kitchen. "I'm already ready."

I wasn't too sure of that, so I went downstairs to find her and Sam sitting at her little table in the corner of the kitchen. She was wielding the hot-glue gun like a professional with Sam sitting across from her watching carefully. He was selecting intact shells from the pile on the table and laying them in a row for her to glue onto the design she was making.

As I approached, Sam looked up and smiled. "Bet you didn't know we have an art class in progress."

"See this, Miss Lady?" Latisha said, pointing to the sheet of poster paper in front of her. "I don't have another frame, but Mr. Sam say I can make designs on this paper an' later on I can frame it like a picture."

"What a good idea," I said, and looked admiringly not only at her design—which I would call abstract modernism in the extreme—but at Sam for coming up with the suggestion. "But we should be on our way. You need to go to the bathroom? Wash your hands? They'll be expecting us soon."

Sam stood up then and, saying that he needed a little getting ready himself, left to go upstairs.

Latisha put the glue gun down and stood up. "I'm jus' gonna leave everything right here, an' let them shells get glued on real good. Great-Granny say we goin' home tonight, but don't worry, I'll come back tomorrow and finish it. Besides, Mr. Sam, he say artists need time to think. So that's what I'll be doin' tonight."

"Good idea," I said again, for who could argue with an artist's need for creative thinking time?

As Sam drove us to the Pickens house, I said, "Did Lillian tell you about James?"

"What's he done now?"

I laughed. "Not what he's done—except try to get Lillian to cook supper for him—but what Mr. Pickens has done. Don't be surprised when you see James guarding the front door with a shotgun on his lap."

"Do *what?*"

"Oh, it's not loaded, but Mr. Pickens wants anybody passing by—especially anybody in a big, black car—to think it is."

"Well," Sam said with a wry smile, "I guess James is safer than Granny Wiggins would be. It wouldn't surprise me if she kept a few shells in her pocket."

"Shells?" Latisha asked, perking up in the backseat. "Did Miss Granny go to the beach, too?"

"Different kind of shells, honey," Sam said, glancing at her in the rearview mirror. "Not the kind that you can glue."

"I bet I could," she said. "That hot-glue gun'll glue anything to anything you want."

"Here we are," Sam said, turning into the Pickenses' drive and pulling up beside a familiar SUV. "Looks like Coleman and Binkie are already here. And there's James, armed and ready. Better put your hands up."

As we walked up onto the porch, Latisha edged close to Sam at the sight of James with a shotgun. And James himself greeted us warmly without stirring from his chair.

Smiling broadly while straightening his shoulders, he said, "You folks real welcome. Jus' go right on in. We been 'spectin' you."

"Good to know you're on duty, James," Sam said, acknowledging James's important post. James, in turn, visibly stiffened and tightened his grip on the long gun.

"Yessir, I'm the lookout. And, Miss Julia, I got to 'pologize for wantin' to put supper off on Miss Lillian. They wadn't nobody else but Miss Granny, an' she cook so slapdash you wouldn't wanta eat it."

So it had been James's idea to maneuver Lillian into the kitchen, probably to keep Granny Wiggins from edging into his domain.

"Arrangements have been made," I told him, "so don't worry about it. But, James, have you seen any black cars go by? And maybe slow down as they pass?"

"No'm, nothin' like that, but I'm watchin' for 'em."

Latisha, still eyeing the shotgun, asked, "How long you got to sit out here with that thing?"

"Mr. J.D. say till he say to quit. An' when Mr. J.D. say do something, I drop my cookin' an' moppin' an' dustin' an' everything else, an' hop to it."

"You and me both, James," I murmured as Sam held the door for me to walk into the Pickens house. "You and me both."

Chapter 45

Hazel Marie, wearing one of the sundresses she'd bought at the beach, hurried out into the hall to welcome us. She looked lovely, as she always did, the tan she'd worked so assiduously to acquire contrasting with Velma's expertise in the field of hair color.

"Come in, come in," she said, her face glowing, not, I suspected, because we were visiting, but because Mr. Pickens was home. "Binkie and Coleman are here, drying out, they say. Sounds as if it rained more over in Pisgah than around here. Latisha," Hazel Marie went on, "Gracie and the twins are with Granny Wiggins in the study. You want to run back there with them?"

"No, ma'am," Latisha said, looking around at the gathering of adults. "I'll stay with Mr. Sam an' Lloyd. An' that black-haired man with the mustache, jus' in case somebody still lookin' for my shells."

And there he was—Mr. Pickens himself, broad and powerful—standing behind Hazel Marie. He gave Latisha a reassuring pat on the head, then reached for Sam's hand, adding his welcome to his wife's. "Sam," he said, "good to see you. And, you, Miss Julia," he went on, turning to me as his black mustache twitched, "I don't know what you're doing, but you just get younger every time I see you."

I immediately took umbrage, stiffening at his carelessly offered and patently untrue compliment. But that's the way he was, always with the teasing remark that made you look ridiculous if you challenged him.

So I didn't. Instead, I said, "We're glad you're home, Mr. Pickens. Has Hazel Marie told you what's going on?"

"Yes," he said, frowning slightly as he put on his business face, "but I want to hear it again from everybody who's had any contact with them."

"You realize, I hope, that we're not even sure who 'them' are. But finding that out is in your hands now, and I hope to goodness that you're up for it."

"Oh, I'm up for it," he said, his black eyes gleaming enough to make me wary of another unwelcome comment. Instead, he urged us into the living room, where Coleman stood to shake Sam's hand and Binkie slid over on the sofa to make room. Mr. Pickens made sure that we were all comfortably seated, proving once again that he could, on occasion, be quite gentlemanly. From my viewpoint, however, those occasions were few and far between.

Yet, I found myself feeling as if a burden had been lifted—actually feeling almost euphoric—because Mr. Pickens was finally on the job. Even though he could aggravate me beyond endurance, I had total confidence in his investigative skills and his ability to get things done. And with Coleman around to back him up if need be with a crew of deputies, I could rest assured that we'd soon learn why we'd attracted the attention of shell-stealing strangers.

He didn't, however, jump immediately into what I had assumed would be an interrogatory session. The little twin girls came running in and climbed into his lap, so we had to wait while he played with them.

Then Granny Wiggins appeared in the doorway, announcing that Gracie and the little girls had had their supper and that she was ready to put them to bed. Gracie sidled up to her mother who assured her that it wasn't yet her bedtime. The two little girls, however, created a firestorm of wails as Mr. Pickens carried them both upstairs.

Latisha, covering her ears with her hands, said, "I never heard such a racket in my life."

Lloyd shrugged. "You get used to it." Then he grinned at her. "I mean, if it's a fact of life, you learn to live with it."

When Mr. Pickens returned to the living room, Lillian announced that dinner was served. Noticing how tired she looked, I moved beside her and whispered, "You are not to do another thing but eat your dinner, and that's it. No dishwashing, no putting food away, no pot scrubbing, not one thing! Leave it all for James."

"James say he got to guard the door."

"Guard the door, my foot! Nobody's going to come in with all of us here. James can either clean the kitchen tonight or he can do it in the morning."

As we finished eating Lillian's banana pudding dessert, Mr. Pickens stood up and invited us back into the living room. "I want to hear from everybody who met the people on the beach or who saw them later, as well as those of you who've seen the suspect car. Come on in and have a seat."

So we did: Hazel Marie, Latisha, and I on the sofa; Sam in an armchair on one side of the sofa; Binkie, with Gracie in her lap, in one on the other side, with Lloyd on an ottoman beside her. Mr. Pickens brought in chairs from the dining room, and Lillian and Coleman took those. Lillian, I noticed, heaved a sigh of relief as she stretched out her left foot.

Mr. Pickens took his usual large wingback chair that faced us and the television set. "Start at the beginning," he said, "which I believe was the morning of the Great Money Haul. Did anybody see or hear anything unusual before money started washing up on the beach?"

"I wasn't even on the beach that morning," I said, "and knew nothing about it until Lloyd came running up to tell me."

Sam said, "The first I knew of it was when people started running into the water—sort of everybody at the same time a little farther south of where we were."

"I didn't notice anything," Hazel Marie said. "At first, I mean, because Lily Mae had sand in her mouth."

"Me, either," Binkie said. "I was trying to get some sun."

"And," Mr. Pickens said to jog our memories, "what about Etta Mae and Mrs. Conover? You think they might've noticed anything?"

"I've spoken with Etta Mae," I said, "and she's not seen anything unusual. As for LuAnne, well, she's had her mind on other things."

Then Sam added, "Either one would've mentioned anything unusual—Etta Mae, especially. She's used to being observant. We can check with them later."

"Okay," Mr. Pickens said, leaning forward with his arms on his knees. "So the next thing was seeing the three people wandering on the beach. That same day?"

"Yessir," Lloyd said, "that same afternoon while everybody was dancing at the house. Miss Julia and Latisha went for a walk on the beach and I caught up with them."

"Yes," Latisha said, "an' you an' me saw 'em at the same time 'cause nobody else was on the beach an' they didn't have no bathing suits on."

Mr. Pickens's eyebrows shot straight up. "Nudists?"

Lloyd doubled over, trying not to laugh. "Street clothes, J.D. Which made them stand out just as bad, but in the opposite direction. Too much instead of too little."

"All right then," Mr. Pickens said, suppressing a smile. "Now the three of you tell me exactly what was said."

"Well," I said, starting the account, "one of them was friendly—Rob was his name, but he didn't introduce himself. One of the others called him that—the woman, I think."

"He tole me I could buy a scooter," Latisha said, recounting her most vivid memory. "An' that I could go to the bank an' they'd give me a good sand dollar instead of a broke one. I didn't b'lieve it then, and I don't b'lieve it now."

"I'll tell you the truth," I said, wracking my memory to fill in the blanks, "I didn't think too much of that meeting at the time. I mean, it was obvious that they weren't from around there. The way they talked, for one thing. And for another, Rob was almost too familiar with us, while the other two would've passed by without speaking at all." I stopped as I pictured again the meeting with the three strangers, then went on. "It was Lloyd who had a bad feeling about them from the first."

Mr. Pickens looked at Lloyd and said, "What was it you didn't like, son?"

Lloyd shrugged. "I'm not sure, J.D. They just made me feel they were up to something. One was too interested in us, and the other two were too busy scouring the dunes for money to pay us any mind at all. And this was *hours* after the money washed in. It seemed like a lame excuse for what they were really doing."

"Maybe," Sam said, "they were looking for something else."

Mr. Pickens nodded. "That's what I'm thinking."

After another thirty minutes or so of questions and answers, we'd given Mr. Pickens a blow-by-blow account of Lloyd's seeing the woman in a big, black Suburban on the interstate, seeing what we assumed was the same vehicle at least four times—twice near the Pickens house, once passing by ours, and once following Lillian and Sam. And maybe again as a black flash in a rainstorm after Latisha and I had been ambushed by two hooded thieves.

"Yes," Latisha said, her black eyes glowering at the thought, "an' one of 'em stole my best shells, an' I prob'bly won't *never* get over it."

Hazel Marie put her arm around Latisha and whispered, "Next summer, we'll get some more."

"Looks like," Mr. Pickens said, sitting back in his chair to give a summation of the situation, "we ought to assume for now that the car most of you have seen is the same one every time, and it's the same people you saw on the beach—Lloyd recognizing the woman might confirm that. And if it was one of them that went through Hazel Marie's car and found our address, they didn't have to actually follow us home—they knew where we'd be. The problem is, though, just what is it that they want?"

Well, my Lord, I thought, that's been our question all along.

Lillian, who'd been sitting quietly throughout the interrogation, said, "Maybe they was something special 'bout Latisha's shells. A prize or something."

Everybody turned to look at her as we considered for the first time such an unlikely possibility.

"If that's the case," Latisha said, "then I *really* want 'em back."

Mr. Pickens rubbed his fingers across his mouth, thinking and pondering. "Well," he said after a while, "I can't think what it could be, except that it's obviously *something*. Coleman, what do you think?"

"Beats me, but they could be casing us—or rather, your house and Sam's—setting up for what they think could be a major haul. I'll make sure we patrol both houses on a regular basis, but we're stymied, legally speaking, until they make another move."

"But they've already stolen something," I said, thinking again of that frightful incident in my car.

"I know," Coleman said, nodding sympathetically, "but could you or Latisha identify them?"

I shook my head, knowing that the hooded, rain-streaked figures we'd seen had been effectively disguised.

"Here's something else," Coleman went on. "I'll put out a Be-on-the-Lookout for black Suburbans first thing tomorrow. We'll stop every one of 'em, check the occupants, and run the license plates. Can't make any arrests, but it'll narrow the field and maybe give us a line on who it is."

"That's good," Mr. Pickens said, nodding, "and I'll go out at first light tomorrow and drive through all the parking lots of hotels and motels—they've got to be staying somewhere. I'll take down the plate numbers of every black Suburban I see and get them to you to run."

"I can help with that," Sam said. "We can divide up the B&Bs in town and the motels out along the interstate."

"That'll work," Coleman said. "Count me in."

"Me, too," Lloyd said.

"Good deal," Mr. Pickens said with his usual confidence. "By this time tomorrow we should know who we're dealing with."

"Lots of tourists in town this time of year," Binkie said, slightly dampening my surge of hope, "but it's worth a try."

"Only thing we can do, honey," Coleman said, patting her knee. "At this point, anyway."

Mr. Pickens stood, nodded toward the hall door, and said to

Sam and Coleman, "I've got a county map in the study, and a list of tourist accommodations. Let's plot our rounds so we can check as many parking lots as we can before guests start getting up."

As the three men and Lloyd went across the hall to the study, I leaned my head back and closed my eyes in gratitude for capable and willing friends. Then nearly jumped out of my skin as Latisha threw herself back against the sofa and howled at the top of her voice, "*Oh, no-o! I forgot my pocketbook!*"

Chapter 46

"*Latisha!*" Lillian sprang across the room, took Latisha by the arm, and said, "Hush that up! What you mean yellin' like that? You wake up them babies an' scare everybody to death. What's wrong with you?"

"But, but, Granny, I left my pocketbook at Mr. Sam's house. Miss Lady's house, too. An' I *need* it!" Tears flooded down Latisha's face as she sobbed and gasped for breath.

"We goin' back over there tomorrow. You can get it then."

"No, Granny," Latisha said, shaking her head, "that won't do. I need it *now*."

"Well," Lillian said, firmly, "it'll have to do, 'cause I'm too tired to be drivin' all over creation tonight. We goin' home an' you goin' straight to bed."

Latisha put her head in her lap and sobbed piteously, pleading with Lillian to take her back to our house. But Lillian's face was set in stone, and I had no doubt that her surgically altered foot was bothering her as well. She was of no mind to limp out to the car and make an unnecessary trip just to retrieve a little red plastic pocketbook.

"I'll take her," I said, getting to my feet. "Besides, I need to move around a little. Sam will be awhile, I'm sure. So I'll run Latisha over to the house and we'll be back before he's through. You sit down and rest, Lillian, and let me do this."

Lillian tried to discourage me, and I had to put up with a chorus of "Let me," and "I'll do it" from Binkie and Hazel Marie. But I'd had my fill of sitting around waiting for the men to decide who would cruise the parking lots of the Holiday Inn, the Quality Inn, the Motel 6, and Stewart's Rooms for Rent.

"Come on, Latisha," I said, taking her hand. "We'll take Mr. Sam's car and be back in a few minutes. You remember where you left your pocketbook?"

"Yes, ma'am, I think I do." Latisha sniffed wetly and wiped her face with her arm. "And, Granny, I promise I won't never forget it again."

"They Lord," Lillian said with a roll of her eyes, as she gave in and sank onto a chair. "I sure do thank you, Miss Julia, an, Latisha, you better thank her, too."

"I will," Latisha said with another loud sniff, "jus' as soon as I get my pocketbook."

Glancing in through the study door, I saw the men bent over the desk, intently studying a county map, marking the locations of hotels, motels, and inns, and deciding who would go where. I dangled my key chain, which also held Sam's electronic key, so he would know I was leaving, and mouthed, "I'll be back."

Night, helped by the cloud cover, had fallen by the time we walked out onto the porch. And James was still sitting on guard, his empty plate beside his chair.

"Y'all goin' home already?" he asked, blinking alertly, but I thought he'd been dozing.

"We'll be right back," I told him, as Latisha and I carefully maneuvered the steps to the walk.

Sam's car was bigger than mine, so I had to adjust the seat before starting the engine. Looking back at Latisha in the backseat, she seemed twice as far away as when she was in my car.

"Will you go in with me?" she asked, sounding small and uncertain.

"Yes, of course."

"Good, 'cause I don't like goin' in a dark house by myself."

"I don't, either. But we'll switch on the lights as soon as we get there."

"Uh-huh, 'cept we got to get in 'fore we can switch 'em on."

I smiled at her quickness. "We'll just have to watch out for each other. Here we are," I said as I pulled into our drive and parked behind my car. I turned off the engine, unbuckled my seat belt, then watched as the headlights went off, wondering why in the world we hadn't left a few lights on, the yard lights especially. The night was as black as pitch.

Holding hands, we stumbled to the back door, which took an eternity to unlock, doing it by feel rather than by sight. Reaching inside as soon as it opened, I felt for the switches on the wall, flooding the kitchen with light.

Latisha edged past me as I turned the deadbolt on the door. She dashed across the room, yelling, "There it is! Right where I left it!"

And, sure enough, there the little red purse hung by its shoulder strap from the back of the chair, right where she'd left it. And right where she'd also left her new shell design, piles of mostly broken shells, and Hazel Marie's hot-glue gun.

Latisha slipped the strap over her head and one arm, then sat down and unsnapped the clasp. She began rummaging through the fully packed pocketbook, checking, I supposed, that all was as it should be. Although who would've disturbed anything with all of us away for the past few hours, I didn't know.

Noticing the blinking light on the answering machine, I punched the button to hear the message. "Julia!" LuAnne's voice sounded so stricken that it unnerved me. "I have to talk to you. Call me! Please call me as soon as you get home. This is just *awful!*"

Fearful, as I'd been so many times before, that some tragic event had occurred, I turned to Latisha. "Honey, I'm going to run up to the bedroom and return this call." As well as to use the bathroom, which I didn't mention. "We'll be ready to go back in just a few minutes."

She nodded, busily pulling out a few things from her pocketbook, making sure everything was there. Making my way upstairs, turning on a few lights as I went, I felt my nerves thrumming away at the distress I'd heard in LuAnne's voice. *What could've happened? What had she done?*

After relieving myself—the most urgent calling—I dialed LuAnne's number from the phone beside our bed.

"LuAnne? It's Julia, what—"

"Oh, Julia, thank goodness you're home. I just needed to talk to somebody, because I can't take this anymore. Nothing's working right. I can't find an apartment that I like or can afford. And I'm all packed up with nowhere to go, and Leonard just goes on about his business like I don't even exist! And now I'm having second thoughts, because you know, in spite of everything, I do love him."

I knew no such thing. But, as I listened to her begin to cry, I did know that I'd had enough of listening, commiserating, and sympathizing—none of which had done any good. Her cries for help had always drawn me in, while she'd done nothing to help herself. *Duped again*, I thought, as I recalled the fright I'd felt at the distress in her voice. My shoulder felt permanently damp from all the times she'd cried on it, and all of a sudden, I'd had enough.

"Get hold of yourself, LuAnne!" I stormed. "I am not going to listen to you moan and groan about Leonard another minute. Either live with him or get rid of him—I don't care which—but I've had enough of it. And another thing—"

A long, piercing shriek from downstairs ripped through the house, sending a sudden shock through my system. *Latisha!* I slammed the phone down and ran, nearly breaking my neck on the dim stairs.

Chapter 47

My heart banged against my chest as I missed a step and slid halfway down the stairs, then scrambled to my feet and ran through the downstairs hall toward the kitchen whence screams and banging and crashing noises emanated.

Yelling for Latisha, I dashed into the room, nearly tripping on an overturned chair. Regaining my balance, I couldn't believe my eyes. Latisha, her arms flailing away, hung by a red strap held by a hairy-legged man in Bermuda shorts who was swinging her around, scattering shells, glue gun, salt and pepper shakers, a Dawn dish detergent bottle, and various kitchen utensils around the room.

"Put her down!" I screamed, running toward the man. "What're you *doing*? Turn her loose!"

I grabbed Latisha by the waist as another revolution brought her within reach, and before I knew it, I, too, was swung off my feet. Crashing into the peninsula counter, I lost my grip on her and so did he. Latisha slid across the floor, curling up beside the refrigerator. Breathing hard, the man turned his attention to me. As I scrambled for anything to fend him off, all I could see was the dark, determined look in his eyes as he raised a fist with a gold-ringed finger.

Rob, I thought, and wondered where the other two were—but not for long. I dropped to the floor just in time to avoid a blow to the head.

"*Run, Latisha, run!*" I yelled, scooting to the other side of the peninsula.

Expecting Rob to be on me, I hoisted myself to my feet only to see him leaning over Latisha, tugging at her.

"Get away from me!" she yelled, kicking wildly at him. "Help, help, Miss Lady! Don't let him have it!"

But that's exactly what I intended to do—if I could find something to let him have it *with*. Coffeepot! There it was, a glass coffeepot on the counter, half full, cold as yesterday's, but with a handgrip for convenient pouring—or swinging.

Snatching it up, I headed for Rob, who now had Latisha cornered next to her little shell-strewn table. Still screaming and kicking at him, she scooted under the table. He dropped to his knees and crawled in after her.

Raising the coffeepot, I braced myself, getting ready to brain him as soon as his head poked out. Then another, deeper scream overrode Latisha's, and Rob backed out so fast that he almost knocked me over.

Screaming and high stepping, he danced around, scrubbing at his face. "Get it off! Get it off!"

Leaning over, he brushed frantically at his naked legs, and I saw my chance. Drawing the glass pot way back to work up momentum, I swung hard and caught him on the side of the head—cold coffee sloshing over him and the refrigerator. A dazed look swept over his face as his eyes rolled back in his head. His legs slowly giving way, he crumpled to the floor.

"Come on, Latisha! Run!" I yelled, reaching for her.

She came crawling out, her red pocketbook dangling from the strap across her shoulders, and a gun pointed at Rob.

"Good Lord!" I gasped. *"Where'd you get that!"*

"From Miss Hazel Marie," Latisha said.

Glue gun—of course! With the aid of a coffeepot, Rob had been hot waxed into submission.

Knowing there were two others somewhere, I grabbed Latisha's hand and pulled her toward the door. She screeched as the glue gun's cord slowed her until it popped out of the receptacle. At the same time, my foot touched something that skittered toward Latisha, and she, being closer to the floor, scooped it up without missing a step.

I almost missed one, though, as I slid on shattered glass from the window on the door. Rob had just *broken in* with Latisha sitting right there and me in the bathroom—the nerve of him!

Seeing the car keys on the floor, I swept them up and ran,

dragging Latisha with me and throwing her into the front seat of the car with no thought of seat belts or backseat safety.

Ramming the key into the ignition and the gear into reverse, I stepped on the gas. The car spurted backward onto the street at nine miles an hour, helpfully engaging the door locks.

"Are you all right?" I screamed at Latisha, my nerves twanging as my eyes switched back and forth between the rearview mirror and the windshield. *Two others on the loose. Got to move! Got to get to Mr. Pickens and Coleman.*

"Yes'm, I guess," she said, sniffing. "At least I got my pocketbook, but I'm hopin' you won't tell Granny on me."

Giving her a quick glance as I took a corner a little too fast, I asked, "For what? You were wonderful, Latisha. Nobody could've done better."

"Well, yes'm, I coulda, 'cause Granny tole me not to never leave the glue gun plugged in. An' looks like I did."

The urge to laugh surged up so unexpectedly that I had to grip the steering wheel to keep it down. I might never have stopped if I'd given in to it.

"Well, this one time, Latisha, I'm glad you did. We might never have fought him off if you hadn't hot-glued him."

But they surely weren't done with us. *Where were the other two?* As we sped through a residential area, getting closer to safety, I became aware of a peculiar beeping sound.

"What's that noise?" I asked, glancing at the dashboard for a warning light.

"That man's smartphone," Latisha said, holding up a black rectangular object that was not only beeping its head off, but blinking off and on like crazy. "Look like somebody callin' him."

"Well, don't answer it." Not knowing a smartphone from a dumb one, I didn't like the sound or the look of it.

Whirling the car into the Pickenses' drive so fast that I took out part of a forsythia bush on my way, I had a notion to grab the black box and throw it as far as I could sling it. Who knew what it was? Did bombs beep and blink?

Before I could do anything, though, Latisha was out of the car and running for the porch, the box beeping and blinking in her hand and the glue gun's electrical cord trailing behind her. I sprang out after her, yelling for help.

James jumped up, his eyes wide and the shotgun at port arms. "What's goin' on? You folks all right?"

"Stay alert, James!" I didn't stop, just dashed inside where help awaited. "They may be following us."

"Oh, Jesus," he said and snapped to attention at the head of the steps.

"Looks like part of a tracking system," Mr. Pickens said, turning the little boxlike device over in his hand. "It's not a cell phone, that's for sure. I'd say it's a scanner of some kind, probably operating on radio frequency identification or RFID." Which didn't mean one thing to me, but it was obviously operating on something because it was still blinking and beeping up a storm.

Coleman was on the phone, calling in the cavalry from the sheriff's office. "Yeah, on Polk Street. Home invasion, child endangerment, assault on a female—*two* females—attempted robbery, and that's for starters. And spread out, there're two more of 'em somewhere, maybe in a black Suburban."

Everybody who'd come for dinner had also come running to the study, when we, wild-eyed and frantic, burst in. Between us, Latisha and I told what had happened, gasping out the details of our close-quarters encounter with Rob.

Sam kept rubbing my arm and saying, "Julia, Julia," and Hazel Marie wrung her hands, while Binkie and Lillian searched Latisha for signs of injury.

Coleman hung up, saying, "A car's there now, and more on the way." He frowned at the madly working device, still in Mr. Pickens's hand. "Whatta you think?"

"Well, it's operating on a signal from something that enabled them to track us not only from the beach but from one house to another, that's for sure. Only thing is, we don't know where the signal's coming from."

"Got to be close," Sam said. "Somewhere around here from the looks and sound of it."

"James may need backup," Coleman said, reaching for his service weapon under his shirttail and heading toward the porch. "An empty shotgun's not gonna cut it."

My nerves were still on edge throughout all of this. In fact, as relieved as I was to have given the slip to Rob, it now seemed that worse things were in store. Strange people after us and strange devices tracking us—this we knew. What we didn't know was why.

Looking around the room, I saw anxiety or puzzlement on one face after another except Latisha's. Gazing up at Lillian, she asked in a pitiful little voice, "Granny, I sure could use some more of that 'naner puddin'.'"

"I could, too. Come on, baby girl, let's go to the kitchen an' get some." Lillian took her hand and they walked out, crossing the hall, going through the living room and the dining room, and on into the kitchen.

Mr. Pickens, still examining the device in his hand, suddenly said, "Sam, look at this. It's slowing down. Still going strong, but not as fast or as loud as it was."

Both Sam and Mr. Pickens stood watching the black device, then they looked at each other. "Lillian!" Mr. Pickens yelled as he left the device with Sam and ran toward the kitchen. "Take Latisha out in the yard. Take her out to the garage!"

Good grief, I thought, *he'll scare them to death*. But I knew she'd do whatever he told her without question.

Mr. Pickens came back into the study, then leaned over again to stare at the device. Even I could tell that the beeping was quieter and less urgent. The blinking red light was as bright as ever, but it, too, was settling into a slower, regular rhythm.

Mr. Pickens and Sam stared at each other. "*Latisha!*" they said at the same time.

And to prove it, Mr. Pickens went to get her, bringing both

Lillian and Latisha back to the study. And, the nearer to us they got, the louder and more agitated the device became.

Lillian was almost as agitated, having been sent outside then called back in so precipitately by Mr. Pickens. "What we done, Mr. J.D.?"

"Not a thing, Lillian, not a thing. We're just thinking that Latisha may have picked up something besides this little box. Did you, Latisha? Did you bring anything else from Miss Julia's house?"

"No, sir," Latisha said, her eyes wide. "I mean, yes sir. I brought back Miss Hazel Marie's glue gun an' I got my pocketbook."

Her *pocketbook*! I'd thought that Rob had been after Latisha herself. But instead of wrestling *for* her, it had been her pocketbook that he'd been trying to wrest *from* her.

Chapter 48

Mr. Pickens squatted down in front of Latisha so that they were face-to-face, or, rather, eye to eye. Suspiciously frowning at him as he reached her level, she edged closer to Lillian. As he gazed steadily at her, Latisha squinched up her face and clutched her little red pocketbook tighter.

"Latisha," he said, fairly gently for him, "may I see your pocketbook?"

She stared right back at him, holding his gaze defiantly for several seconds until his mustache began to twitch, and a little smile started to curl at the edge of Latisha's mouth. "I guess," she said, slowly handing it to him. "If you'll be real careful."

"Oh, I'll be careful," he said, standing. "You can count on that." Putting the pocketbook on the desk, he opened the clasp and began to carefully pull out what it had been stuffed full of—one thick white sock after another. Three of them.

We all leaned over the desk, ignoring for the time being the crazily active black box, fascinated with what might be in the pocketbook besides socks.

"Uh-huh," Mr. Pickens said as he laid out the socks in a row and felt the toe of each one. "Feels like something more than toes." Glancing at Latisha, he went on. "Socks're good hiding places for something you want to take care of."

Latisha nodded. "Yessir, that's where I keep ev'ry cent to my name."

Taking great care, since Latisha was watching his every move, Mr. Pickens held up one sock by the toe and shook out into his hand a chipped sand dollar. He laid it beside the black device. Then he shook out another sand dollar from another sock, this one cracked almost in two. Then finally the last sand dollar—smooth on the surface and along the edges, thicker in the middle and a little larger than the others—fell out into his hand. He laid it beside the black device and you would've thought every first responder for miles around would be responding to its demands.

"That's it," Mr. Pickens said. "That's the tracker. A signal, probably from an embedded chip, is going from it to the scanner." He first tapped the perfectly formed sand dollar, then moved his hand to the little black box. "These days, chips can be as small as a grain of rice, which this one would have to be."

Lloyd leaned over to look at the sand dollar. "How'd they get it inside the sand dollar without breaking it?"

"Feel it," Mr. Pickens said. "It's not a real shell. Some kind of plastic material maybe, but made up to look like a sand dollar."

Latisha's face fell before it began to screw up in dismay. "*It's not real?* But I found it on the beach!"

"I'm figuring," Mr. Pickens went on, "that it went overboard along with the money—whether on purpose or by mistake, there's no telling. But I'm betting this is what the three on the beach were looking for."

My hand flew to my throat as I recalled that both Latisha and I had as good as told the three beachcombers exactly what they'd wanted to know. Latisha had volunteered that she'd found *hers* right where they were looking, and I had offered clarification by saying that what she'd found was something besides hundred-dollar bills.

With a shock, it occurred to me then that we'd been fortunate that Rob and company had not put two and two together on the spot. At some later point, they'd obviously figured out that what Latisha had found could only have been the manufactured and preloaded sand dollar—especially because, all unbeknownst to us, it was signaling every step Latisha made after she'd put it in her pocketbook.

Lloyd, who'd been eyeing the fake sand dollar, said, "I don't get it, J.D. What good would it have done them to get the sand dollar? They already had the scanner—this little black box—to tell them where the sand dollar was, but now that we have both of 'em, we don't know any more than we knew before we had either one."

"Right," Mr. Pickens said, "you're right. So I'm thinking there's something else in the sand dollar—maybe another chip that sends a different signal. Coleman," he went on, turning as Coleman returned from the porch, "come see what you think."

The two men put their heads together, occasionally glancing up to include Sam and Lloyd. I heard words like transponders, radio frequencies, RFIDs, satellites, and a few others of like electronic origin, none of which I understood.

Coleman straightened up and said, "Let's get the Coast Guard in on this. They know what goes on offshore, and I'll bet they've seen something like this before. Oh, and by the way," he went on, turning to look at me with a grin, "the guy you left on your kitchen floor, Miss Julia, is being looked at in the Emergency Room. He's got a concussion and some burns on his face and legs, but he'll survive."

"I'll take credit for the concussion," I said, "but Latisha gets it for the burns. I do, however, hope he'll be all right."

"All right enough to go to jail," Coleman said. "J.D., let's go to the sheriff's office and contact the Coast Guard. They're gonna be *de*-lighted to hear about this."

"Yeah," Mr. Pickens said, a pleased look on his face. "And if we're right, and there's another chip in this thing, it'll be sending a dedicated signal programmed for a specific scanner, maybe to coordinate with an offshore boat. With a setup like that, two or more boats could meet without using GPS navigation or radio traffic—both of which could be picked up by the Coast Guard. Of course," he went on, scratching his head, "that could be too high tech for a bunch of smugglers, but I wouldn't bet against it."

"Why?" Lloyd asked. "Couldn't they just meet at port somewhere?"

"Not if they're transferring unlawful goods—drugs, cigarettes, people, whatever. Cash, even. Whatever the plan is, the payoff has to be worth enough for the three stalkers to go to a lot of trouble to get the sand dollar back. So what we're seeing here," Mr. Pickens, nodding at the device, went on, "is a backup signal simply to locate the sand dollar in case of loss or theft or a double cross."

"Oh, my goodness," I murmured. Then aloud, I said, "But what about the other two? The other man and the woman? Since Rob's out of the picture, won't they still be after it?"

"Looks like they've flown the coop," Coleman said. "We have an APB out on 'em, but so far, nothing. J.D., let's get these things out of Latisha's purse and our hands. They'll be safe in the evidence room until we can turn 'em over to the Coast Guard. If we're right, and the sand dollar is set up to draw in another boat, somebody's gonna have a big surprise waiting for 'em."

Mr. Pickens grinned at the thought. Then, squatting again to Latisha's level, he said, "Latisha, honey, we have to turn in your sand dollar, but I think you need some compensation for taking such good care of it. How does a nice, new twenty-dollar bill sound to you?"

She studied on that for a few seconds, then said, "Sound like a pretty good swap to me, 'specially if it get rid of all that beepin' an' blinkin' goin' on. I'm tired of it."

Mr. Pickens laughed and stood up. "We all are." Then, with a wave of his hand, he said, "They're all yours, Coleman."

Gathering the beeping and blinking scanner and the sand dollar that was causing all the fuss, Coleman said, "The Coast Guard will want to talk to you, too, J.D. Let's get these things to the sheriff's office, then put in a call. We can see if anybody's sighted the other two, as well. I want to be sure they're gone for good and not still hanging around here."

Mr. Pickens agreed as he began stuffing the little red pocketbook with two socks holding chipped sand dollars and one sock that was empty. He snapped the clasp closed and handed the purse to Latisha.

"Here you go, honey," he said. "I'm sorry about your sand dollar, but you've been a big help to local and federal law officers tonight, which means you're one of the good guys."

"Yessir, I know," she said, taking the purse and putting the strap over her shoulder—right where it belonged. "But what I want to know is where's that twenny-dollar bill you promised?"

Chapter 49

"Julia?" Sam said, as he came into the library. It was the Monday morning after our tumultuous weekend, and I'd been reading the newspaper article about it. The reporter had gotten almost everything wrong, but then, I was still trying to straighten out the weekend events myself.

It was nearing lunchtime, and Sam had just returned from one of his downtown jaunts, which usually included talking with Len Burnside about property values. But that morning he had other property on his mind. "Have you been by Thurlow's house lately?"

"No," I said, lowering the paper. "Why?"

"You should see what's going on. There's a crew up on the roof, carpenters working on the windows, and somebody with a sling blade cutting weeds. And the front door's open with workmen going in and out. That house is being remodeled or refurbished or re-something. And about time, too. Thurlow let the place turn into an eyesore."

"That means," I said, sitting up straight, "that Helen is on the move in more ways than one. But that's so typical of her. She doesn't fiddle around when something needs to be done."

"Helen Stroud? What does she have to do with it?"

"Come sit down," I said, patting a place on the sofa beside me. "I'll explain it to you as Lillian explained it to me."

"Enlighten me," Sam said, as he sat down.

"Well," I said, pleased to be able to instruct him since it was usually the other way around, "did you know that it's not uncommon for a single woman to essentially give up her life, including her own home, and move in to take care of somebody who's old and decrepit? And in exchange she'll inherit everything the old person has?"

Sam's eyebrows shot up. "You mean, Helen and Thurlow?"

"Apparently so," I said and belatedly told him of seeing Helen and the Delmont lawyer after they'd met with Thurlow. "I expect she made it plain that she wouldn't live in a pigpen. Thurlow may have two broken legs, but it sounds as if his feet are being held to the fire, as well."

Sam smiled. "He must've broken more than his legs."

"Broken his pocketbook open at least," I said, somewhat wryly. Then as the clouds in my mind suddenly cleared, I clamped my hand onto his arm. "*Oh!*"

"What?"

Springing to my feet, I declaimed, "I have had an epiphany!"

"A what?"

"You know—one of those things you've been having." And I headed for the phone on the desk, punched in LuAnne's number, and, when she answered, said, "LuAnne, it's Julia, and—"

"I'm not speaking to you, so you can just hang up."

"No, wait. Listen, LuAnne, call Helen. Call her right now before—"

"Forget it," she snapped. "It's not Helen. It's Totsie, and you can stay out of it."

"No, listen," I said, wanting to shake her. "Helen is moving. *Moving*, LuAnne, to Thurlow's house, which means she's vacating her condo."

There was a long silence on the line as LuAnne digested the ramifications. "Her condo?"

"Yes, so if you want it—"

"Get off the phone, Julia. I have to make a call."

I declare, with all the climactic turmoil we'd just been through—running from a hurricane that followed us home, fighting off Rob in my kitchen, and learning that Latisha's beach find was the target of the stalkers—it was about time that I had some relief by the way things had worked out, but I didn't. A general sense of unease continued to unsettle me, and LuAnne's coolness just made it worse.

The house was still and quiet later that afternoon—Lloyd was at his mother's house, Lillian and Latisha at their newly roofed home, and Sam off in the hills somewhere checking property lines. Alone, I had walked around the yard, looking at the state of waterlogged plants on the first sun-filled day we'd had in a while. Then, back in the library contemplating a nap, I had sat down to organize my thoughts.

Sam and I had gone to church Sunday morning as was our wont, but, for all the good it had done me, I might as well have stayed home. I couldn't even recall what Pastor Ledbetter's sermon topic had been. The events of the previous evening kept running through my mind, while one seemingly minor incident played havoc with what should've been a satisfactory close to a week filled with storms, both atmospheric and emotional.

It was LuAnne in the midst of a raging storm of her own who was weighing heavily on my mind. I shivered at the memory of how I had had my fill of her vacillating over Leonard and had rudely ended a phone call by both telling her off and cutting her off. No wonder she hadn't wanted to speak to me even though I'd been relaying the good news of a vacant condo.

Objectively, I'd had every reason to point out that the dillydallying and wishy-washing she'd been engaged in—and constantly burdening me with—were keeping us both in a state of turmoil. But, as a friend, I should've better understood her situation—after all, who better than I who'd been through the same? So it behooved me to have been able to put up with it without flying off the handle at her. LuAnne and I had too much history between us for me to have cut her off so rudely.

The doorbell jerked me out of my self-critical reverie, so I hurried to answer it. And found myself set back on my heels.

"LuAnne!" Lord, I didn't know what to say. After just beating myself up for telling her off, I was now covered with shame at seeing her face-to-face on my doorstep. "Come in, I'm so glad to see you. Oh, LuAnne, I am so sorry—"

"Oh, don't bother," she said, breezing past me as she entered. "That's what I came to talk about. Can we sit down? I have a lot to say."

I was in for it, I knew, and well deserving of whatever she wanted to dish out.

"Yes," I said, indicating the living room, which was more suitable for a formal meeting than the library. "Let's sit in here. LuAnne, let me explain—"

"No, don't," she said, cutting me off again. "I spent most of last night being furious with you. I couldn't believe you'd be so cruel, but I finally went to sleep at about four and woke up in a different frame of mind. Julia," she went on, leaning toward me, "I came to thank you. You made me see that I was doing just what you said— going back and forth and making everything worse. You helped me see that I had to make a decision on my own and stick to it. And now I have, and I will."

"Thank you, thank you," I said, immeasurably relieved that she wasn't taking my head off. "I shouldn't have been so short with you, LuAnne. Your call, well, it came at a terrible time, and I just unloaded on you. But I am glad you've made a decision." I wasn't really glad, because it would be just like her to keep on putting up with Leonard, regardless of his playing footsie with Totsie. So it wouldn't have surprised me if she'd found some fault with Helen's condo in spite of my efforts on her behalf.

Then she floored me.

"Yes, I'm leaving him, and I know in my heart that it's the Lord's will for me, in spite of what the Book of Ephesians says. Julia, you won't believe how it's all working out, because I see now that my call to Helen was predetermined, as yours was to me. It all goes to show that I'm being *led*, because Helen's already packing up even though Thurlow's house won't be ready for a while. But she wants to be there to oversee the work, so see how it's all falling into place?"

"Uh, well, I guess," I said. "You've talked to Helen?"

"Yes! And it was perfect timing, because she doesn't want to sell her condo. She's going to rent it to me just to have somebody take care of it. It's not very fancy, because she couldn't afford the best." LuAnne stopped and laughed. "Of course she can *now*, but, Julia, it's perfect for me! She's even leaving a lot of her furniture, because, listen to this." LuAnne's face lit up with the thrill of telling what she knew. "She has total access to everything Thurlow has! Can you believe that? He must've been at the end of his rope to go that far."

"Oh, my goodness," I said, even though I already knew it. LuAnne, however, hated it when anyone knew something before she did. "You mean, Thurlow's turned everything over to her? That's hard to believe."

"Isn't it, though?" LuAnne said, a dreamy look on her face. "She is just so lucky."

Well, I wouldn't go that far by a long shot, so I didn't say anything. But if anybody was lucky in that particular arrangement, it was Thurlow. Which I'd have to think about another time. For the moment, though, I was relieved to have repaired a friendship.

"So," I said, "you really mean to leave Leonard?"

"You better believe it! He wanted solace? I'll give him solace and have some myself! Just think of it, no more cooking three meals a day if I don't want to, and I hope to goodness I never see another blueberry pancake. Because now, thanks to Helen or maybe to Thurlow's fall off the roof, I have an affordable place to live. I tell you, all the signs are right and I know it's what I'm supposed to do. So I have to thank you, Julia, for opening my eyes."

"Well," I said, trying for humility, "I'm glad to've been of help."

"You were. Although," she said, rising and going toward the door, "you could've been a little nicer doing it."

That evening after Sam and I had exhausted all we knew about the Thurlow-Helen arrangement, as well as the LuAnne-Leonard pending dis-arrangement, Sam went up to his study in the sun-room to check in again with Coleman. The two still-missing stalkers were weighing on his mind, especially since Lillian and Latisha were no longer under our roof. Coleman had been good about keeping us abreast of the investigation, and had, in fact, called us early the day before to let us know that the Coast Guard was on the case. They had been so eager to get their hands on the sand dollar and the other little device that they had flown two officers to Abbotsville to get them. And to get Rob, too.

As for the other two stalkers, they seemed to have disap-peared. The black Suburban had been located in the lot of the Quality Inn with no corresponding guests. As it was a rental car, the thinking was that they'd abandoned it and rented another. Which would've made for an easy trace had anyone known their names, but nobody did except Rob and, so far, he wasn't talking.

I thought to myself that I knew a way to loosen his tongue, but nobody asked me. The problem of Rob and company was now in the hands of the Coast Guard, and, since we no longer had any-thing of value to smugglers or stalkers, we were told to rest easy. But I intended to learn how to wield a hot-glue gun as soon as Latisha could teach me—just in case.

And, speaking of Latisha . . . Lloyd came bouncing in after school one afternoon a few days later to tell us about his classes and about Latisha. According to him, she'd finally presented her surprise—the fairly evenly shell-covered frame—to Binkie be-cause Binkie had given her the little red pocketbook that now accompanied Latisha every day to second grade.

And the shell design—the one that Sam had encouraged her to create on poster paper, and which turned out to be that of a huge foot to commemorate a recent surgery—went to Lillian be-cause she'd missed the beach trip.

Then, Lloyd continued, Mr. Pickens had heard Latisha mention a scooter, so he'd bought her one as a reward for uncommon bravery in the face of danger in a kitchen.

"And like it was no more than what anybody would've done," Lloyd went on, "she said, 'Well, he was tryin' to get my pocketbook.'"

Lloyd couldn't help but laugh as he went on to tell us of Latisha's reaction when she saw the scooter. "She tried to be excited when J.D. gave it to her," he said, "but her face gave it away. See, all along she was thinking scooter meant *motor* scooter—like a moped. She was planning to ride it to and from school."

"Oh, no," I said, "surely she didn't think she could ride it on the street."

"Well, she did. So when she saw it didn't have a motor and she'd have to push it with her foot, she was pretty disappointed. But I told her it was the prototype of a skateboard—a kind of Early American model—and she perked up at that. And now she loves it. I kinda do, too, whenever she lets me have a turn."

"*Good* morning, ladies." Sam, rubbing his hands together, strode into the kitchen a few mornings later. Beaming with anticipation, he pulled out a chair and took a seat at the table.

He'd had another bright idea and couldn't wait to spring it on me.

"Mornin', Mr. Sam," Lillian said, turning from the stove. "Scrambled, over light, or hard fried?"

"Anything, any way, Lillian," Sam said, holding out his cup as I picked up the coffeepot—a new one since the old one had been put to another use. "I'm easy to please this morning. Julia, I've been thinking—we ought to be making some Christmas plans."

I smiled, almost laughed, and reached over to take his darling hand. "I'm not surprised. You're always thinking of something. But let's not worry about Christmas until we've gotten over summer. Why, Sam, the school year's just started. Let's at least get through Labor Day before we start thinking of Christmas."

"Can't start too early, especially if we want to go somewhere popular, like, maybe Williamsburg? Or, think of this, Julia." He leaned forward, eager to tell me. "What about renting a lodge at Greenbriar or Wolf Laurel or somewhere like that for a week of skiing?"

"*Skiing?*" I couldn't believe he thought I'd risk life and limb on a ski slope. Or that he would, either.

"Wel-l-l," he conceded, "the children would enjoy it. And so would everybody younger than us." He grinned. "Which is all of them. You and I could sit by the fire, drink hot cider, and people watch."

"We can do that here," I said. "I'll even wear a fur hat and a pair of tights if it would help."

Lillian's shoulders began to shake as she listened to us. She knew what a homebody I was, and what a gadabout Sam was. But I smiled, too, for I knew what Sam was up to. He'd proposed a ski holiday, knowing it wouldn't suit me, but hoping I would agree to Williamsburg instead, which was probably his first choice.

"That," Sam said, squeezing my hand, "could make me want to stay home. But let's be thinking about Christmas."

To tell the truth, I didn't give Christmas another thought for the rest of the day—too happy to be home, too glad that the sun was shining, and too grateful that we'd survived unharmed, being the focus of a seafaring crime syndicate.

Sam, on the other hand, must've been thinking about it all day. We'd just crawled into bed that night when he turned on his side and said, "I've had another idea."

Speaking up into the dark room, I said, "Sam, I am not flying anywhere."

He laughed softly. "I know, but how about New York to see some shows—just you and me? We can have a big Christmas here, ask them all over for dinner, play Santa Claus for the children, then take off for the big city." Then, to really tempt me, he added, "We'd take in some museums, too."

"I'll think about it." And for a few minutes, I did, along with all the things that could go wrong. "But what if we ran into another storm? At that time of year, we could have a blizzard."

"Ah, honey," he said, turning and wrapping his arm around me, "we've weathered a hurricane with no ill effects. What's a little blizzard to us? You can't not do something for fear that the worst could happen—chances are that it'll happen, anyway."

"I know," I said again, whispering against his neck. Then I began laughing. "Remember what we used to say as children—'Let it rain, let it snow, ain't nobody out in it'? Or maybe it was 'Let it rain, let it pour,' I don't remember. But I don't want to be in any kind of storm, be it hurricane, blizzard, or LuAnne's anger at Leonard. And, on that note," I went on with sudden recall, "let me suggest that if you ever have the urge to bring home some black lace step-ins, find a better hiding place than a shaving kit."

Sam started laughing. "I can do without black lace, but a pair of tights and a fur hat? That's another matter entirely."

"Oh, you," I said, laughing as I slid closer to him. "I'm going to stop worrying about storms. As you said, they're coming whether we like it or not. But as long as you're around, I can weather them all."

"Oh," he said, running his hand down my back, "I'll be around all right."

And he was.

Miss Julia Raises the Roof

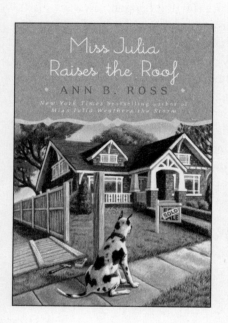

When Miss Julia discovers that nosy do-gooder Madge Taylor has embarked on a mission to buy up a vacant house down the street, she suspects that something is afoot. She soon learns that a much larger plot is unfolding, one that threatens the existence of their quiet neighborhood. Now Miss Julia must band together with friends and neighbors to take on Madge, in another entertaining installment of Ann B. Ross's bestselling series.

VIKING

PENGUIN BOOKS